deliver
ME FROM
DUVAL

ME FROM
DUVAL

The Duval Series: Book I

CHASSILYN HAMILTON

Jacksonville, FL

DELIVER ME FROM DUVAL

ISBN: 978-0-578-85762-6

Published by Chassilyn Hamilton
Jacksonville, FL

Printed in the United States of America
First Edition March 2021

Cover Design by: Fresh Designs
Interior Layout by: Make Your Mark Publishing Solutions
Editing: Make Your Mark Publishing Solutions

acknowledgments

S o! I have a *long* list. I just want to say that I would literally need a book to thank *everyone* who has done anything to get me here. If I've missed you, please know that my heart is pure, and it is not intentional.

My Lord, The Trinity, Father, Son, and the Holy Spirit, You've kept me for this long. You've never let me go. With You, I've never felt alone. You sent Your children to speak Your words into my life to ensure that I hear You. I pity those who haven't experienced You as I have because I know I would be so lost without You.

Byron (deep breath), my best friend, my biggest supporter, you are precious. I didn't realize how blessed I was long ago, but baby ... I know. Thank you for being my rock. Always protecting me and taking on my problems. I'm obsessed with you. I hope to retire you one day because you deserve it!

Mom, Dad, you never questioned my dream. I've never had to prove you wrong, which is something I am realizing I took for granted as I type this. I wonder how hard it would be to step out if the people closest to me didn't believe in my dream. Thank you for not showing me what that feels like.

My advance readers: You held it down. I love the messages. I live for the discussions. So many nights I pushed myself beyond my limits because I knew you were waiting on that email

(Message! ... LOL). I hope I didn't burn you out because this is one of many. (Yep, surprise!)

Crissa "Crystal" Brisco, my sis, I appreciate your obedience. You put yourself out there that day, and in the moments when I'm unsure, I think about that conversation, and I know this is what I'm supposed to do. I couldn't wait to get here to let you know that one call got me here. Thank you.

Deuce, Tiara Symone, are the words even needed? Let's have a moment of silence to let our vibe convey what I want to say (shhhh ...). Talk about a *day one* (fights this thug tear that's trying to fall). You inspire me. No matter the story, the best friend is always an extension of you. Chile you are *stuck* stuck with me!

Jordyn (waves ... Hey, girl!). After I left the job, I went through an uncertain period. I hadn't picked up a book in years and hadn't written in so long. One day, you posted about a book club, and I thought, *What the hell? Seems like just a good a time as any.* Ten days and seven books later, I was hooked. That was the domino that started it all. Thank you. Book clubs matter! Everyone, go check out @hottgirl_booktalk on IG and have your wine ready for Wednesday!

Dwinique, you are so pure. I hounded you with questions, and you always responded with an abundance of knowledge. Your guidance really simplified a process that I dreaded, and your willingness blessed me so much. I can't wait to be able to pay it forward. Check out her work: Author Chaunee on Amazon.

To my Penthouse crew, your conversations helped me through some tough times. Thank you for the laughter and the support. You all are the MVPs.

dedication

To my babies, everything I do is for you. I hope I make you proud.

To every supporter, I do this for you. I am overjoyed to share my imagination with the world, and my only dream is to write quality work that makes you want to turn the page.

One

Tyree smiled as she admired herself in the bathroom vanity of her hotel suite. Her pressed hair flowed softly past her bra strap. The layers her hairdresser convinced her to get framed the sides of her face perfectly. She applied minimal foundation, a nice matte lip color, and lashes to accentuate the natural beauty of her cinnamon-brown face.

Her black lace La Perla cut-out bra, matching lace thong, and black sheer robe flattered her naturally curvy body. Her full breasts were sitting just right, and the lace of her panties gave a seductive sneak peek of what was to come. Victoria's Secret usually got the job done, but for the occasion, Tyree decided to drop five hundred dollars on her ensemble. She needed to shoot straight to get things between them back to normal, and it was going to take more than a little booty rub to accomplish that. She accessorized with the platinum Cartier bracelet watch and Etincelle de Cartier ring Kamaal gifted her. Both pieces continued to promote her confidence. She wasn't sure if they felt *that* good or if it was the price tag she enjoyed more. A firm believer in "If you look good, you feel good," Tyree felt like a candidate for *People* Magazine's coveted Most Beautiful issue.

She recognized she had fucked up; there wasn't any way around it. Knowing that action brings reaction, she hadn't objected much to the distance he'd put between them. Now, however, she was ready to get past it. They had things to do, and once she revealed what she'd been up to, they would be able to get to them after tomorrow's game.

She planned a sexy surprise for them and felt that making her move on neutral ground would even the field. At their home, Kamaal was king, and she wanted him off his familiar turf. Kamaal, her man, played in the NFL as a star wide receiver for the Jacksonville Jaguars while they were in town for a home game.

The entire team, as well as some of the coaching staff, were required to stay at the same hotel on the night before a game to ensure everyone was in on time. So shortly after Kamaal left for the team's hotel downtown, Tyree followed.

She asked for a kiss when Kamaal bid her goodnight at the conclusion of what he most likely thought was their routine call. It was time to put her plan into action when he told her he would love to but couldn't because of work.

"I would if it wasn't for curfew," Kamaal responded with a sigh.

Unable to keep the smile out of her voice, Tyree said, "Well, come down the hall and give me one. Room 1001." She knew he'd been caught off guard by her response when he asked her to repeat herself. "You heard me. Room 1001. I'm waiting."

After a final once over in the mirror, Tyree approved her look. "Perfect," she said to her reflection. Moments later, she held a champagne-filled flute in her hand while getting comfortably situated on the plush, king-sized bed that had a soft-as-clouds coverlet.

Only when Tyree sipped the chilled Moet did the fluttering butterflies in her stomach begin to calm.

"Why are you so nervous?" she asked herself with a soft chuckle.

It was as if she was waiting on a first-time Tinder date instead of the man she had loved for the past two years.

With her eyes closed, Tyree got lost in the sensual vocals of Ginuwine's "So Anxious" coming from the Bose speaker next to her on the bedside table. She glanced at the clock, and just like the song, she was anxious. It was an hour past the team's 11:00 p.m. curfew, and Kamaal was due to show up any moment. It wasn't uncommon for a teammate or staff member to drop in before they retired to bed. Tyree had been on the phone with him plenty nights before game day when someone stopped by for a quick conversation, so she didn't object when Kamaal told her he wanted to wait a little bit in case an unplanned visitor turned up.

With the Moet having taken its effect and her nerves finally calmed, Tyree's confidence boosted. She grabbed her phone and began playing with her angles so she could send Kamaal something to look forward to. The first picture was of her covering her kitten. In another picture, she gave him a full view of her barely covered essence cupped in her diamond-dripped grip. She wished she could be there to see the look on his face when he saw her spread thighs. Diamonds and her thighs were two things Kamaal liked to indulge in, and she couldn't wait until he got his fill that night.

She looked down at her right hand and studied her ring. It was beautiful, but it was just *a* ring . . . not *the* ring. And that was the problem. They'd been on opposite ends of the spectrum, debating over things that truly went hand in hand—a baby for him and a wedding for her. Instead of meeting in the middle, both refused to relent, which put them at odds. Tyree didn't understand Kamaal's aversion to the thought of marriage; she was sure he probably thought the same about her being against having children out of wedlock. Maybe it was time to tell him about what happened before. She hoped she was finally ready to let him in on one of the most devastating moments of her life. She pushed those thoughts away as she finished her drink. They could revisit that another time. Tonight, she had sexing on the mind.

While tying her robe closed, she walked to the room's door after hearing a soft knock. Her heartbeat sped with each step she took. Her temperature instantly elevated a few degrees at the bright emerald-green eyes staring back at her through the peephole. She'd anticipated this moment all day, and her body reacted as if it had been on a timer and it knew the ringing was soon to come. Tyree opened the door and salivated at her man.

Kamaal Omari Duval leaned in the room's doorway, with his arms crossed over his strong chest and his coconut-sized biceps bulging out of his muscle shirt. His presence was commanding and demanded her full attention. Tyree's breath caught in her throat as she tilted her head back to look up at his smooth pecan-brown face. His hair, which he sported in textured coils at the crown and a fade on the sides, glistened as if it had been recently washed. When he cut his long dreadlocks last year, Tyree never thought she would recover from the change, but surprisingly, it hadn't taken long for this look to grow on her. She was convinced he could look good in anything.

It amazed her how she still responded to him. They'd spent over seven hundred days together and she still felt giddy whenever he called. He could melt her with the lightest touch. Just the thought of him caused her panties to saturate.

Being with Kamaal intimidated her at times, not by any of his doing; her limited experience made her question herself. She felt that she was no match for the powerful force he was on and off the field. Kamaal did what he could to include her in his world. The way he took care of her made her want to please him in every way. She remembered feeling this way when they met and wondered when the honeymoon phase would end. She was still wondering that very thing today.

"You know, I could get in trouble for this," Kamaal warned. "If coach finds out that I snuck out after curfew, I'm benched." His words expressed his concern for the risk, but his eyes gave away that he knew it was worth it. She watched as his gaze swept over her body and lingered on the skin that peeked through the material of her robe. He wanted her, and tonight he was going to get her. The thought sent erotic chills throughout her body.

"I know. That's why I came to you. However, technically, you are still in the hotel, so you aren't really breaking the rule, right?" Tyree pulled him into the room and placed the Do Not Disturb sign on the door handle before she closed and locked it. "We've been fighting, and I wanted to make this right before you got on the field tomorrow. I would hate for you to play with all the pent-up energy that needs to be released. Let me take care of you, baby." A cocky smile curved her red-painted lips, which Kamaal returned, showing his perfect teeth.

She led him through the separate sitting area furnished with two chairs, a table, and a television. There wasn't any need to stop, as their business would take place a few steps beyond there in the bedroom. She threw an extra switch in her steps, knowing he was watching her ass. She could feel his eyes as they roamed her body in a heated skim.

She was slimmer than she'd been when they met, but she still had plenty to show. Being constantly surrounded by build-a-WAGS had her insecure when they first began dating, and she immediately went into action to change it. Now, she was a proud size eight, two sizes smaller than when they'd met. She would shoo Kamaal's words whenever he told her she was fine the way she was. Losing weight was something she needed to do for herself, and she was very pleased with the improvement. After her transformation was complete, Kamaal let her know that he admired her for her determination and agreed that she had improved, not in size but in confidence, and that shit turned him on. He often repeated that sentiment. She was happy to be a single-digit size, and he made it known that he was happy her ass was still sitting. He liked having something to hold on to. It was a win-win.

Tyree turned to Kamaal once they entered the suite's bedroom. It was dark except for a small lamp on the desk in front of the window. She opened her mouth to begin the speech she rehearsed all day, but her words were lost when, without warning, he lowered his head and his mouth took possession of her lips. His soft lips held firm to hers before he pushed his tongue inside. The kiss was urgent and full of passion. Their tongues tangled as they tried to make up for lost time. She grabbed a handful of his thick, black beard and held his face close to hers.

Seven days without making love was the equivalent of seven months for them. Their passion was palatable and needed to be tended to daily. It had been hard sharing the same bed yet not feeling welcome to touch him.

Tyree broke the kiss, leaning back to pull his shirt over his head. Her hands roamed over his hard chest while she gained control of her breathing. The tips of her acrylic nails skimmed the indentions of his muscles that were covered in ink, starting at his chest and traveling downward. She loved the feeling of his muscles contracting under her touch. He'd put up a good front these past few days, but he couldn't suppress this; he was hers. She worked her fingers down his abdomen, taking a detour to graze every abdominal muscle until her hands reached his waistline, slipped past the hem of his shorts, and she took a hold of *him*. He was massive, erect, and ready for her. That was a good sign.

Kamaal untied the belt of her robe and brought her body flush against his. His strong, calloused fingers tucked her hair behind her right ear before he used that hand to cup the back of her neck. They stared in each other's eyes as her hand slowly stroked him inside his pants. She loved the velvet skin beneath her fingertips. She gripped and squeezed him tightly, just how he liked, and watched him quiver. Seeing him react drove thunderbolts to her center. Kamaal was the strongest man she knew; he made a great living out of smashing niggas on the field. She'd seen grown men run into him, not causing so much as a budge, yet her soft touch disarmed his vigor. Kamaal was Goliath, and Tyree's touch was the slingshot. Her green-eyed giant, her Hulk.

She sucked in a sharp breath and wrapped her legs around Kamaal's waist as she was lifted from the floor. His hands palmed her ass, and he nibbled on her neck as he stepped toward the bed. Her eyes rolled upward as he trailed kisses down her body the moment her back met the covers. Her breath hitched when he tugged her underwear to the side.

"Shit, Chelle," he hissed, using the name he only used during their intimate moments. Derived from her middle name, Machelle, it was personal and powerful, and it usually caused her to lose control.

She couldn't prepare herself for his wide tongue as it flicked her pearl then traveled down her oozing slit, telling of her longing. She quivered when his tongue pushed through and reintroduced itself with her insides. Her back arched from the mattress, and she bit down on her lip to hold back her groan. She didn't know how she'd survived the past week. Kamaal's skilled loving had become an obsession of hers. She needed it every day.

Her mind was empty of words. Her spiel vanished. She had no thoughts. All she could do was feel. She jerked when his lips surrounded her sex, sucking like she was a piece of fruit, and he wanted every last drop of her nectar. She grinded back and forth on his thick fingers. This needed to happen now. They needed to clear the fog. They'd talk . . . after.

The next morning, Tyree sat up in the bed, not bothering to cover her bare breasts. They made love throughout the night, and Kamaal scrambled to gather his things so he could get back into his room. Game day check-in was in an hour. They talked, but not how she planned it. Instead of using words, they used touch, kisses, and responses. *Kept this man up all night. Hope I didn't do more harm than good.* The tense expression defined his strong jaw and made him look sexier. He pulled his shirt down his frame, causing his biceps to flex. Tyree's tongue swept her bottom lip; she would prefer to taste his skin instead, but she knew he didn't have the time.

She changed the subject before she was tempted enough to try for a last-minute quickie.

"I was thinking we could try again the week after your game in Oakland?"

Kamaal stepped into his shorts. "Try what again?"

"The trip to Baker," she answered.

He paused before he responded. "Naw, that's all right. I'm not on that anymore," he answered, finally pulling his shorts up on his waist.

Her heart sank. It had taken her bringing it up for almost a month before Kamaal had finally agreed to visit his dad at the Baker Correctional Institution. She thought back to how relentless she had been in getting him to agree. Kamaal had finally agreed to go but only under the condition that she accompanied him.

Now, after all the time she'd put in, he had changed his mind.

"You're willing to go the rest of your life without having a relationship with your father? And rob Karl from having a relationship with him?"

Kamaal frowned. "Him shooting up in my mama to make me doesn't make him a father, and I am not dragging my son up the road to visit a murderer."

"He isn't a murderer, and you know it," Tyree challenged.

An eyebrow lifted. "You checked the DOC website lately?"

She sucked her teeth, annoyed by his sarcasm. "I know what the conviction is for and you know what I mean."

Kamaal's dad and his uncle were doing what should have been a quick robbery when an unanticipated security guard surprised them. Kamaal's uncle, who was the accomplice, was shot and killed. Now Kamaal's father was serving a life sentence for felony murder. He'd lost his freedom and his brother at once. Double murder.

"What about our future kids, Kamaal? I want them to know their grandfather."

Fully dressed, he stood at the end of the bed with his arms crossed over his chest again. This was him withdrawing, using his brawniness as a buffer between the most vulnerable parts of him and everyone else, including her.

"You're not trying to give me a baby right now, so we have time to figure it out, right?" The nonchalance in his tone agitated her. She hated that she disappointed him.

She decided to end that conversation there. They'd just made up, and she didn't want to throw him off before work. She honestly wasn't sure if they really made up or if they only made up for the days of no sex. Either way, it was a step in the right direction, and they would soon reach their destination of concord. She was sure of it and would see to it, starting tonight. She was counting the hours.

two

"Girl! I want your life!" Toni squealed as she and Tyree settled into her new Mercedes AMG coupe. Toni melted into the red and black soft leather seat. "Oh!" she squealed again as the seat massaged her back.

Once Kamaal left to go back to his room, Tyree got dressed and picked up her friend before she headed to the stadium.

"That's nice, isn't it?" Tyree said, smiling over at her best friend.

Toni's eyes were closed, and the expression on her clay-brown face exuded enjoyment. Tyree had reacted the same way when she and Kamaal purchased the truck the other week. They spared no expense and bought her the top of the line. There might've been a lot of these coupes on the road, but when Tyree's ruby-red bad bitch pulled up, there was no question that the bag was bottom-less. The black-glossed Forgiato rims with the chrome lip always earned a second glance. Kamaal tried talking her into getting obnoxious-sized rims, like sixes or eights, but twenty-three was her favorite number, so that's what she got.

Tyree loved being able to share these moments with Toni.

When they met years ago in the fourth grade, they were anything but friendly to each other. It all started when Tyree accidentally tripped Toni with her foot, causing her to chip her tooth on Tyree's desk. Toni had it out for her ever since until their teacher completely shook up fifth period science class. For a partner assignment, Mrs. James paired up the children by first name as opposed to their last as she usually did. It took them being forced to work together on a class project to realize they had a lot in common. And once Toni's parents had her tooth fixed, their beef became old news. They'd been besties ever since.

"Shiiit. Nice isn't even the word," Toni complimented as she ran her hands across the shiny chrome dashboard. "You are so lucky! You have a man who loves you, takes care of you, and he's getting major paper! It's all your MASH dreams come true."

Tyree nodded; she agreed with her friend. When they were younger, they mapped out their lives with their favorite childhood game: mansion, apartment, shack, or house.

"Who woulda' thought, right? As long as I'm not in a shack, I'm good."

"True, but this is definitely better." Toni finger-combed her naturally curly hair that she wore in a short pixie cut.

Tyree felt the same way. Sometimes it felt like things were too good to be true. Quite often, she would find herself in awe of the beauty and luxury that oozed through all forty-five hundred square feet of the beautiful waterfront home they purchased a year ago. Her parents would've been proud.

Losing her mother when Tyree was a young girl crippled the Morris household. Her dad had a hard time, but Tyree was thankful he did what he could. They were two people living with shared pain only they could understand, and it made them closer. Father and daughter—a delightful duo. Tyree sometimes thought being alone had been too much on her father, because not long after she moved away to start her life as an adult in college, he became addicted to drugs and died from an accidental overdose.

"Tell me, did my dating advice work?" Toni asked as she applied a new layer of lip gloss while looking in the mirror.

Tyree smacked her lips and turned to her best friend. "Toni, I hardly think a quote from Uncle Luke and Poison Clan really counts as dating advice."

"Did you shake what your mama gave you?" Toni asked over the rim of the Celine squared sunglasses Tyree bought her for her birthday.

Tyree sighed. "Yes."

"And did it work?" her friend followed up.

Tyree didn't readily answer as she checked the road next to her and switched lanes. After turning off her blinker, she turned to an expectant Toni, who awaited her response. The straight face Tyree fought to keep still transformed into a silly grin. "Yes, it worked."

"Hell yeah! I told you. There is power in that poon!" The two women laughed and high-fived each other.

"You're right about that. Kamaal still seemed a little bothered about me missing the visit with his dad but nowhere near how pissed he was the other day." Tyree rolled her window down and presented her all-access pass to the guard.

"But come tonight, once you tell him you're off birth control and ready to get pregnant, all will be forgiven."

"That's the plan."

Kamaal had been furious the day she went to her appointment, so Tyree figured she would tell him about it another time. After he hung up the phone on her, he ignored her calls and texts and stayed out way past the normal 8:00 p.m. time he usually made it home each day. When her doctor's office called to push her appointment back due to an emergency C-section her provider had to cover, she opted to reschedule. It was then that she was advised her doctor was booked up and wouldn't be able to see her for six weeks if she did not take the time slot that was available later that day. Tyree was assured her procedure was routine and she could be in and out within an hour. She hadn't counted on the applicator breaking in two inside of her arm and the extra time it took to remove it, making her too late to meet Kamaal. She knew his reason for staying out later than usual was in hopes she would be asleep when he got home, but she had been wide awake, unable to drift into dream world with Kamaal out of the house and angry. She feigned sleep when he walked into their bedroom and was able to drift off while he showered. She could rest once she knew he was all right.

"You're really about to make me an auntie, Ty?" Toni eagerly asked. Her excitement warmed Tyree, who responded with a small smile and a nod. "I can't wait to spoil my niece or nephew."

The instrumental to Lil Duval's *Smile* began playing. "Oh shit, turn this up! This your anthem, girl. You are most def living your best life!" Toni turned the volume knob to the right, causing the song to blast through her Bose speakers.

Tyree chuckled while singing along with the hometown hero. She couldn't wait to give Toni a niece or nephew to spoil. The thought of a baby brought joy; it was amazing. No matter if they would be celebrating the first game and win of the season or if they needed a pick-me-up after a loss, the news would, without a doubt, be the means to the perfect ending of the day. Like Uncle Snoop said, she had a lot to be smiling for.

Three

"Duuuvalll!" The crowd inside the stadium erupted as the attendees began cheering at the customary call. Everyone was out of their seats, clapping and yelling. The city had showed up for the season opener against the Bengals.

"That's it, Jacksonville! Show your love for your Jaguars. Give it up for your starting lineup!"

The commentator announced the team with enough energy for everyone in attendance to catch it. Fireworks lit the sky as the football team ran onto the field. Tyree was amazed by the sea of gold and teal that shook the grounds. The array of towels, pom poms, signs, and other cheering accessories lit the gigantic scoreboards. The fans weren't fazed by the blistering heat, even though the high for the day was in the low nineties, average for early August, and it was about ten degrees warmer inside the stadium. Still, they celebrated as if it was a cool day. It was impressive.

Jacksonville, Florida, was the city, but the residents claimed the county. Duval County, once nicknamed Da Bangem, was one of the grimiest, laid-back mixtures of suburbs, hoods, and trailer parks. Contrasts in wealth separated the social classes, but the home team was something the residents had in common. Jacksonville was a football city through and through. What the team lacked in age or experience, being the youngest team in the league, they made up for with a strong fan base and tons of support. The people of Jacksonville bled teal and gold.

The commentator began again. "And now, let's give it up for your fourth-year wide receiver, responsible for the most receiving yards last season, and future Hall of Fame inductee, Mr. 904 himself: Kamaal Duval!"

"Mack Truck! Mack Truck! Mack Truck!" the crowd chanted the nickname Kamaal was given during his rookie season. The way he pulverized the charging competition while he took the football down field birthed the moniker. Instead of leaping over the defenders like Ezekiel Elliot or impressing the crowd with jukes like OBJ, Kamaal beat his defender by doing just that: beating them. It didn't take long for the league to recognize his power. At 6'5", 225 pounds, her Hulk was an intimidating giant. Players who had the unfortunate experience of coming up against him described being run over by Kamaal as similar to being run over . . . head on . . . by a big rig going max speed. Pedal to the floor.

He was King Leonidas, leading his team of skilled soldiers to combat, and she, Queen Gordo, sat on her throne, her back erect as she peered from the sky box above the stands. She surveyed the faces of her army; they were absent of smiles and laughter. This wasn't a comical matter. To the sixty-five thousand supporters, this was a game. To him and his team, this was war. This was Sparta. Kamaal was a born leader, and the role looked natural. This was his city, which also made it hers.

"I see Daddy, Tyree, look!" Kamaal's son, Karl, jumped up and down excitedly. His small left hand, sticky from the cotton candy he'd been snacking on, encased her fingers, and he used his other hand to point at the sideline. Kamaal's aunt Brenda met her there with his son right before kickoff.

Kamaal stood there and waved in their direction. He was too far away to actually make her and Karl out in the crowd as they sat up high in the sky box for the team's family, but he waved anyway because he knew they were there, and he wanted to let his baby boy know he knew he was watching.

"Hey, Daddy!" Karl waved hysterically. Others in the box laughed and cooed at his response. Karl was his father's biggest fan and self-appointed backup receiver. He was always ready to step in for his dad whenever he needed help in a game and saw to it that he dressed the part. Each week, he came prepared with a helmet and pads, dressed in a kid version of his dad's jersey.

Tyree couldn't help but smile watching Karl react to his father being on the field. His joy could not be imitated. It was pure, genuine, and infectious. Without trying, he had the power to lift her worst moods, even ones his father couldn't brighten. Kamaal and Karl brought light into her world when she hadn't even realized she was in the dark. They brightened her existence with an acceptance and belonging she'd forgotten about. The strength of the love they showed her lit the path to a lifestyle she couldn't imagine living without.

As Kamaal led the team onto the field, adoration from fans caused Tyree's chest to inflate with pride. He took charge without it being asked of him. He stood tall and strong, and seeing him in his element excited her. She squeezed her thighs together and pressed down in her seat to relieve the sensations she got from thinking about the things they'd done earlier. After the National Anthem and coin toss, the game began.

"Move those chains! Move those chains!" Cheers erupted as the Jaguars earned another set of downs. Jeremiah Canning ran the ball for twenty-five yards, giving his team a great field position. What was almost diminished to a three-point field goal attempt had been turned into another opportunity to score a touchdown for a larger lead margin in the game.

Jeremiah's girlfriend jumped out of her seat. "You go, boy!" she yelled proudly. "That's my man!" She pointed to the number eighty-eight on her jersey, making it known to everyone in the suite that she was proud of her guy.

Tyree watched the players go over the next play before hurrying to the line of scrimmage. The ball was hiked, and the quarterback Malcolm Watkins took a moment to survey the field before he sent the ball in Kamaal's direction. The player that covered Kamaal jumped and swung his hand in the air a second too soon, and the ball flew over his head. Kamaal bent his knees and exploded upward, snatching the ball down and rolling in bounds.

"We have another Jacksonville first down!"

An animation of a gold and white Mack truck with the number ninety-nine, Kamaal's number, shot across the jumbo screens. The crowd went wild.

Karl jumped up and down excitedly. "That's my daddy!" he shouted.

Kamaal's teammate, Hakeem Sanders, stood over him and extended his hand to him. Kamaal reached up for his help; however, Hakeem withdrew his hand, causing Kamaal to fall back on the ground. Tyree watched the exchange on the scoreboard screen and waited for the men to crack a smile to give a clue that it was nothing and they were joking, but that didn't happen. Hakeem said a few words and walked off, leaving Kamaal sitting in the same spot. Tyree frowned.

"Uh oh, looks like we have trouble in paradise," the sportscaster commented on Hakeem's taunting of Kamaal. One of the televisions that hung on the wall in the box showed the game as it played on ESPN.

"Yes, it does," the man's partner chimed it. "Someone should tell Sanders that him and Kamaal are now on the same team, and it's time to play nice."

Hakeem Sanders was a two-year vet who was traded from Jacksonville's biggest rival, the Tennessee Titans, during the off season. They had been down a receiver when the last one retired after eight years in the league.

The ball was hiked, and again, Malcolm briefly checked all his options. The players on the field dispersed to their assigned spots for the selected play. The offensive line kept the defenders from getting to their quarterback, and the extra time allowed for a chance at a big play as both star receivers made their way to the end zone. As a Bengal slipped past Malcolm's protection, he sent the ball flying. Kamaal kept his eye on the football while shifting on his feet and dodging his opponents.

The football was thrown to the corner end of the field where Kamaal was headed. Hakeem read the play and did a spin move, breaking his coverage. He sprinted in Kamaal's direction, and both men jumped simultaneously as the ball reached the five-yard line, causing them to collide and slam to the ground.

A harmonious "oh" filled the space as the crowd reacted to the hit. The contact was strong, and the clacking noise of helmets crashing into shoulder pads pierced the microphones and echoed through the speakers.

"Daddy!" Karl cried out for his father in horror as he watched him lie on the field. Hakeem laid still, only for a moment, before he slowly stood.

The stadium became eerily quiet. Everyone waited for a signal that their star player was all right.

"Get up, Kamaal," Tyree urged under her breath. She stared at the jumbo screen without blinking, repeatedly willing him to stand. She whispered the words over and over so quickly that they ran into each other and the sound mimicked a ritual chant.

Toni shot to her feet, squeezing Tyree's other hand in hers. In what felt like an eternity later, Kamaal rolled over and braced himself on his knees. Tyree blew out the breath she was unaware she was holding and looked toward the sky, thanking Jesus. Everyone in attendance applauded; the thunderous sound caused the stands to vibrate.

Relief gushed through Tyree, and she clapped as hard as she could, turning her palms red as she blinked back tears. This was the part of the game she hated the most. These moments reminded her how fragile a professional football career really was. A man of colossal stature, whose job required extreme conditioning and keeping his body in the best shape, could lose it all on any given Sunday. It didn't matter if he could bench-press five hundred pounds or run a forty-yard dash in four-point-something seconds. One hit could snatch away a dream he worked his entire life for. She could deal with the two-a-day practices, away games, and mandatory appearances, but the injuries that could end a career or take away his ability to walk or even his life were too much at times. From the stress of it all, she was sure that she now had a few gray strands. An appointment with her hair stylist Peaches was in her near future.

After being knocked down by Hakeem, Kamaal sat out a few plays to get his bearings. Coach benched Hakeem for the entire third quarter, and Tyree agreed with the decision. Hakeem could use a reminder that he wasn't the enemy anymore, and he needed to act that way. The camera focused on the two receivers on the sideline as they sat on opposite ends of the bench. Kamaal kept his attention on the game, while Hakeem kept his attention on Kamaal. They weren't sitting close to each other, and Tyree watched as Hakeem spoke in what she assumed was a loud enough voice to make sure his words reached Kamaal.

She turned her stare from the field to the television that was closed in on them. It appeared that the newcomer had been engaging in meaningless competitive banter until he made a statement that got a reaction out of everyone who was in earshot. Hakeem's back was facing the camera so there was no way to know what he said, but whatever it was, it ruffled feathers. Kamaal snatched his helmet from his head and stomped to Hakeem's side of the bench before he was cut off by several team members. Tyree watched in horror, thankful that enough people intervened before a brawl broke out. *What the hell is that about?*

"Did you see that?"

Tyree faced Toni. "Yes, I saw." She was turning back to look at the national game coverage playing on the TV when a figure in the corner of her eye caught her attention. She clashed eyes with Hakeem's wife, Simone, who was staring at her. Tyree tried to read her expression but was unable to decipher a single mood. She saw many. Fear, amazement, shock. She was sure the woman's face mirrored her own.

Tyree watched the rest of the game in a daze. Every now and then, as she caught the glances of sympathetic onlookers, she flashed the plastic smile she had perfected. Throughout the game, she got lost in her thoughts and she knew she had done the right thing by getting off birth control. Kamaal and Karl were her everything, and she was ready to solidify their unit with a new addition in their family. Tyree couldn't wait to get him home and tell him the exciting news.

four

Toni and Aunt Brenda had already left the game when Tyree and Karl went downstairs to meet Kamaal. Karl kept his eyes glued on the locker room door while he waited for Kamaal to walk out so he could congratulate his dad on the win. Tyree looked at the people in the waiting area, scanning everyone's faces in search of Simone. She'd only been introduced to the woman once briefly but wanted to speak with her to let her know that whatever issues their men had didn't affect them. However, upon surveying the room, it appeared that Simone had either left or decided to skip the reception.

Tyree heard a familiar voice approaching and turned around.

"Excuse me, ma'am. Visitors aren't allowed. So, you," she said, pointing to the woman's protruding belly, "and you have to wait beyond the doors." Her words were full of authority she didn't possess.

Cherise Watkins, wife of quarterback Malcolm Watkins, rested her fist on one hip while she used her other hand to rub circles on her belly. "OK, you heard her. You gotta go," she fussed at her protruding stomach. She turned her head to the side and placed her ear closer to her stomach as if she could hear words coming from her womb. "He said he needs to chill in there for about another month, so you're just going to have to deal with it."

Tyree laughed as she closed the distance between her and the woman. "I guess we'll give y'all a pass." The women embraced. "How are you feeling? I'm surprised you're still making it to these games."

When they'd seen each other last at Cherise's baby shower two weeks ago, she'd stated she had opted to support her husband from home until she delivered their son.

When Tyree and Kamaal began dating, Cherise was one of the only team wives who welcomed her. Unlike a lot of the others, Cherise never judged her appearance or lack of NFL knowledge. She even went so far as to help her adjust to the football life.

Tyree took note of all the changes her friend went through with pregnancy. Her nose spread, her face looked puffier, and her feet had swollen to where she could only wear flip-flops. But regardless of all the many changes Cherise's body had endured, Tyree knew for certain that she thanked God for it. Cherise had shared more than once how she and Malcolm had almost given up hope when they'd received the news they'd prayed for. Tyree was genuinely happy they were getting what they'd wanted for years. The prenatal glow of her golden brown skin was sure to match the happiness she exuded from within. Her journey was a beautiful one.

"I know, I told Malc I was going to stop coming once I hit thirty-six weeks, but I couldn't miss the first game of the season. But this is it, you can believe that. My feet have been asking me 'Is we finished?' or 'Is we done?' since the second quarter."

The two friends spent the rest of the time laughing and

catching up. Malcolm Watkins walked out of the locker room and found his wife. He responded to those who spoke to him without breaking his stride. Once he approached Cherise, he bent down, brushing his sandy-brown locks from his face, and kissed her belly before he straightened to kiss her lips.

"What's up, M-Dubb? Congrats on the first win." Tyree saluted the quarterback, giving him a sideways church hug.

"'Preciate that, Tyree." Malcolm tugged her shoulders in a friendly squeeze.

"First of many, right?"

Malcolm nodded. "You damn right."

"Daddy!" Karl's hand was out of Tyree's and he took off, his feet barely touching the ground as he ran. He didn't slow his speed when he approached his dad. Kamaal braced for his boy, hooked his armpits, and threw him up in the air. He caught Karl and held him up so they were eye to eye.

"You won!"

Kamaal smiled at his son. "*We* won, my guy. I did what you told me, and it worked."

Karl radiated in pride. "That's what I'm talking about."

He got a few laughs out of those around, including Tyree. She always stayed back to give her two fellas their time. Their interactions could cause the Grinch's heart to grow instantly. They were beautiful, and Tyree cheesed as she watched. This was family, her family. She'd gone without and tricked herself into believing she didn't need one. That was easier for her. She found her missing pieces when she hadn't been looking, and she was grateful.

"Congratulations, baby." Tyree lifted on her toes and met Kamaal's quick peck on the lips.

"Aww. Isn't that sweet?" Kamaal's teammate Josh teased while walking up. "I think you grabbed my bag, Mack." He held up a black Nike training duffel bag with the initials KD stitched on its side.

"My bad, Josh. Here you go." The men switched bags, and Josh walked off.

"Still taking things that don't belong to you, huh, KD?"

Tyree turned to find Hakeem standing behind her with a wry smile on his full lips.

"That's the word on the street," Kamaal shot back dismissively and turned his attention to Tyree. "I'm ready."

Kamaal moved around Hakeem with his son still in his arms and Tyree at his side. Not so much as a goodbye was uttered in Hakeem's direction, and he didn't seem bothered. The energy shifted as it did during the game. Hakeem seemed to enjoy meddling with Kamaal, and she wanted to know why.

Thirty minutes later, the three of them walked toward the exit. Kamaal was ready to leave but was detained by a coordinator who wanted to discuss their schedule to prepare for next week's game.

"Hakeem, there's no question that there is some tension between you and Kamaal. Do you care to share why that is?" Tyree heard a reporter's inquiry. She glanced to the left and saw the post-game interview as it played on a television that hung on the wall.

Tyree watched Hakeem raise his massive shoulders. "Just a little friendly competition." His smug expression revealed the duplicity of his words. What he said warranted no pause, but the way he spoke made her cautious. Kamaal seemed disinterested; instead of tuning in, he kept walking.

As they proceeded, Hakeem's words bounced in the hall. Hearing Kamaal's name again made their ears perk up, and instinctively, they slowed their stride and tuned in right outside the door where Hakeem was conducting an interview.

"After you and Mr. Duval were sidelined during the game, we

saw what looked like a heated conversation between you two. It appeared you said something that got everyone's attention. Would you mind sharing what that was?"

The audience of journalists was quiet as they waited for his response. This was the number one question that needed answering. Hakeem stared into the face of the reporter who asked the question. His eyes squinted and his jaw twitched as different emotions washed over his face. He appeared to be playing a mental game of tug-of-war. Say it or don't say it? His fingers drummed the podium.

Kamaal regained Tyree's attention by tugging her arm. "C'mon, let's get home." He'd seemed to have had enough of Sanders for the day.

As if their movement caught his eye, Hakeem turned his head and made eye contact with Tyree. She stopped walking and waited along with the room filled with media experts. His piercing eyes held hers as if waiting for her input. The right side of his lips lifted into a cynical grin, and he began to speak the words directly to her.

"I told Mr. Duval that I was taking his position since he took my bitch."

five

Tyree stormed inside the house after Karl. She kept her head forward while she ignored Kamaal's pleas for her to listen to him. He'd been trying to talk to her the entire thirty-minute ride from the stadium to their home on the beach, and she hadn't been trying to hear it. He knew that her mouth could be reckless, and there was no putting a lid on it once it was uncapped. While he wanted her to speak to him, he appreciated that she didn't spazz out on him with his son in the backseat.

"Tyree, chill." Kamaal caught the door she attempted to slam in his face.

"Go Jags!" Aunt Brenda walked in from the kitchen, wiping her hands on a towel. Her smile was replaced with an expression of concern, her eyes bouncing between Tyree and Kamaal. "Everything all right?"

"Everything's fine," Tyree uttered as she breezed by and went upstairs.

"AB, could you take Karl home with you tonight?" Kamaal asked his aunt.

"Sure, son," Aunt Brenda answered. Concerned eyes followed Tyree, who huffed upstairs after she mumbled goodnight. "Karl, grab your things so we can head out." The door to the master suite upstairs slammed loudly. "Now," she urged.

Karl slowly headed upstairs with his gym bag hanging from his shoulder. He always had clothes at Brenda's and didn't need to pack any, so he only needed to grab a few other items he needed.

"Looks pretty serious," Brenda stated.

Kamaal took a deep breath. "It's not. Just some dumb team beef that got personal today." He leaned back against the wall beside the L-shaped staircase.

Brenda nodded. "Doesn't sound like too much for you to handle."

"Nothing more than a misunderstanding we need to talk through. That's all."

After seeing Karl and his aunt out, Kamaal took the steps to the second floor, hoping what the last words he said to his aunt would end up being true. The scent of eucalyptus and spearmint found his nostrils when he stepped in their bedroom. The bathroom door was closed, and the sounds coming from beneath it let him know it would be a while before she would speak to him. Tyree was in her Zen zone, and he knew better than to interrupt. He could picture her soaking in the massive, stark-white soaker tub, her stress relief candle flickering in the windowsill giving a minimal amount of light to the room, her hair pulled up because she was not about to ruin her fresh blow out, and head back and eyes closed as Mary J. Blige belted another sad love song. He was sure she was sipping on something nice from the wine fridge she had installed right beneath her vanity. It was going to be a while.

An hour later, Tyree walked out of their en suite as Kamaal sat on the bench at the foot of their bed. His head was bowed with his fingers laced and shoulders slumped. He didn't look like a man celebrating his first win of the season. He looked up at her. Her light-blue satin chemise stopped mid-thigh. Kamaal turned his attention to his hands and thought about the weather to force the blood to leave where it rushed to before he stood from the bench. *Down, boy.*

"Are you ready to talk now?" Kamaal asked.

"Are you ready to tell the truth now?" Tyree shot back.

"Baby, I'm telling you the truth. There's nothing more to talk about. Hakeem just—"

"Hakeem just what, Kamaal?" she interrupted. "Hakeem just got up there and lied his black ass off on stage. I'm supposed to believe that?" She cocked her head to the side. Her high ponytail swayed as the long strands brushed across her shoulders.

"He's feeling some pressure because he's in a one-year contract and he is trying to build some static around his name." Kamaal stopped there as if he'd explained enough.

"Static?" she asked incredulously. "You're saying he needed to build static by accusing *you* of messing with his wife? Make it make sense, Kamaal." She placed both hands on her hips and watched Kamaal's eyebrow lift in curiosity. Those gestures combined with the tightening of her lips illustrated she wasn't buying the story he was trying to sell. She wasn't even accepting a free sample. She passed by his explanation with a not-so-polite "no thank you."

"Baby, there's a lot on the line for Hakeem this year, and he's grasping at straws, trying to create drama so eyes will be on him. Because I'm the franchise player who has the same position as him, I got pulled into it. That's all there is, Ty, you trippin' for nothing."

Tyree tightened her eyes and silently stared at Kamaal as she looked for any clue to let her know if he was being truthful or not. What he said made sense. She'd seen plenty of housewives keep mess going by starting stupid fights or carrying bones to other cast members for an opportunity to get a peach. Why would it not work with football also? She didn't know Hakeem well—or virtually at all. Did it make sense for her to take his word over the man she loved? Her man? The more she thought about it, the more the rigidness in her shoulders faded. She hated that she was turning so easily, but she was starting to believe him. His eyes bore into hers, and his mouth stayed shut. He was waiting on her.

"Yeah, but why that accusation, Kamaal?" Tyree took a step toward him. "Out of all the ways to get a buzz going, why would he involve you in that way? Why involve his wife in that way?"

"Only thing I can think of is because I gave her a ride home one night after practice."

"Excuse me?" Her hands were back on her hips. He needed to come the eff again.

Kamaal sucked his teeth as if Tyree had no reason to be bothered. "It ain't nothing like that. She came to watch practice and had car trouble. I saw her as I was leaving, and I knew Keem was staying behind for some one-on-one with the coordinator and couldn't get her home. She stayed right up the street, so I gave her a lift. It was dark, and you know it's not safe to walk around that area at night."

Tyree inwardly agreed. The stadium wasn't in the best area, and she would feel a way if Kamaal knowingly let anyone walk home alone, let alone a woman. But she hated having to find out this way. Finding out this way felt like she would have never known the truth; this situation forced him to be transparent.

"Why not tell me, Kamaal? It doesn't look good for me to find out like this." She pouted her full lip.

"You see how you're acting now? This is why I didn't tell you. It wasn't anything major, and it wasn't worth mentioning. Now, I'm sorry Hakeem's crazy ass decided to bring my name up, and I'm going to straighten that. I need you to believe me, a'ight?"

Kamaal stepped to Tyree and placed his hands on her hips. He stared into her eyes and didn't blink. She felt that he wanted her to see the sincerity he exuded. Tyree felt herself swoon under his smolder. He wasn't running from her inquisition; there was no deflection. *Maybe he is telling the truth,* she thought.

"*Please* tell me I can believe you." She hooked her arms around his neck. The last words trailed off into silence, expressing her vulnerability.

"Baby, you can believe me. I promise you." He bent down and pecked her lips. A jolt was sent to the apex of her thighs.

"If anything happened, we could work through it. You *have* to be real with me. If you're lying to me, Kamaal . . ." She gave him one last chance. She offered an immunity she didn't know she could spare.

Kamaal placed his finger on her lips, silencing her. He took her waist into his grip and lifted her up, placing her legs around his waist before he took slow steps to their bed. Tyree admired his strong shoulders as she gave them a light squeeze. Another jolt caused her pussy to moisten. His strength supported her through her angst and weirdly turned her on. He sat on the side of the bed and looked up into her eyes. "I'm not lying to you, baby. I know what I have with you, and I'm not fucking that up."

His golden eyes bore into her as if they could peer into her soul, and she bit back a smile. Packaging was everything. Something about an apology coming from a chocolate masterpiece of a man made it even more soothing to receive. He was fine—too fine. It distorted her senses, even the common one.

Tyree smiled and didn't try to fight it this time. There was no need to put on that tough girl mien; the moment didn't require any mechanisms for preservation. Kamaal had said the words that were needed to plow through her insecurity. She believed him and knew he was worthy of her trust. Whatever publicity stunt Hakeem was angling would be left to Kamaal to remedy.

She reached to grab the hem of her gown then pulled it over her head, leaving her naked in his lap. He rubbed his hands up and down her back while admiring her body. Leaning forward, he drew a taut nipple into his mouth. She hissed and pushed her breast further into his jaws. His tongue swirled around the bud before his mouth clamped down and sucked. He moved to the next mound and gave it the same attention.

He stood from the bed and gently laid her down, never taking his mouth from her breast. Kamaal never rushed this part; he knew how much she enjoyed it and always gave her girls their time. He moved his kisses from her bosom down the center of her abdomen. Tyree swallowed her excitement. Her pulse quickened as she anticipated the pleasure that was near. Kamaal settled between her thighs and placed her legs over his shoulders. He bent his head down and kissed her clit.

"Damn, Chelle, you're so wet." The warmth from his breath created a zing that went straight to the bottom of her belly.

"Ahh!" she called out.

His tongue flicked her button before his mouth took possession of it. His cheeks flexed as he sucked. Tyree wound her hips on his face, causing the pressure to build in her midsection. Kamaal used his tongue to lick up and down her slit before he began to thrust it in and out of her, mimicking the moves she was sure he would put on her as soon as he had his fill of her taste. Using two fingers, he opened her lips and sucked on her clit again.

"Yes, baby. That feels so good," she groaned. She used her fingers to pinch her nipples, which heightened the pleasure Kamaal gave her.

Tyree peered down at him, loving the sight of Kamaal looking up at her. She knew he enjoyed seeing her play with her breasts. He sucked harder and didn't waver. He felt her legs begin to twitch on the side of his head and knew she was almost there.

"I'm about to . . ." she breathed out, unable to complete her sentence. She could only yell out as an electric sensation shot through her. She let out a continuous moan as the waves continued to soar. Kamaal didn't let up on his oral assault, which caused her orgasm to intensify. She called out his name as another current overtook her.

Once her tremors subsided, Kamaal eased from between her legs and undressed. Tyree scooted back on the bed as he leaned over and positioned himself above her. He took his length into his hand and guided himself inside. Tyree sucked in a quick breath as his impressive girth filled her, leaving no room for even air to fit. Kamaal bent down and took her lips with his as he began to slowly thrust in and out. Their tongues pushed back and forth with the same speed as their hips. Tyree lifted her pelvis and met his thrusts. She broke the kiss and moaned in his ear. Her hands clawed at his back as his strokes assaulted her spot.

"Yes, right there," she whispered in his ear, letting him know he was right where he needed to be. Kamaal responded by intensifying his pumps. He pressed her button repeatedly until she erupted. She threw her head back and called out his name. He continued to move inside her as he quickened his pace, a signal he was nearing the finish line.

Tyree brought her head upright and looked up at Kamaal. She stared at him; the passion she saw in his vibrant gaze matched hers. She knew he was feeling just as good as she was. They excelled when it came to sex together. After her first, Tyree thought there would never be a lover who could compare, but Kamaal proved he was more than capable. Her body betrayed her when it came to him. He was able to pull things out of her with little effort. It was as if her body spoke a language only he could understand. He had the type of dick, fingers, and mouth that could make her cut up in the streets. She was glad Hakeem was only popping shit to create drama because it meant she didn't have to let her crazy bitch side come out to play.

He bit his lip as he suppressed his explosion. She could tell he wanted this to last a little longer, to be in that space with her a little longer. Tyree flexed her inner muscles and nestled his thickness inside of her tighter. Kamaal groaned as she clamped down on him; she was trying to take him there and he was following without protest. A tingling sensation crept up his legs and settled in his middle.

"I love you," he breathed out. His lovemaking told her what his mouth did not. This was home.

"I love you too, baby," she moaned out. His profession of love sent a wave of warmth over her skin. Even if he hadn't said it, she discerned his sentiment. She could feel it. His face contorted into a blissfully painful scowl, and his breathing became shallower. She bit her lip and purred sweet commands as she ushered him into his capstone.

He pumped a few more times before he slammed into her once more, his lips forming into an O. He squeezed his eyes shut as she'd done when euphoria rushed through her moments ago. He collapsed above her with his weight braced on his knee. They said nothing. The sound of their decelerated breathing filled the air. Kamaal closed his eyes. He remained still with the side of his face planted on her chest. She could feel her heart thump behind her ribcage and wondered if he felt it too. Tyree listened as his breaths took longer to expel. She knew he'd drifted to sleep once his exhales evened out.

Today had been one hell of a roller coaster ride, full of astounding elevations and far-rooted dives. From the football game to the events that took place both before and after it, the start of the season was packed with more excitement than Super Bowl Sunday.

Tyree exhaled a weighted breath. Her and Kamaal's exchange felt ceremonial. More than a carnal release had taken place, and they'd taken an unfolded paper clip and activated the reset button. Tyree glided her fingers through her hair as she listened to his light snores. *Guess I'll tell him about the surprise tomorrow.*

Six

"Kamaal," Tyree called, nudging him to move his leg and arm from around her so she could get to the restroom.

"Hmm . . ." Kamaal turned over on his side, still asleep. She pulled her leg from under him and slid out of their California king-sized bed, careful not to wake him. He deserved his rest. If Kamaal had worked the football field as hard as he worked her body before *and* after the game, there was no doubt he was drained.

Tyree stared into darkness as she found relief. "Ssss," she hissed at the sting she felt when she patted herself dry. She welcomed the discomfort as it reminded her how hard he'd explored her body. "So worth it," she whispered with a smile.

As she made her way back to the bed, Tyree was still grinning. Kamaal had been in rare form tonight. She wouldn't be surprised if he'd placed a baby inside her; it was that intense. Her flat palm rested on her stomach; the thought sent hopeful chills through her. She couldn't wait to share the news of what she'd done. If he didn't have such a long day, Tyree would have woken him up to tell him the news so they could get started on their journey to conception.

She was almost to the bed when Kamaal's cellphone chimed, and she knew from the sound it was a text message. She read the clock on her nightstand. *Two fifteen in the morning.* She wondered who could be texting at this hour and went to find out. She typed in his passcode and went to the message sent from an unsaved 615 phone number.

I'm so sorry about everything. Please call me when you have a chance.

Tyree frowned and pulled down the top of the touchscreen to read more texts. The thread didn't budge. There weren't any other messages before that one. She read the few messages that came after the initial apology.

I hope Tyree isn't mad at you.

Oh? Saying my name. Mighty comfortable, are we? she thought.

I feel bad that we took things as far as we did. But I also want to take things there with you again.

I dreamt about you. Does that make me a bad person?

Please call me. No matter how late.

Tyree didn't give herself a chance to second-guess her decision when she hit the button to place a call. The screen indicated she was calling a number from Nashville.

"Hello?" a woman's voice answered. "Maal? I'm glad you called. I was worried."

"Who the fuck is this?" Tyree barked into the phone.

The woman hurriedly ended the call, and Tyree was tempted to call her back but decided not to. She'd gotten all she needed from the greeting. Her eyes snapped shut, and her grip on the phone tightened until the tips of her nails pressed so hard into her palm that they almost broke her skin. She stalked over to the bed and stood over him. The expression on his beautiful face was of contentment—the opposite of what she felt. That pissed her off more. It was time to wake up.

SLAP!

Kamaal bolted upward. The shock of the blow pulled him out of his slumber without the slightest warning.

"Yo! What the fuck, Tyree?" He rubbed his cheek and jaw.

"I'm sorry, did I wake you?" She tossed the phone in his direction. "You missed some text messages while you were sleeping."

Kamaal leaned over to the left. The phone barely missed his head before it hit the padded headboard where his head was resting moments ago. He read the messages and jumped out of the bed and started toward her, his long erection pointed at her.

"Are you going through my phone and calling people now?"

He got some bitch's nose wide open and that's what he asked?

"The fuck? She said to call no matter how late. So, ring ring, bitch!" Tyree threw her hands in the air. "Who was that, *Maal?*" The moniker was said with cynicism. "That's her, isn't it? That's Hakeem's wife, Simone." She answered her own question.

Kamaal sat on the side of their bed. He rotated his neck and dropped his head between his shoulders.

"Yeah, that's her," he quietly confirmed.

Tyree scoffed. She had follow-up questions she didn't even have to ask. The first "yes" confirmed the responses for her remaining queries. Her heels vibrated and sent tremors up her body. His offense had been loud and now his remorse was quiet.

"*When* did you fuck her?"

He lifted up his head, his emerald eyes bulging at her question. "Ty, I really don't remem—"

"When?!" she screamed, saliva sprinkling his face. Her voice cracked from the burn in her throat. She held him in her regard and willed herself not to crack. She'd never give him the satisfaction of seeing her break. As King Bey said, it would be suicide before he saw her tears fall. She forced air to creep from her nostrils to conceal her irregular breaths.

Kamaal's eyes widened at her outburst, and she knew why. They'd had plenty of arguments, but she had never responded so strongly. She never had to—until now.

"It happened on the day we had that bad fight."

Bad fight? she thought. Her mind went into a frenzy as it attempted to recall what fight he was referring to. It was unable. There was only one of those she could recall, and it was a nasty one.

That fight.

He fucked another woman the day she took herself off birth control for him. She laughed; this was comical. She was a believer of coincidences, but this one seemed extreme, even for her.

While basked in the sensuous aftershocks of their lovemaking, she thought their deep connection had been a way to signal they were going to be OK. Now that the fog of multiple mind-blowing orgasms had cleared, she was able to see it for what it was. It was their farewell. They'd been so in tune that their bodies communicated the adieus without them understanding what was taking place. How complicated the heart and mind were. Too intense and detailed to see the picture in its entirety, too sophisticated to recognize what their flesh easily translated. They were over.

Seven

Tyree's vision blurred after her eyes pooled with tears again. She tried to blink them away, which pushed them out onto her cheeks. Using the sleeves of her Versace hoodie, she wiped the wetness before she put her hands back on the steering wheel.

She felt so empty. Lost. How could he look her in her eyes with a straight face and tell her a lie? Who was he? Her Kamaal wasn't a man who deceived her. He wasn't the man to betray her trust. He wasn't the kind of man who would sleep with another woman, then come home and get into their bed as if nothing had happened.

"Hey, Siri, play 'Stranger in My House.'" She leaned her head back on the headrest and closed her eyes for a moment.

He was good; damn, he was good. His skills were deserving of a standing ovation at the Academy Awards. *Fake-ass tears.* The truth was there in her face, and she hadn't believed it. All he did was blink those big, beautiful eyes at her and give her the good dick she loved, and she threw her common sense out of the penthouse window.

"Shit!" The force at which she hit the center of her steering wheel caused the horn to honk, the loud sound making her jump. "I let him lie to me then fuck me right after like it was a reward." *How could I be so stupid?* She felt pain she had never experienced before.

Tyree drove to the W, and before getting out of the car, she pulled her visor down and checked her reflection. She looked exactly how she felt—a mess. Her eyes were swollen and red, and tear stains streaked down her puffy cheeks. She flipped down the sunglasses compartment, pulled out her Moncler aviators, and slipped them on her face.

It wasn't until she went to the check-in desk that she realized she'd grabbed the wrong purse. She left the clutch she wore to the game at home, and it had her wallet in it. She grabbed her Louis Vuitton weekender bag off the floor beside her and rushed outside, hoping to catch the valet before they took her truck to the parking garage. Once she was back in her car, she thought about the only other place she could go. She pressed the telephone button on her steering wheel to activate her vehicle assistant.

"Call Living Legend."

The phone rang until the voicemail picked up. She disconnected the call and proceeded to her best friend's house. It was a few minutes past three a.m., and Tyree was sure her best friend was asleep since she had to be at work at eight that morning. She felt bad for waking her friend up so late at night, but she couldn't go back home. She hated Kamaal in that moment and was afraid of what she may do if she had to see him again. It was best for them both that she stayed away that night.

Twenty minutes later, Tyree pulled into the driveway in front of Toni's condo and cut her engine. She sat there for a bit to enjoy the quiet. The entire day had been loud, from the fans at the game to the commotion caused by Hakeem's outburst, and she'd contributed by screaming and fighting with Kamaal. She needed a moment of silence. Once she'd gotten herself together, she grabbed her bag and rang Toni's doorbell. After waiting a minute, the porch light turned on, and the door swung open.

"Tyree? What's going on? Is everything OK?"

Tyree sniffed. She looked up and down the street, happy it was late. "I hate to show up like this, but I'm in a bind. Could I crash here tonight?"

Toni stepped aside. "Of course, come in." She locked the door behind her. "What happened?" she asked once Tyree was inside.

"It's Kamaal. He lied to me about Simone." She took a deep breath. She could feel the levy was about to break, and she didn't want to break down and cry again.

"Everything all right, Toni?"

Tyree looked over Toni's shoulder and watched the tall figure as it approached. She tilted her head back slightly to see his face. Once she recognized who Toni's late-night visitor was, she had to blink a few times, hoping her eyes were playing a trick on her.

"I know you're fucking lying. What are you doing here, Malcolm?" She turned to Toni, and that's when she noticed her friend was only wearing a bathrobe, her wavy hair wild. She turned and noticed the quarterback's shirt was halfway on and his pants weren't zipped or buckled. "Really, Malcolm? The whole team just ain't shit, huh? What, y'all like to sit up and tell stories about all the bitches you're fucking while your women and children are at home thinking you love us?"

Malcolm stood there stunned and said nothing. Tyree advanced on him with one hand on her hip and poked him in the middle of his chest using her long, coffin-shaped nail.

"I wonder how Cherise, who is near the end of a difficult pregnancy, would feel knowing about what you're doing."

Malcolm's face was consumed in horror at the mention of his wife finding out about his affair.

"OK, Tyree," Toni said, as she stood between her friend and her lover. "Look, go get settled in my room, and I'll be right there."

Toni turned apologetic eyes to Malcolm, who appeared to read her loud and clear. He put his hands up in the air in surrender and shook his head. Tyree glared at the man one last time before she did as Toni asked.

———◇———

After he was fully dressed, Malcolm walked toward the foyer.

He turned around before opening the front door. "I hate to ask, but ya girl . . . she's gonna be cool, right?"

Toni felt a jab to the chest; his question injured her pride. She cleared her throat and gave him an assuring smile after she recovered.

"Yes, she's cool. You don't have to worry about her telling Cherise."

Malcolm smiled, and Toni could tell he liked her response. He stepped away from the door and brushed her chin with his thumb before he leaned down and placed a quick kiss on her lips.

"Thanks, baby. I'll call you in a few days."

Toni locked the door and peeked through her blinds, watching him get into his car that was strategically parked on the street two units down. She inwardly groaned, and her stomach sank as she watched him leave. As always, when Malcolm left, he took a piece of her heart with him.

Once Malcolm's Range Rover pulled off, Toni headed back.

She reached her bedroom as Tyree stepped out of the master bathroom.

"Is he gone?"

Toni crossed her arms over her chest. "Yes, he's gone."

"That man is married . . . *to my friend.*" Tyree scowled at her. "Do you know what kind of position you put me in?"

Toni walked over to her with her hands on her slim hips.

"Excuse me, *I'm* your best friend, and this has nothing to do with you. I understand that Cherise is your friend *too*. That's why I didn't intend for you to find out."

Tyree looked at her. "What are you doing?" she asked in a low, uneven voice.

Toni's eyes prickled. It was the same question she asked herself every day for the past year. Tyree wasn't asking her what she was doing that night; that part was obvious. But what was her plan, her end game? Affairs always had an expiration date, and they usually ended up in a mess with both participants at odds; she knew it. She also knew the way her body responded to being around him. She knew she hadn't imagined the longing looks he snuck her way when the attention wasn't on him; the wanting in his depths had matched her own.

"I'm just following my foolish heart," she sighed out. "Now, enough about me. What are you going to do?"

Tyree's eyes clouded with sadness. "Kamaal cheated on me with Hakeem's wife, Simone. We're done. I can't be with him after this. I can't trust him." She winced as if the saying those words caused her physical pain.

Toni shook her head. She hated seeing her friend so hurt by Kamaal.

"I think it's a good idea to get away for a while, but are you sure you and Kamaal are finished? You are so in love with him, and I know for a fact that he loves you."

She tilted her face upward as she leaned back on the wall. "If only that were enough for him to stay faithful to me. And to think, I broke my own rule and got off birth control without us being married, just for him to cheat on me. I guess I should be thankful this happened now and not while I'm at home pregnant."

Toni frowned, once again feeling the sting of Tyree's words. Her friend spoke of her predicament, but it also applied to the one she was caught up in. She'd just been on top of a man who belonged to someone else while his pregnant wife was at home. Toni wondered if Cherise believed whatever story Malcolm gave that granted him permission to be away from home so late on a Sunday night. She never asked what reasons he provided Cherise because she never cared. What she wanted with Malcolm trumped everything else. Marriage and babies included.

Toni went into her closet and put on a nightgown. She stepped back into the room and spoke to Tyree, who leaned on the wall next to the bathroom.

"You're free to do what you want, but I'm going back to sleep. My alarm clock isn't waiting for anybody."

Tyree nodded. "I understand. I'll grab a blanket from the linen closet and crash on the couch."

Toni frowned at her remark. Tyree and Toni weren't shy with each other and weren't above sharing a bed. They'd done that since they were children. They knew how to respect each other's space by staying on their side.

Tyree must have deciphered her look because she stated, "Bitch, I know you don't think I'm sleeping in there with you after you and that man were doing God knows what in there."

eight

The smell of bacon welcomed Tyree when she made it to the front of the condo. Her stomach growled; the aroma awakened the hunger within her. After the eventful day and night with Kamaal, she needed to refuel.

After eating as much of her breakfast as she could, Tyree scraped her untouched food into the trash can and began washing the dishes. She grinned when she felt Kamaal's arms wrap around her waist. A sigh escaped her parted lips as she leaned her back into his front, and her lower abdomen fluttered. Tyree smiled when she felt Kamaal drop his head and place a soft kiss right below her ear. His arms moved from her waist and rested on top of her flat stomach.

"When are you going to give me a daughter, Ms. Morris?" he whispered in her ear.

Tyree turned her neck, meeting Kamaal's eyes with hers.

"Whenever Ms. Morris turns into Mrs. Duval," she challenged. "The title of Kamaal Omari Duval's baby's mama is taken. I'm trying to be your wife." *Not wifey.*

Kamaal tilted his head back and squinted his eyes. He chuckled. "All right, little baby, I got you on that wedding, then you gotta give me like three jits." He rubbed her stomach as if his seed already took shelter there.

"Yeah, we'll see about that," Tyree laughed. She turned back to the dishes that sat soaking in the sink.

―――――∽∘∾―――――

Tyree opened her eyes and welcomed a new day. Already, she missed the pleasantries of dreaming about one of her favorite memories with Kamaal. The whimsicalness of her dream waned, and her depressing reality was a stark reminder of how she'd been blindsided by the two people closest to her. A blow blasted through her chest when she thought about Kamaal's treachery. His cheating and bold-faced lying about it competed to be the most detrimental hurt she'd experienced that day. She didn't have the time to determine what hurt her more. Toni's compliance with Malcolm's treason against his vows had been the second letdown. Yesterday had been Snaky Sunday. She was surrounded by strangers.

She raised her arms and stretched before checking her phone. Her eyes bugged at the sight of her notifications bar. There were thousands of updates from one app alone. Blog posts and comments about Hakeem's interview had her timelines in a frenzy. After being fed up with the constant chiming, Tyree had silenced her phone and was able to get some sleep with one less thing impeding that process.

She could hear Toni moving around in the kitchen, most likely in a rush because everything she did had to include a dramatic flair. That's who Toni was. Tyree wanted to speak to her before she left for work and, with much effort, forced herself from the couch and into the bathroom.

Tyree completed the morning grooming routine that consisted of relieving herself, brushing her teeth, washing her face, and throwing on clothes. She didn't have anything to do today so she put on a plain tank and pair of leggings. Her foot had just touched the hallway when Toni called her name.

"What's up?" Tyree answered while she made her way up front.

"Package!" Toni hollered back.

Tyree walked into the great room. "What are you doing here?" she asked Kamaal, who was standing in Toni's living room. A plain white tee stretched across his wide solid chest; the sleeves could barely contain his robust biceps. Two carats of the clearest diamonds glistened in each ear. His impressive print bulged in his grey sweatpants; he was on a mission. She moved her eyes from his pelvic area to his face. His expression was sorrowful, his golden eyes full of remorse. Him popping up without notice didn't afford her the opportunity to prepare herself and secure the lock on the security wall she erected around her heart and libido.

Toni retreated into her kitchen and Tyree walked over to him for auditory purposes only. She preferred to relay the tête-à-tête to her friend later rather than her being a silent participant. Toni obviously caught her drift because she turned on her speaker to help drown out their discussion. The historical instrumental that sent NWA to fame began, but instead of Eazy-E telling the story about him cruising down the street in his six-four, Trina "The Baddest Bitch" told the tale about trying to figure out why a nigga was at her door.

Kamaal squinted; she knew he hadn't missed the motive.

"Fuck Boy" was his diss track. Tyree kept her face humorless and acted as if the song choice was purely coincidental.

"I figured you needed this." He held up her Prada galleria tote. "And I wanted to talk to you."

Tyree stepped forward and took her purse, glad that he thought to bring it because she refused to go to his house. Now she didn't have to offer to transfer money to Toni so she could have cash on hand.

"Thanks for bringing my purse, but I don't think there's anything else we need to talk about."

The volume of the song turned up a few notches. Subtle but noticeable. The Baddest Bitch continued to berate Mr. Duval on the track. The line about an ex crying on her voicemail was timed perfectly.

"I understand you not having anything to say to me, but if you would please listen, Ty. I—"

A loud bang sounded, immediately followed by the sirens of a car's alarm system. Kamaal looked out of Toni's window and growled.

"What the hell was that?" Tyree asked. Kamaal walked past her without blinking in her direction as he advanced to the front door. He snatched the handle back and rushed outside, still ignoring Tyree who called his name.

Toni walked out of the kitchen. "Did you hear that?"

"Yes, Kamaal went outside, and I think I should go check on him."

Tyree gasped in disbelief once she stepped outside. Her eyes were like a pinball, bouncing off each point of interest before flying to the next object in an attempt to process what was happening. Beside Tyree's car was Kamaal's truck, which was blocked in by a sleek orange Audi sports car that was parked at a crooked angle, with the front axis slanted across the driveway. The back half of the car stuck out in the street as if the owner had driven erratically.

"Damn," she hissed, noticing the front bumper of the car dented from the impact of colliding with her friend's mailbox.

Tyree didn't have a clue who the driver was, but it was obvious that Kamaal knew. He stomped down Toni's driveway, a hostile scowl on his face. The driver's door opened, and Hakeem Sanders stepped out and appeared to be prepared for an altercation.

"Fuck this shit!" Kamaal pulled his pants up on his waist and uttered a string of vulgarities.

Tyree hadn't seen this side of Kamaal before. Yeah, he was a beast on the field, but this was way more threatening. There were no rules, no penalties, no referees, only anger and opportunity. She grew increasingly nervous. The animosity in Hakeem's eyes told her he should not be underestimated. He looked like a man with a score to settle, like he was about to confront the man who fucked his wife.

"You put that shit out, didn't you?" Hakeem walked toward Kamaal, not bothering to close his car door. "You an ol' tit-for-tat ass nigga, huh?"

Tyree made her way to the men. She didn't know what Hakeem was talking about, but she for sure didn't want a fight to happen, not here in her best friend's front yard first thing on a Monday morning. Some of Toni's neighbors had caught on to the melodrama as it unfolded. This wasn't good.

She rushed to the guys, who were now face-to-face, and begged, "Please don't do this!" Her screams went ignored as the men continued to charge at each other. Feeling like she had no other choice, she risked it by standing between the two behemoths. She wrapped her arms around Kamaal's neck and urged his head downward until their eyes met. "Please, Kamaal, you've done enough."

"Hakeem!"

The wail captured the attention of all three. Tyree looked back and saw that Simone had also pulled up. She didn't appear as the well-put-together football wife who sat in the same box as her yesterday. Her hair that was in messy wand curls the day before was now tangled and stringy. Her warm, brown face was ashen. She looked like she hadn't slept. She looked the way Tyree felt: like shit.

Seeing his wife near the man she had an affair with seemed to push Hakeem beyond his limits. Taking advantage of the brief distraction, he snuck a fiery fist, snapping Kamaal's head to the right. Kamaal blinked hard twice before regaining his composure. He ate the punch like it was one of Karl's playful jabs he was known to throw when they wrestled around. In a flash, he'd picked Tyree up, moved her out of the line of fire he was about to start, and advanced toward Hakeem. He rushed him and wrapped his arms around him before slamming him to the concrete. You would've thought he was the best defensive tackle in the league. Tyree stood stock-still as she watched the fight happen. She wished she would wake up from this nightmare.

The men tousled on the pavement, both throwing punches and insults. Kamaal had the edge and beat Hakeem's attempts round for round. A few neighbors who had been watching came over to try to break up the fight. Hakeem snatched his arm from Mr. Domino, a retired mailman who lived across the street, and the force sent the poor man flying. He landed face first, the lens of his glasses shattered on the ground.

A few other bystanders came over to assist Mr. Domino before trying to break up the battle. It took five men to pull Kamaal and

Hakeem from each other. With much effort, the group of guys were able to get them to either side of the driveway.

Toni appeared at Tyree's side.

"Aw shit, there goes the property value." Her gaze turned to Simone, who stood crying at the end of her driveway with her gaped mouth cupped in her hands.

"Don't look so shocked. Y'all did this shit. Close your mouth like you should have closed those legs, bucket bitch."

Tyree looked at her friend in bewilderment. *If this ain't the fuckin' pot judging the kettle right here.*

Simone was visibly disturbed by Toni's remark. She closed her mouth and squeezed her eyes shut. She reopened them and turned toward Tyree and took a step.

"I'm so sorry."

"Don't." Tyree held up her hand to cut off any more words. "You feel bad, but you want to take things there with him again, right?"

Simone snapped her head back. The recognition of the words she'd sent to Kamaal hours ago flashed across her face.

"That bitch said that?" Toni's head cocked to the side. Tyree instantly recognized that the persona her best friend kept hidden wanted to make an appearance. Nene only showed up in extreme circumstances, one that required showing one's ass. The metamorphosis was on its way.

Toni scurried to the end of her driveway where Simone stood when two chirps from an approaching patrol car halted her advance. Realizing her opportunity had been missed, she stepped back. The police car was now parked on the curb right beside Simone's car. Toni had never been so relieved to see a police officer until she saw it was one she knew.

"Toni, is everything OK here?" Officer Janine Banks asked as she approached. She and Toni met each other in a hip-hop dance class at their gym and grew to be friends. "We received some complaints about a disturbance. When I heard your address on the radio, I decided to take the call just in case."

"Oh no, not too much of a disturbance. A few choice words, but that's done with now." Toni gestured toward the back of her driveway.

Janine lifted an eyebrow as she surveyed the scene. There were two towering athletes, each with a handful of neighbors huddling around them, no doubt trying to convince them to avoid any more fighting.

"That's good to know that things didn't go further than that and we can all leave this here, but anyone who is not residing at this residence must leave now."

Toni's neighbors dispersed immediately. It was Monday morning, and no one woke up with a booking at county on their agenda. However, Hakeem and Kamaal needed a little more encouragement to get going. Janine coolly made them aware of the scene they caused. All movement on Toni's block ceased; all eyes were on them. They were center stage. Kamaal winced at some of the disapproving looks that were sent their way. It seemed like everyone had their cellphones out recording them. It was time to go.

Simone attended to Hakeem, who had to remove his shirt and use it to stop the blood gushing from his nose and mouth. She tugged on his arm, and thankfully, he followed. He got in his car and pulled off, and Simone followed in hers.

"I don't think I'm needed here anymore," Janine said to Toni. "I'll get going now."

"Thank you for coming. Things could've gone a lot worse if you hadn't been the one to answer the call."

Janine opened her patrol car door and paused before getting inside. "Hey, no problem. Will I see you in class Saturday?"

"9:30 a.m. sharp!" Toni confirmed while waving off her friend as she drove away.

Toni turned back to her house to see Kamaal walking toward his car.

"I'm sorry, T," he muttered.

Her phone vibrated in her pocket, and she pulled it out to check the message.

"See what you did?"

Toni heard Tyree call out to Kamaal's back.

"Tyree . . ." Toni cautiously called. Her eyes stayed glued to the screen.

Tyree ignored her and kept speaking to his back. "This is your fault. Stay the fuck away!"

"Tyree!"

"What, Toni?" Tyree snapped her head back; her face wore aggravation as she yelled back.

"I think you need to see this," she responded, holding up her cellphone.

Tyree took the phone, and Toni watched her crumble right there. She blinked once, then twice as she watched. Her face contorted into a pained scowl as she passed Toni her phone back and rushed inside with her arms cradled across her middle. Toni stood there staring at Kamaal, hoping that every smidgen of disgust and disdain she had for him was legible.

"A hoe gon' be a hoe, and a lame gon' be a lame."

nine

Tyree released the deep breath she'd inhaled as she sank lower into the large tub inside her hotel room. The deep breathing was a technique she used to help her de-stress and decompress. Breathe in peace, clarity, and strength. Breathe out insecurity, sadness, and fear. Inhale relief. Exhale bullshit.

Ten breaths in and out, and she wasn't feeling any lighter, so she decided to go for another round. She had yet to figure out what exercise, breathing technique, or journaling could keep her mind occupied enough to stay away from the awful memories made a week ago.

Inhale. Exhale.

If only she had a magical genie in a lamp. She would ask that the hands of time be turned back to eight days ago, the day before her world had been rocked. The last day she'd gone to sleep happy. She would gladly forfeit her other two wishes for a chance to go back to that oblivious bliss.

Enjoying the way the hot water filled with bath salt made her body feel, she hopped on the express train that navigated to more pleasant times. She thought about the day she met Kamaal. Her and Toni walked through the Jacksonville Fall Fair one late November night, laughing together as they indulged in fatty fair foods. Tyree had just finished up her funnel cake topped with an obscene amount of sweet toppings when a fight broke out in the bumper cars line they were in. Tyree knew there was a risk something like this would happen and turned around when the sign on the fence next to the entrance advised that tonight was teen night.

When the dust settled, all that was left was a sweet little boy, sad and scared. Tyree notified security and waited the twenty minutes it took to locate his father. She refused to leave until she knew he was safe with his parents.

Swift movement out of the corner of her eye made her curiously turn her head to the left. This was his father; the mixture of fear and relief was a tell. And what a sight he was. The man came from the place dreams were made, like he walked off a sex-filled page of a steamy Brenda Jackson novel. He was a walking cliché: talk, dark, and handsome as fuck. Tyree drank him in as he rushed to where she and Toni stood with his son, waiting on him. His mocha-colored skin was rich and smooth, and she suddenly had a taste for hot chocolate. It was obvious he took care of himself. His strong shoulders couldn't be concealed by his pullover. His jet-black hair was cut into a high-low fade, the longer locs on the crown of his head were thick and wavy. His beard and mustache were trimmed close to his face, giving him a rugged yet sophisticated look.

Kamaal was so grateful to Tyree for making sure his son Karl was safe. He repeatedly thanked her for looking out for his child. While he gushed about how worried he'd been, she tried not to fall under the spell his vibrant eyes unintentionally bewitched on her.

She snapped out of her trance when he offered her a wad of

cash from his pocket. It had to be at least five thousand dollars. Tyree refused to take the money, and Kamaal refused to give up. The back and forth lasted for a while until Toni came up with an idea that he take them out to eat as a token of appreciation. Tyree and Kamaal had been inseparable ever since.

Their relationship blossomed into something greater before they realized what took place. Kamaal shocked her when he confessed his feelings to her over a random dinner a month after they met. His confession forced her to deal with the feelings she'd been battling. She warmed as she accepted the fact that she'd fallen hard for him but shuddered when the realization hit her that being in love put a lot at stake. Being in love was a beautiful, painful reminder of what bad can come from it. It was a reminder of how much she lost the last time she gave her heart away to Aiyden. How many times was she going to learn this lesson?

Inhale. Exhale.

A thumping sound on the door pulled her from her reverie. She turned down the volume on the speaker and listened. After a few seconds of silence, she turned the music up a little and proceeded with her soak.

Having strolled enough through her recollection, Tyree ended that trip into her past and vibed with the music she presently listened to. Her head rocked side to side on beat with the sorrowful hit "I Remember." It felt like Keyshia was the only one who knew what she was going through.

I remember when my heart broke.

Tyree remembered that moment; the moment Kamaal dropped his head and shoulders was when she felt it. A blow in the center of her chest took her breath. His nonverbal admission made her heart shatter, the pieces of it scattered at her feet. Then, the fiasco at Toni's house did further damage. She was beginning to know this pain too well. This pain was punctual, appearing when things were going too well to keep her on her toes, to remind her that happiness is temporary.

Another knock.

Tyree stepped out of the tub and took her time to dry off before she dressed in a baggy sleep shirt and leggings. Whoever interrupted her bath was going to have to wait. Five minutes later, she walked to the door, hoping that whoever knocked had gotten the idea and left.

Her pulse quickened when she leaned over and checked the peep hole. Unlike the last time, it was nervous agitation that flowed through her. She wanted to get this over with and begrudgingly opened the door.

"You can't keep doing this, Kamaal," Tyree sighed out. She stood with the door cracked just enough for her hand to tightly grasp the knob.

"I know, it looks crazy, but I need to talk to you, Ty. One talk."

The "crazy" was him showing up to every hotel she stayed at. He took a page out of her book and upped that ante triple-fold. He used his celebrity and his agent's connections to get around the rules and into her business. Kamaal made his presence known wherever she decided to lay her head. When he wasn't present physically, he extended himself through lavish gifts. In the past week, she'd received flowers, purses, steak dinners, and jewelry. She had politely declined all but one. She didn't have the heart to let a good massage go to waste when the masseuse arrived; she gifted it to the newlyweds across the hall.

She gave a tight, polite smile and small nod to a trio of young guys as they walked by in the hallway. Recognition flashed over their faces as they glanced at Kamaal. Once they passed, Tyree spoke.

"Then talk."

Kamaal's shoulders dropped. "I was hoping we could speak in private."

Tyree fixed her mouth to tell him she didn't give a shit what he hoped when the same group of guys came strolling their way again, this time their strides slower.

In awe, the guy stated, "That *is* him. Mack Truck, I am a huge fan. Could we get a picture?"

Kamaal appeared to appreciate the expectant expression the admirer wore, and Tyree figured he felt it only right to oblige him.

"Sure, man." Kamaal's answer was no surprise to Tyree. She'd witnessed him taking time with his fans countless times.

The man's face lit up as he pulled out his phone to take a few selfies. His two friends stood on either side and posed while he alternated angles. Tyree tried to keep the annoyance from her face as she looked on. Kamaal caught her eye and mouthed a silent apology. After a few more pictures, Kamaal politely thanked the men and told them to have a good night.

He turned to her. "Now, could we go inside and speak privately?"

Tyree rolled her eyes and snorted at the arrogant wiggle of his brow as she stepped aside. Kamaal took a seat in the high-back accent chair beside the console table, and Tyree chose to lean against the dresser that doubled as an entertainment center. She crossed her legs at the ankles, and the movement drew Kamaal's attention to her toenails, which were painted a sparkly lilac. She watched his gaze travel up her legs, and she shifted when his eyes lingered on her hips and settled on her middle.

His slow observation caused her to second-guess her choice of clothing. She chose the understated white loose T-shirt because it was comfortable. Tyree looked down at herself and noticed that her bra could be seen through her shirt. The white lace brassiere transformed a plain, uneventful garment into a sexy teaser. Kamaal's approval couldn't be subdued. Even in serious matters such as this, he wasn't too preoccupied to show the desire he had for her. She sighed; that was not her intention.

"Well?" she asked dryly. One brow lifted.

Kamaal sat up straight and got right to it. "Shit ain't right with you not being home, Ty. I know I hurt you and it will take a lot of time and work, but we can get back to where we were before all of this."

Tyree frowned. What was he talking about? He didn't make a little mistake. What he'd done hadn't been a measly petty offense. He'd committed a flagrant foul that resulted in him being ejected from their relationship with no chance at extending that contract. His hopeful grovels frustrated her. Where was this nigga when she gave him his chance?

"I looked you in your eyes and asked you, I begged you, to tell me the truth. I could've forgiven you. I could've learned to trust you again if you had. All you had to do was tell the truth!"

She flinched. He'd made his mistake—a grave one—but one that with work and time could be moved past. He'd crippled her trust by cheating. The attempted cover-up was worse than the crime.

She focused on nothing as her surroundings blurred and she relived the moment where she begged him to be someone she could trust. He'd gazed into her eyes, unflinching, and told a lie. He did it with an ease that only came with much practice and experience. While being introduced to who he really was, she realized she didn't know him at all.

Tyree and Kamaal remained planted in their spots on either side of the room. East Coast versus West Coast in '94. They were back in the Biggie and Tupac beef era. Each side experienced pain but was too prideful to fold, so they remained there and faced off.

"All you had to do was be there!" Kamaal jumped up and challenged with a base so strong she felt it pass through her. A small vein she'd never seen before began to protrude from the center of his forehead. "You knew how hard it was for me to go see him. I couldn't even talk about him, but *you* made me. Always bringing that shit up. You wouldn't stop until I said yes, and I did. All you had to do was be there for me."

Tyree winced from the sting of his words; his outburst alarmed her. Here was what he had kept bottled up. His arms were at his sides. He was being open and vulnerable; she knew he was speaking from his heart. She walked to the other side of the room and sat on the sofa. Being close to him was suffocating her.

"I'm always there for you. Cheering you on at your games, tending to your needs at home, keeping your belly full and your sacs empty." Her teeth clenched; she continued as she spoke through them. "Taking care of your son when you're away. Don't do this to me. Don't act as if I don't live to be there for you." Tears raced down her face. One wrong was more impressionable than a hundred rights. His selective memory was blindly misleading.

She cut her eyes to the side and looked back at him. She needed to break that trance to continue. "Even when I wasn't there with you, I was there for you."

Kamaal didn't respond. His eyes questioned her meaning.

"I didn't make the visit because I was at the doctor, Kamaal. Like I always do, I caved and gave you what you wanted. I got off birth control. The procedure took longer than expected and you left for Baker before I got home. I was going to tell you that night after your game, then everything got crazy."

His head tilted back until his eyes were adjacent to the ceiling. Tyree heard his deep breaths. She watched him lift a robust arm and pinch the bridge of his nose.

"Baby, I am so sorry. I was so messed up that day that I fucked up." He looked down at her. Redness lined the white of his eyes. "It was one time, and I want to make it work with you. I can't lose you, baby. We can't lose you."

He took her hands in his and pulled her forward as he walked backward. His expression softened as he poured from his chest. Her feet betrayed her as they took the steps he urged. He sat on the foot of her bed and leaned forward. His face was buried in the fabric of her shirt that rested over her stomach.

"Kamaal, please." Her voice cracked. Her arms rested on top of his strong shoulders. He ignored her and took a deep breath. He sighed as if her scent pleased his senses.

"Tell me. Tell me what do I have to do? Whatever I can do to make this right, Chelle, you got it." His wide eyes bounced erratically as they searched hers. His nostrils spread as he expectantly perked up. He reminded her of Karl whenever he tried to convince her to give in to his request.

She nudged his chin with bent fingers until they looked in each other's faces. "I need you to be truthful with me."

"I am being truthful, Ty. I messed up, but that's a wrap," he spat out quickly.

"Have there been any others?" The dip in his brows told her he wasn't prepared for the question. "I need to know, Kamaal. There's no way we can move on without me knowing everything. Please don't lie to me again, baby. Tell me." She cursed herself when the corners of her eyes spilled. *Suck that shit up!* She couldn't let him see how he broke her. Where was a rope?

Kamaal pushed air through his nostrils. Again, his hesitation did the damage before the words were spoken. His naked truth was an ugly one. She fought the urge to look away. *Chin up, this is what you asked for.*

"Yes."

One word. One syllable. Three letters dismantled her.

"But that was before." He followed up on one breath. "In the beginning. I know it doesn't make sense, but I had to know if what I felt was only with you. I figured out it was and that all I needed was you."

"Until . . . her," she added.

His shoulders slumped beneath her fingers, causing one defiant tear to slip from her lid. Kamaal had finally done what she yearned for him to do. He opened up to her. He was naked. His every wish would've been her command had he done it sooner. It wouldn't have taken her as long to make the appointment had he shown her he was all in. She could see the promises lingering in his gaze. Their silent language pierced the room. The way he touched her, the way he looked at her, had said it all. She heard him.

Tyree wrapped her hands around his arms and urged him upward. He stood without hesitation, his hands on her waist, and Tyree shook at the recognition of his touch. They were joined front to front without anything to separate them, but Tyree never felt so disconnected, so distant. With his cheeks cupped in her hands, his face followed their command as they pulled his face down until they were inches apart. Two troubled souls shared the space. Their exhales became the other's inhales.

His emeralds were the window to within, and they bore it all. She saw them together; she saw their future. Her walking down the aisle, eyes cloudy and full of love as he stood at the altar. His mini-me at his side. She saw her family. She blinked and could see her belly swollen, his hands rubbing her stomach whenever they were near because he wanted his seed to feel how loved they were. She wept at the future. She could see all the things she wanted, but . . . she could also see more.

She couldn't see the good without the bad. She'd learned this lesson before; Aiyden had been an excellent teacher. The strongest love was the deadliest. Something that could do so much good could also be as prominent in the opposite direction. She also saw what she wished she could un-see: him and *her*. Expectant faces. Frisky hands. She could see him dressing at the foot of her bed, a satisfied smirk on his face. Nothing in his countenance conveyed conviction.

The images that played across Toni's phone would forever haunt her. How could Kamaal be so careless to let the world in? To let Simone in? Elation danced in his orbs as he looked down at her. She knew that look; she saw it many times after they'd had each other. He had been satisfied sexually. Gestures she fancied herself having exclusive rights to were lent to the next woman so freely. She could hear the smacking of lips as he offered quick kisses along with promises to call.

She knew she couldn't do this. She saw herself wave the crisp, white flag.

"I want your lying ass to leave."

ten

Kamaal leaned forward, bracing himself on the shower tiles in front of him. He bowed his head and welcomed the hot water to flow down his body. The high temperature soothed his muscles as it washed his aches down the drain along with the sweat and tiny tire bits that stuck to his damp skin. He closed his eyes, grateful for the peace he found in the moment.

Practice was both physically and mentally grueling. No one came right out and said it, but his coworkers weren't fucking with him in any sense. He'd committed the ultimate sin against his brethren, and he'd paid the price by losing their respect. Teammates who he spoke to daily, both on and off the field, breezed by him as if they could see right through him. His suggestions and feedback went ignored. A sixth-round pick rookie on the practice squad received more favorable treatment than him, and Kamaal didn't blame them. He foolishly allowed his libido to stroke his bruised ego, and it caused him grief in every aspect of his life. Work was hostile as hell, home wasn't home, and even

Karl hadn't taken Tyree's absence well. He had multiple problems to fix with no solution in mind.

After washing off, Kamaal prepared to head home where he could take a real shower. He twisted the water nozzle to its off position and stepped out. He dried off, slipped on his Rick Owens boxers along with the Nike athletic pants he endorsed, and went to collect his items from his locker. On the way out of the shower area, one of the defensive backs bumped Kamaal as he walked in. Kamaal caught himself from his stumble and found his footing. He looked up at the player who stood scowling as he sized him up for seconds before turning away. Both corners of his mouth turned downward in a knowing grimace. He closed his eyes and took a deep breath to gain control of his anger. There were only so many passes he was willing to give, and he was almost out.

"Ain't that 'bout a bitch?" He shook his head and chuckled; he needed humor to tame his anger.

"Not the warmest reception, I see." Malcolm walked in and sat in a chair backward. His chin rested on his folded arms that were propped on the chair's back.

"Icy like ten-seventeen," Kamaal chuckled again. Malcolm lifted his hand and gave a light squeeze of his shoulder.

"It'll wear off, just takes time."

Kamaal appreciated his friend's optimism. "That's what I'm hoping." He pulled his shirt over his head and down his torso. "I need that to be the case here *and* at home."

Malcolm nodded. "No headway with Tyree, huh?"

Kamaal lowered himself onto the padded seat in front of his locker and swiped down his face with his large hands.

"Naw, if anything, I made things worse." His brows bunched and met in the center of his forehead. He thought his relentless pursuit would flatter Tyree, but instead, it pushed her further away. "I just want her back home," he admitted.

"Shit, man. I didn't know it was like that. Where is she now?"

"She's staying at Hyatt out by the airport now. She can't stand me, bruh. She's not accepting the gifts I send her; she checks into another hotel if she finds out I know where she stays. And the last time I saw her . . ." He paused. The flashes in his memory provoked agony in his abdomen. "I don't think I can make this right."

Kamaal and Malcolm didn't notice the man that entered the room and stood on the other side of the wall listening to every word. He had been coming to shower up and head home, but he slowed when he recognized the voices coming from the locker room.

He made a mental note of the details Kamaal provided Malcolm, knowing the information would prove most helpful with his plan. He left with a confident smile. He would shower at home. He wanted to leave immediately, knowing what needed to be done.

eleven

The warmth provided by the sun comforted Tyree's skin like a wool blanket. Today's weather was near perfect, and she didn't want the eighty-degree temp with virtually no cloud coverage to go to waste, which was what led her to the hotel's poolside. She lifted her head and took a sip of her frozen blue margarita.

Tyree lowered her eyelids and listened to the urban romance novel by her favorite author, Chassilyn Hamilton, playing through her earbuds. The voice actor did a phenomenal job bringing the audiobook to life, and she became lost in the story. Her surroundings had been drowned out by the undivided attention she gave the audible literature until the climate cooled.

An object stood above where her head laid, blocking the sun and instantly dropping the temp by a few degrees. Figuring someone walking by had stopped for a second, she ignored it and kept her eyes closed. Another minute passed and the figure that obstructed the sunlight hadn't moved. She lifted her Chanel shades to the top of her head and peered upward, surprised to find the area above her empty. She looked both directions and didn't see anyone in proximity close enough to have been overhead.

Tyree sat up and observed other guests until it was time to meet Toni for lunch. After some time passed, Tyree exited the pool area to return to her hotel room. She walked through a hallway and called for the elevator. A quick look to the left and right confirmed she was there alone, and she continued to listen to her audiobook when, suddenly, her left wrist was grabbed and twisted behind her back, her elbow bent into a ninety-degree angle. Her knuckles were forced below her spine, causing her to flinch. She was then driven forward and crashed into the wall. Her shades shattered on impact.

"What do you want from me?" Tyree hissed through clenched cheeks as the attacker's other hand mushed her face against the wall.

A large rigid body pressed into the back of her. The man was substantially taller than her. His hold on her told her she wouldn't be able to put up much of a fight against his strength. She accepted her fate and silently hoped he was the type that left his victims alive when he was finished.

"Shhh, don't be scared, baby," a rugged voice said, unsuccessfully trying to calm her. "Me and you can give them both a taste of their own medicine." One of his hands circled her and rubbed up her shirt. His cold fingers were rough, and the gritty skin scratched where he caressed her. "Shit, baby. I can treat this body right."

Tyree gasped. She was chilled by the proposition, disgusted by the contact, and confused by the familiarity of his voice. Had she heard it before?

"Hey, man, what the hell are you doing? Get away from her!"

The family Tyree had seen in the pool walked up on her

assault. The attacker, spooked by the unexpected witnesses, ran off and left Tyree stuck against the wall. She didn't know what to do; she was just thankful for the intervention. Without any words to say, she crumbled and slid down to the floor as a hotel attendant rushed to help.

After her attacker had been scared off, Tyree was escorted to her room, where the hotel manager called the cops and waited there with her. Tyree was still in a state of shock, and the manager thought it was best to call someone to come be there. Luckily, she already had plans to meet Toni, and she showed up right as the police officers did. Due to the nature of the attack, the officer suggested she leave the hotel and go somewhere else, preferably not alone.

Toni immediately suggested that she move in with her until things died down, giving her time to figure out her next move. Tyree declined the invitation, reminding her of the mess that was made when she stayed there last time. The videos bystanders took of the fight between Hakeem and Kamaal had gone viral before lunch time. Every local news outlet reported from the street in front of Toni's home. When she'd called the police for them to intervene, they advised that the street was public property and the reporters unfortunately weren't wrong as long as they did not cross the threshold to her driveway. For two days, there was some type of news coverage reported from her block. Toni had been approached by journalists asking for a comment whenever she left and arrived home.

"Absolutely not," she declined verbally, in case the eager shake of her head wasn't convincing enough.

An eye roll accompanied her frustrated breath. "And why not?"

"I refuse to bring drama back to your front door, T. There was already too much going on between Kamaal, Hakeem, and the reporters last week. Now, I have to hope that crazy man doesn't come after me again. I don't want my mess taking over your life, and I won't do that to your cousin."

She trembled as she thought about the attack. She wanted to believe it was random, but the words the man breathed on her said otherwise. She couldn't put her friend at risk by staying there.

Seeing that Tyree was set in her decision to not move back in with her, Toni offered a plan B by way of a room at her cousin's house in St. Augustine, a neighboring city. The money Kamaal previously deposited into her account was dwindling down with each night she stayed at the hotel. At the rate she was going, her funds wouldn't make it to the end of the week.

"Tyree, trust me. It's no big deal. St. Augustine is far enough from the chaos around here but not too far where you're out of reach." Her arms waved as she presented her case. "I've already talked to my cousin, and it's fine. Please take the time away from this mess to figure out your next move."

Tyree's leg bounced as she pondered. In eight measly days, she went from waking up in a six-bedroom, seven-and-a-half-bathroom mini mansion on the beach to living out of suitcases like she was on the run. Nothing had been the same. She felt that saying she was homeless was a reach, but when she thought about it, it was the truth. She had no home—literally or figuratively.

She still wasn't sold on the idea; the way she nibbled on the corner of her mouth translated her indecisiveness.

"I don't know. I need to think about it. I would feel better talking to your cousin before I made my decision."

"That's fair." She checked the time on her watch. "We can call later today; he should be off soon."

Tyree's head jerked back, and she swore she heard a snap. "*He*? Toni, you never said he was a *he*!" Her nibble had been for a reason. Her senses picked up on the bullshit before it had been made known.

Toni rolled her eyes and smacked her glossed lips as if Tyree had overreacted.

"I never said he was anything. I merely said my cousin."

Tyree scrutinized her friend's words. Toni had purposely not used any gender-revealing pronouns when proposing her plan. *Slick ass.*

Tyree swallowed and looked away. She focused on the magazine that offered the hotel's amenities and hoped the distraction would overtake the hopelessness that crept up her spine. "That's not going to work, T."

"Why not?"

Tyree slumped on the desk chair. "Because I can't stay with some random man. Plus, I'm not working now, and I can't really help with bills." She hissed through clenched teeth.

Toni waved off her words. "He's not a random man; he's my cousin. You don't know him only because he didn't grow up here. He moved down from Chicago a few months ago for work." She tilted her head to the side and sent her a pointed look. "And as far as money goes, I told him this is a favor to me. You are not expected to pay any bills. Only take care of you and get on your feet."

Tyree contemplated the offer. After a quick inventory of her options, she recognized there weren't any others. Kamaal showing up with the ratchet convoy had threatened the property value in Toni's neighborhood, and now she had a lunatic to worry about. She needed distance. Sometimes it felt like the walls were caving around her. She thought about the only other place she could go and instantly dreaded the idea. She would sit outside a shelter downtown before she asked for her mother's family for help. They ended any chance of a relationship with her when they disowned her mother for getting pregnant at sixteen. They could forever kiss her ass.

"The only other place you could go is Texas, and you know you're not going there," Toni replied as if she could hear what Tyree had been thinking.

Tyree squinted. "Get out of my head."

"Sorry, toots, I can't. Blame it on the vibe." She cocked her head before walking to stand beside her. "T-N-T?"

Tyree studied Toni's unfolded pinky finger with the letters T, N, and T in permanent ink down the length of its side. Bored at Tyree's house, they helped themselves to her dad's rum and came up with the bright idea to commemorate their friendship and celebrate Toni's nineteenth birthday at a tattoo shop. The nickname was birthed from Toni's mom, Mary, who used to say the twosome didn't play about each other. When you tried one, you had to deal with the other, and that wasn't an easy feat. Both girls were passionate and protective over each other, and when they fought a battle, you were met with an energetic force of substantial proportion. It was like dynamite.

Tyree hooked her matching finger with Toni's.

"T-N-T," she repeated.

The matter had been settled. Their initials were their safe word—not as a relief from sexual experiments but as a promise. They didn't swear to God, but if they did, T-N-T held that weight. It was of the caliber of "on my mama"; there was no going back. A shake of a finger said, "Bullshit aside, I got you." Toni wanted to let Tyree know that while her proposal wasn't one of the usual sorts, she felt it was a necessary one . . . and that, Tyree knew she could trust. She was close, but she needed more time for consideration.

"We'll see."

"Where is she?!" a deep voice demanded from outside Tyree's hotel room door. She could hear someone trying to calm the man down. She knew the attempt hadn't worked when the baritone yelled, "Fuck all that. I need to see her *now!*"

The officer who took Tyree's statement half an hour ago walked over to the door to assess what was happening. The bass in Kamaal's voice boomed louder into her room now that the door was left slightly ajar.

"Officer," Tyree called out and the man turned to her. "You can let him in; he's fine."

The officer appeared happy to oblige her and opened the room's door wider in time for her to see Kamaal snatching his arm from another policeman before turning around and stepping toward the man. Kamaal invaded the officer's space as he towered over him by at least a foot. Her pulse quickened when the cop's hand went to his waistline.

"Kamaal!"

He snapped his head up in her direction and ran into the room, bumping anyone who stood in his way without so much as a sideways glance. All his attention was on where Tyree sat. He didn't even regard Toni who was standing right beside her.

He took Tyree's hands into his and clasped them against his firm chest. His only movements were the soft rise and fall of his chest as he took breaths. His eyes scanned over her, completely taking inventory of her. She knew he had to see she was fine.

"Are you OK?"

She swallowed while nodding in affirmation. She didn't trust herself to speak. She was rocking on the edge. *Keep it together.*

For the first time, he turned his attention to someone else in the room. "Do you have the guy who did this?"

The officer cleared his throat once he recognized he'd been asked the question.

"Not yet. We're working on identifying him, then we'll begin our search."

Kamaal's brows met in the center of his forehead. "Can't you just look at the security camera footage?"

"Yes, that's where we will begin; however, in most cases, the camera footage is grainy and doesn't help much. We're working plans A *and* B until we determine the most efficient way of going about this. We're putting all of our resources into shedding light on this situation."

Toni gathered her things and turned to Tyree. "I need to run; you'll be all right here until I make it back later?" She searched Tyree's face for any sign of opposition to being left alone with Kamaal.

Tyree stood up and hugged Toni. "Yes, I'll be fine. Take your time," she answered confidently.

She would never pick up the phone and ask that he come, but the relief she felt hearing Kamaal outside her door let her know this was OK . . . for now.

"My bad, Toni," Kamaal said, having just noticed her presence. "Thank you for coming. Malcolm drove me here and can walk you to your car."

Toni's shrug in response to Tyree's raised brow told her she had no idea of her secret lover's presence.

"That's nice of him, and I feel better knowing you won't be walking to your car alone with that crazy man out there. Tell him thank you for me." Tyree was sincere. Differences aside, her friend's safety exceeded all.

The officers finished up their initial reports and left shortly after Toni, advising they would follow up with any updates. Kamaal suggested she go freshen up while he waited, and Tyree didn't object. Knowing he would be there was comforting. She wasn't ready to be alone. She studied herself in the reflection, thankful that she didn't look like what she's been through the past week and a half.

To her, she looked like Tyree, a woman whose pieces were starting to fit together in her puzzle of life, a woman who finally found a love that was all hers, which came with a bonus of two individuals who gave her life purpose. She appeared as a woman who knew what she wanted, and with the love that surrounded her, she had the determination to get it. She recently decided to return to school to get the last few credits she needed to get her bachelor's degree.

She didn't look like a woman whose man humiliated her in both public and private, a woman who'd hopped hotels while on the run from the one who hurt her most. Aside from the bruises from where her neck was squeezed, one wouldn't know how she narrowly avoided an attack in the hallway. Her life had taken an unexpected sharp left turn, and she longed for it to veer back right.

Feeling tired of the dispiritedness she'd been unable to shake off these past few days, Tyree wanted to feel different, to feel better. Genies didn't exist, so it was up to her to make her wish come true, and she had an idea.

twelve

Kamaal fought to keep a cool composure as he watched Tyree glide across the room. She hadn't bothered to dry off after her shower, and his brow began to glisten as her smooth skin did. Droplets of water clung to her body, and the coolness of the air caused tiny bumps to raise on her skin. He never wanted to be two hydrogen atoms and one oxygen atom in all his twenty-four years, but damn did he envy Zephyrhills right about now.

"What are you doing, Tyree?" Kamaal forced out on a craggy breath. *Please don't be playing a cruel joke.* Retribution from Tyree was expected, but he feared he couldn't handle this temptation. His erection pressed against his pant leg, begging for release. It throbbed to the point of pain. He wouldn't survive a tease. Maybe it was best he left. Kamaal's eyes swept Tyree's curves that poked from the bottom of the linen towel, and he dismissed the notion as quickly as it came. He knew he wasn't going any-damn-where.

Her eyes lowered to the twist of the towel that kept it wrapped around her body. A world of possibilities flashed through his mind as she toyed with the fabric of the plush towel that barely covered her body.

"I want to forget about the past few weeks for a little while. I know you can do that for me." Her steps became more certain the closer she got to him.

"Tyree," he muttered. "I don't think this is a good idea. You're upset about the attack."

Her beautiful brown eyes rolled up to him, filled with a desire he was familiar with. Her round orbs showed him the need that swirled through her. It communicated the turmoil that could only be remedied by pleasure.

"I just want to feel better for a little while. Help me take some of the pain away."

Kamaal gnawed at the inside of his cheek. Tyree possessed liquid sunshine between her thighs, and he was all too familiar with the benefits of vitamin D. But even he knew this wasn't the most ethical way to escape the trauma she'd experienced. So, why was it so hard to do the honorable thing by tucking her in and walking out of the door?

"Kamaal?"

He quivered at the yearning that rode on his name when she said it. His mouth filled with saliva as he watched her dainty fingers loosen the knot of her towel before it fell to the floor.

His eyes were stapled to her full breasts. He could see her cocoa nipples pebble under his gaze. He rubbed his tongue across his top teeth, suddenly hungry. The only morsel capable of satisfying his craving stood bare before him, and she unashamedly offered herself to him. He eyed the smooth juncture between her thighs; his tongue twitched with the need to taste it.

"Aw shit," Kamaal uttered as that straw broke the hump day camel's back right along with his resolve. He rushed her, charging toward her the same way his opponents advanced on him in the red zone. The play clock struck zero, and Tyree removing the towel was the hiking of the ball. It was play action.

———◁○▷———

Tyree blinked and she was sprawled out on the bed with her wide receiver hovering over her. His golden gaze penetrated her defense as it wandered over her face. The tenderness moved her. She wondered if he looked at Simone like that.

She forced those insecurities away. Her mission was designed on a path that would ultimately lead to another unfulfilled night for her.

"Does this hurt?" Kamaal cupped the back of her head with his hand and used his thumb to lightly brush across her temple and the quarter-sized bruise there from being slammed against the wall. His voice was calm and steady, but the fury behind his eyes couldn't be concealed.

Tyree shook her head, then placed a light kiss in his palm. The protector in him was assuring but not what she needed in that moment. She needed the tongue master, the well-endowed, long-winded, generous pleaser.

"You feel good for me, baby, OK?"

He nudged her head to the side and sucked on the delectable skin there. His tongue traveled down her neck, tracing the areas she'd studied in the bathroom mirror. He gave special attention to the bruises with his firm sucking. It was then that Tyree realized what he was doing. He was replacing old bruises with new ones. He concealed her pain with pleasure. The realization caused her nose to feel a prickle that she quickly sniffed away. *Why couldn't he have cared this much when he broke my heart?*

His kisses journeyed down the center of her chest until his mouth sat between her breasts. He turned right and indulged in the mound he favored. He quickly lapped around her chocolate areola before pulling her nipple between his lips. He flicked the bud with his tongue and blew a low breath, the coolness of the breeze meeting his saliva, causing it to constrict. He kissed to the left and gave the same treatment to the twin. Quick kisses continued down her stomach, and Tyree's anticipation grew with each peck.

He pushed her knees further apart and slid down her body until he settled in her open lap. She grew hot as she watched him lick his lips while openly admiring her. He puckered his lips and blew a soft breath on her opening, the warmth of the air sending chills up her spine. Before she could recover from the sensuous gust, his mouth planted firmly onto her and *bon appétit.*

"Mhmm," Tyree moaned.

He sucked on her as if it were the last piece of sweet potato pie on the day after Thanksgiving. She looked down to see that his face from his nose down was blocked; only the top half of his face was visible as he tasted her. She was wildly disgusted and turned on by it at the same time.

"Ohhh."

She pressed her back into the mattress and thrusted her hips further into his face. He continued to lap her up, alternating his strokes with no method. It was madness. Slow strokes were followed by long licks. As soon as she grew accustomed to his rhythm, he switched it on her, delaying her eruption.

"Fuck, you taste good, Chelle," Kamaal murmured with his lips on hers. Tyree's legs twitched; his audaciousness was an accelerator to her satisfaction.

She reached down and gripped the back of his head when heat

spread from her center and baked her internally. *I can't live without this.* She loved how he loved her this way. Kamaal, being the experienced and generous lover he was, knew that different parts of the anatomy brought about different responses, all important and needn't be rushed.

Kamaal continued to dine on her and brought her to total satisfaction over and over. His tongue drew figure eights, starting at the top of her clit and ending between her cheeks. There wasn't a crevice of hers he hadn't feasted on, and it didn't take long for her to become comfortable with something she once thought was taboo. She squeezed her eyes shut and saw stars behind her lids. Twinkles of pleasure coursed through her, and she held the back of his head tighter as she thrusted her pelvis further into his mouth. Kamaal picked up his pace and didn't relent until he heard her whimpers, the ones she made when she'd given all she had. Her last satisfied cry had been the signal to end the game.

She was descending from her orgasmic high when he positioned himself above her. With her hands, she spread her lips open, giving him unobstructed access. Kamaal swatted her hands away, the knitting of his brows told her he didn't need any help. He'd been on this ride countless times and knew his way around her valley. He held her gaze and entered her with one smooth thrust. Her arms circled his neck, and he followed her urge, bringing his face right above hers. The sea of emotion that swam in his gaze flooded her; the strong waves pushed the torment from her mind. The flame he created in her belly left no space for her to ponder her incident. Nothing else mattered.

Kamaal rolled his hips, and his steel touched every ounce of her with each stroke.

"Gaaaa!" She threw her head back and took off.

She didn't remember much after she came. The bliss had been

blinding, and she had to blink it away to get a glimpse of him above her. He loved her thoroughly, completely. Coition with him sapped her of all her strength. After he jerked from his release, he rained kisses over her face. The touch was soothing and ushered her into the best sleep she'd had in a week.

Through haze-filled eyes, she watched Kamaal return to her with a white towel in his hand. She felt the warm, soft fibers of the towel glide across her skin as he wiped. After he cleaned her, he used a fluffy bath skirt to pat her skin dry. With hardly any effort, Kamaal gathered Tyree in his arms and picked her up to lay her under the covers.

She wasn't ready to face him yet; she wanted to ride the high a little longer.

"I think that it . . . that . . . it was Hakeem that attacked me." Tyree whispered the words without realizing the weight of them. The endorphins caused loose lips.

Kamaal went still. He turned to her slowly. "Why would you think that?"

"I can't say for certain, but I swear it was him because he told me that me and him could get revenge on them both together. I think he was talking about you and . . . her." Tyree couldn't say Simone's name, she refused.

Kamaal grunted and dropped his head in a slow half nod. "Did you tell the police that?"

She shook her head. "I don't think that's enough to give his name to the police."

In these scary days, calling 911 could place one in a life or death situation. She couldn't send an investigation Hakeem's way from a loose assumption.

He's thinking, lost in words she could see zip through his mind. She couldn't decipher them, but she discerned his mood.

He was pissed. She could see he did what he could to tame the beast, needing to leave before he lost his grip.

He leaned over her and placed a peck at her temple. "There's some things I need to tend to. Are you going to be all right here?"

She met his golden stare and nodded.

"Good." He released a breath. He rubbed his fingers over her knuckles, and she was moved by the intimate gesture. "I had to be sure you were all right. No matter what, your protection is my responsibility."

His words floored her. How dare he make a statement about protecting her when this mess began and ended with him? He hadn't protected her heart; he juggled it with his ego, carelessly tossing them about in the air until he slipped up and left her shattered. He hadn't been there to protect her today, and there was no telling where she could have ended up if the assaulter hadn't been spooked. She shivered at the thought of the gruesome possibilities.

The last time they saw each other, Kamaal poured his heart and soul out to her. He left them both at her feet as he finally let her in wholly, completely. He'd given her more of himself in a few minutes than he had ever done during their two years together, and she couldn't help but be moved by his dedication to her. Her eyes prickled. Her throat loaded with emotion. Afraid she would ask him to stay, she opted to keep her mouth closed. A gentle nod gave her answer.

He grinned, and she shifted to rid the pulsing in her pussy. That moment had passed. A subtle lift of his brow told her the adjustment and the reason for it wasn't missed.

"Good. Get some rest and I'll check on you later."

He gave her one last glance before walking out of the room. He looked regretful as if him walking out of her room was the hardest thing he had to do. Tyree pulled on all of her self-control to keep her lips clamped together. She didn't want to be alone, but she couldn't ask him to stay. That would lead to more things she wasn't willing to budge on. She'd already muddied the waters by backsliding into bed with him. This was dangerous.

As if the clicking of the door released the cap she used to bottle up her weakness, she cracked. For an hour straight, Tyree released her despair. She cried until her eyes had nothing left to give. When her shallow breaths returned to normal, she picked up her phone and sent Toni a text.

I'll stay with your cousin.

thirteen

"We as a state must do better."

Tyree adjusted in her seat as she pulled down the sun visor. The two cruised down I-95 while listening to Charlamagne Tha God. He was once again giving the Sunshine State the dreaded title of *Donkey of the Day* due to someone's stupid actions.

"It's just embarrassing at this point."

Toni turned down her radio once commercials began playing.

After she recovered from the humiliation brought on by a weak moment with Kamaal, Tyree squared her shoulders, determined to get away as quickly as possible. The soul tie Kamaal had on her was a double-knotted constrictor with no chance of loosening, not while she was in his midst. Being around him decimated her resolve. She needed to be delivered from Mr. Duval and hoped that moving out of the county with the same name would yield that result. The day after her attack, she sent Kamaal a text asking that he give her the space she needed to heal, and was grateful that he complied and did not contact her. She was able to spend the next week getting her things together in preparation of her move.

She became serious. "I want to thank you again for your help, Toni. You and your cousin really came through for me."

"And again, you don't have to thank me, Ty. You're my sister, and I got you. I know I don't need to, but I want to remind you that you can always stay with me," Toni replied, keeping her eyes on the road.

Tyree kept quiet and kept her self-loathing remark to herself. She tried to not kick herself whenever she thought about her predicament, but there was no one else to do it and she needed a kick in the ass. How had she allowed herself to rely on a total stranger for shelter because she fully let herself go while in her relationship?

She hadn't let herself go in the physical sense; her appearance was a facet that had leveled up. Being taken care of by Kamaal had afforded her the luxury of not needing a job. He was a man who worked tirelessly to achieve the things he wanted and felt he deserved in life.

The word "no" wasn't said to him often. Tyree discovered that when she told him she wasn't available to take an impromptu flight to Cabo for a weekend. He'd shown up at her job and whisked her away to the Caribbean anyway. Tyree hadn't looked back since and fully relied on her man. She'd neglected essential things, like her credit score and employment history, both of which were necessary for her to get a place in her name.

What would her parents think? Would her mother look down from heaven, heart heavy with the guilt of leaving her daughter too soon? For loving a man who didn't have any sisters growing up or any experience that would help him with the things that came with having a little girl, with what it required to raise a daughter? Would her father be disappointed that his baby girl, his only child, hadn't heeded to the lessons he taught her about her worth and being able to provide for herself so no one had the opportunity to hold it over her head?

Before Kamaal, Tyree had been working on establishing herself as an adult. After the death of her father, what was intended to be a semester-long break from school for bereavement ended up being permanent. Her drive diminished and continuing an education seemed pointless, which led to her dropping out of college. Looking back at it, she knew it was depression that caused her discouragement in school. It was time to do what her father taught her: take care of herself.

She brushed her thumb across the two ocean waves tattooed on the inside of her left wrist—one for her father, one for her mother. The beach held some of the fondest memories for her. She thought about them every time her eyes met the inked memorial. Her chest ached at the thought of how she'd let them down; it seemed most of the decisions she made these days lacked good sense. That, she would change as quickly as possible.

"It's not a big deal, I promise." Toni's response pulled her from her mental chastisement. "There hasn't been anyone around there to take pictures since last week, and I'm not finding nearly as many requests for exclusive interviews at my door these days."

"I know it must be hard for your married boyfriend to make drive bys." Tyree crossed her arms and looked out of the window. Toni cut her eyes toward her and narrowed them. "What? Don't get mad at me, T. You know that's some bullshit, right? You know that makes you just like Simone? Even worse?"

Toni's face twisted as she gulped back emotion. The guilt couldn't be concealed. Tyree inwardy sighed, seeing that her friend had some kind of conscience regarding her fault in the matter, even though it may be deficient.

"Look," Toni sighed. "Me and Malcolm just happened, and I know this can't go on forever. I'm just working through some things and would appreciate it if I wasn't judged by my best friend while I try to figure it out, OK?"

Tyree heard the tremble in her voice and knew her friend was at her brink. She would dial back for now because she was sure she would join her in a crying fit and she didn't have the energy.

"OK."

Tyree looked out of the window at a billboard that caught her eye. Her eyes met the verdant ones that she'd fallen under spell of countless times. Kamaal stood fourteen feet high with a growl on his face and a football in his grip. She was captivated by the enlarged face of the man who she'd wanted to run to and from.

Toni followed Tyree's eyes to the billboard as they passed it.

"OK, now, this is getting really freaky. Let's get away." She accelerated the gas and switched lanes as if the billboard was in pursuit of her car.

Tyree shook her head and laughed. Her laughter sobered as she recalled the things she didn't know about Toni's cousin who had agreed to put her up for a while. Dealing with getting her things from the house when she knew Kamaal was away and working with the police on her case had her overwhelmed the past week. She had a lot of questions to ask but knew it was pointless now.

"Tell me a little about your cousin," Tyree stated, deciding that some information would help.

Toni signaled and exited the highway. Once she made a complete stop at the traffic light, she turned toward Tyree.

"He's twenty-three, a year older than us, and he works for a trucking company."

"Is he single?" Tyree watched Toni's eyebrow raise in curiosity.

"Not that I'm looking; I'm not trying to deal with any jealous girl-friend—or boyfriend—drama."

"As far as I know, he's single so there won't be any girlfriend *or boyfriend* drama."

"Good." Tyree nodded. "How long has he lived in St. Augustine?"

"Not long. He got back here some months ago."

"Back here? He lived here before?" Tyree frowned. "Toni, who is this cousin?"

Toni cleared her throat and turned her attention back to the road as the light changed to green. "I need to get some gas right quick." She whipped her car into a gas station and hopped out.

Tyree frowned; she knew Toni was acting weird, but she couldn't figure out why. She thought about Toni's peculiar behavior as the sound of her phone notification intruded her recall. She swiped down her notification bar and read the update. It was Kamaal with a five-thousand-dollar CashApp deposit. Tyree rolled her eyes at the passive-aggressiveness of his giving. He could've transferred the funds with the bank internally, but he knew sending it this way would get her attention. Her theory was confirmed by the memo message that came with it: *Please come home.*

Tyree had blocked him on all her social media accounts. She even set up her inbox to file any emails from him into her spam folder. She hadn't thought of blocking him from the money transfer service, and it was so Kamaal to find a way to get to her. Blog websites ran off in the wind with stories about what happened with Kamaal, Hakeem, and Simone. Tyree knew that her not following Kamaal online would add fuel to the true and fake stories, but she didn't care. She was tired of looking the part for the benefit of his brand. *Fuck that brand.*

She transferred the funds into her savings account with a disgusted turn of her lips. She hated the fact that she needed Kamaal as much as she hated the man himself. Like R. Kelly supporters who refused to give up their two-steps and line dances at family reunions, she would separate the man from his work. One day, she wouldn't need him. She promised herself that.

Toni got back inside the car after she filled it up and pulled back onto the street. She turned the radio up and sipped on her ICEE.

"As you were saying," Tyree said, twisting the radio's volume knob to the left to turn it down.

"We're still on this?" Toni put her drink down in the cupholder and placed both her hands back on the wheel. "What more do you want?"

"His name, Toni!" Tyree yelled. "Why is that so hard?"

"It's not as if knowing his name will change the fact that we are ten minutes away from his house with my truck loaded down with all the red bottoms and Chanel bags you could fit. But his name is Tyrion Weber."

"Tyrion? That's a different name," Tyree observed.

Toni turned down a road that transitioned from asphalt to cobblestone. Healthy palm trees lined the street that dead ended to a huge pond with water sprouting from a fountain that sat in the middle. The neighborhood was new and crisp, every aspect clean and every detail cared for.

"Speaking of your cousins . . ." Tyree unlocked her phone and searched a name she hadn't spoken out loud in years. "I wonder what another one of yours has been up to."

"Aiyden?" Toni's head snapped in her direction. "Why the sudden curiosity?"

She lifted her shoulder innocently. "No specific reason. It's been, what, four years? I'm curious about what he's up to." Her eyes stayed on the passing scenery as she felt Toni's eyes on her.

"He hasn't been up to much; he wasn't the last time we spoke a few weeks ago."

Tyree didn't respond and began her search. She'd gotten over the man years ago and yet her fingers trembled as she composed his name. Not once did she allow her flashbacks to push her to do what she was doing now.

She sucked in a quick breath once the search results populated. The name brought up a page full of results, but her eyes were immediately drawn to the third option. The profile picture was tiny, but she knew it was him.

"What's wrong with his page? There's no profile pic, but I can't see any posts."

Toni glanced over quickly. "That means that you, my dear, are blocked. And we're here."

She parked beside a white Camaro that sat in a driveway of a moderately sized single-story home. The warm tone of the light brown exterior paint and the white and blue accents gave it an inviting look. The house looked like a home for a family of three or four, not the place she would picture for a bachelor.

"You can go ahead and start grabbing your stuff, and I'll let him know we're here." Toni cut off her truck's engine and walked up to the front door.

Tyree exited the car and stretched her limbs. With the running around and the forty-five-minute drive to get there, she needed it. She opened the back seat of the car and pulled her purse and duffle bag out.

"I can't believe that nigga blocked me," she said to herself.

They hadn't seen each other in years, but he felt the need to seek out her IG and make sure she was blocked when he was the one who messed everything up by betraying her? He had the black-ass audacity to behave like he needed to hinder her access to his weak-ass account. Like he was throwing the most lit rooftop party that brought the city out and she was the one who couldn't get past the velvet rope. It bothered her how bothered she was with the development. But it was fine. She'd archive this memory of him like she did all the others and keep it pushing.

Tyree heard the front door to the house open and chose to keep her back to it while she checked on her belongings. Finding out she was blocked threw her mood into a petty funk, and she needed a few moments to shake it off before she met Toni's cousin. She didn't want bitchiness to be the first impression she gave.

Toni met her at the truck and grabbed a few of the shoe boxes that were stacked behind the driver seat.

"He's putting on some shoes, and he'll be out to help us. Go right inside."

Tyree walked to the house and used her foot to push the door open.

"Hello?" she called out into the home while looking around. The house was put together; it looked like a bachelor pad: leather furniture, not enough color; it lacked a woman's touch. Already, Tyree was thinking about how much good a splash of color would do the place.

"Where should I put my things?"

The strap of her duffel bag slipped from her shoulder, causing the bag to thump as it hit the floor. She bent over to check the contents in the bag to be sure her candles and perfumes weren't damaged.

"Right there is fine."

Tyree shot up, and her eyes bulged. The voice that had spoken was as creamy as the unmistakable saxophone chords that danced throughout Sade's "Smooth Operator." The richness of it invaded her dreams and her nightmares all at once. It had more tenor than the octave she'd grown addicted to. Life had given it more swagger, but she knew it; there was no mistaking it.

She took a deep breath and tried to brace herself as she slowly turned around. Time went in reverse as she pivoted. Each degree that passed as she pivoted dialed the year backward. When she completed the 180-degree spin, she faced her past. Her eyes started at the floor where his size thirteen feet were planted and eased upward. The classic Adidas tracksuit pants fit his muscled body perfectly. She could see his chiseled pectorals through the fabric of his white T-shirt. She took her time getting to his face.

"Hi, Ree."

She gulped as she registered the creamy face she'd woken up to and gone to sleep thinking about when they were together and even some time after they'd broken up. Time had been good to him.

His smooth-as-butter mocha skin was without a blemish. His short black wicks were now mid-back-length, well-manicured dreadlocks. The slight smirk of his lips had his deep dimples on full display. Gone was the bare baby face, and now, a full mustache and beard adorned his medium-brown features.

"Hello, Aiyden."

fourteen

Four Years Earlier

Tyree huffed as she rushed up the stairs leading to Aiyden's dorm building, an abundance of possibilities flooding her thoughts. She had been unsuccessful in trying to reach him to give him the dreadful news for hours, and when his phone finally picked up, she'd been unpleasantly surprised to hear not her boyfriend but the voice of a woman, who quietly asked how to hang up the phone. Without considering the risk she was taking by hopping on the highway two hours down the road on a school night, Tyree snatched her purse from the kitchen table and hopped in her car. She hit I-10 by ten p.m. with the same questions repeating in her mind. Who was he with? Why hadn't he called back? *She was about to find out.*

She stomped down the hallway and contemplated what she would do if she saw him with another bitch. It was a toss between jumping on him, her, or, shit, both of them. *The latter seemed more ideal. She could kill two birds with one fist.*

She slowed as she approached the door, not wanting to make her presence known too soon. With her ear pressed to the door, it pushed open. Aiyden complained about how the door jamb was loose and needed to be locked to remain shut. Tonight, his negligence had worked in her favor. Tyree slowly pushed the door back, ready for a fight, and that's when she saw them.

Aiyden sat at his desk with a girl in his lap. They were engaged in an intense kiss that included heavy tongue action. Both of their eyes were closed, keeping them oblivious to her presence. She was surprised they could carry on with an unplanned visitor in the room. Could the loud popping noise that echoed in her ears only be heard by her? She sucked in a quick breath and lost it when Aiyden's hands moved from his side to caress her back. How could he lend their intimacy to the next one so easily?

Tyree's temper was cooled by the anguish that flooded her system. She always said what she would do if ever put in this situation. She fussed at the television as she begged for a woman who had caught her cheating man to beat a bitch's ass. Tyree swore she would never be played for a fool. That get-right was the only option. All that and she stood there stock-still like Cousin Teri when she walked up on her husband with her cousin Faith. Fuck that; this ain't the movies.

She didn't know if she'd thought out loud or if her erratic breathing gave her away, but they ended the smooch abruptly and turned to find her charging at them. The girl's eyes widened, and she threw her hands on her chest.

Aiyden's almond skin brightened a few shades, and his eyes clouded in guilt. He gripped the girl's waist, urging her from his lap. That shit pissed Tyree off to another degree.

"This is why you couldn't answer my calls, Aiyden? Months before I'm supposed to come here, and this is what you do?"

Every few words were broken up by a hard jab she connected with his chest. Her nose burned from the internal fight she had with her tears that eventually beat her efforts and spilled onto her cheeks.

"Stop it!"

Tyree ignored the tug from his lip lover and continued to swing her fist. When she felt another tug, she pivoted, and her fiery knuckles met the woman's nose.

"Don't fucking touch me!" Tyree spat at the woman.

She felt no pity as she watched her use her hands to catch the blood that leaked from her nostrils. Anger flashed in her expression, and she rushed toward her. Aiyden interjected, placing his body between them with lightning speed. His extended arms halted her gait. She gulped her surprise, obviously offended by his defense of her.

"Everything OK in here?"

The three of them turned toward the door where Aiyden's pudgy roommate Eric stood with shock on his face.

"It is now. I'm leaving." Tyree stepped from behind the wall of Aiyden and stomped toward the door. Eric had the sense to step out of her way.

"Can we talk, Ree?" she heard Aiyden ask behind her.

"Talk to that bitch!" Her head remained straight as she proceeded to the elevator at the end of the hall.

After running to her car, she tried to gather her bearings. Her diaphragm inflated every other second as her breaths pushed out of her lungs in rushed heaves. The color drained from her knuckles as she tightly squeezed the steering wheel. Familiar with the saying, "When it rains, it pours," today felt like a fucking category five storm, with constant downpours, high winds, and hail. Her day started off bad and declined from there with no signs of a break in the less-than-desirable forecast.

Her chest burned. Pictures of Aiyden's rendezvous flashed in her mind. She shook her head incredulously, trying to clear the images. She couldn't believe it. The proof had been in the hang-up, but a small piece of her held hope that it was a misunderstanding. Forever hadn't lasted as long as she'd anticipated.

She looked in her rearview to find Aiyden racing toward her car. His hands waved frantically in the air. Her windows were up, but she could make out a muffled "Wait!" from him. Fault lines appeared in her heart when she'd walked in on Aiyden's transgression, and seeing him snapped the thread that held the two halves together. Her hands dropped from the steering wheel and her foot moved from the gas pedal to the brake. A cry came from her lips that trembled uncontrollably.

"Bye, Aiyden," she whispered to herself. And with the heaviest heart, she turned around and pulled off.

These were memories she didn't plan on making when she woke up that morning. It would be known as the day she lost it all—twice.

fifteen

Once Toni made her way back inside the house with a box, Tyree snatched her hand and dragged her to the guest room Aiyden put her in.

"Out of all the ideas you've had in your lifetime, Antoinette Symone Hughes, why would you think this was a good one?"

Toni leaned her back against the closed bedroom door. "I thought this was a good one because you have no other options. You refuse to stay with me, and you know there isn't a hotel you can't go to without Kamaal knowing, so . . . we're here."

"And you thought it was OK to lie to me about who your cousin was?" She stopped pacing and frowned at her friend. "Nigga. Tyrion? I knew that name sounded crazy."

Toni shrugged. "I started watching *Game of Thrones*, and that's all I could come up with on the spot."

Tyree shook her head and made her way to the side of the bed to sit down.

"This isn't going to work, T. I need to go. Now."

"Go?" Toni pushed off the door and sat on the bed beside

Tyree. "I know you guys have a romantic history. I can understand why you've stayed away from each other, but I know you guys can work it out, especially with everything that's been happening. It's been four years, Ty."

Tyree looked into her friend's pleading eyes. What she said made sense, but it wouldn't do. She made it seem as if Tyree still harbored ill feelings about a puppy love that went sour. But what else would she think? She took a deep breath and prepared herself to rehash the third-worst day of her life, a day so awful that the thought of it caused a fierce aching she could physically feel in her core.

"It was more than that, T. He was my first."

"Your first?" Toni asked. "I thought your tutor during freshman year of college was your first."

"No," Tyree sighed. "I told you that to get you off my case about being a virgin. Talking to you about my and your cousin's sex life is weird, hence why I never told you about it."

Tyree kept the details of her and Aiyden's intimacy to herself. Kisses were innocent enough, and Toni walked in on them heading to second base a few times. Anything further was reserved for her and the pages of her diary.

Toni frowned at what Tyree was sure was a mental picture she'd try to spare her friend from years before.

"Yeah, I wouldn't have wanted the details, but I would've wanted to know about you taking that step, no matter who it was with, Ty."

Her lips twisted at the pained expression on Toni's face.

"We thought it was easier to keep things between us, and we planned on telling you more after I graduated. We had it all mapped out. I was going to move down to Tallahassee the summer before I started courses for fall semester, and we were going to get married."

Toni's bottom jaw dropped. "Married?"

Tyree had had plenty of time to prepare for this conversation, and yet, she wasn't prepared for the emotions that were rushing her. She rubbed her hands on her pant legs and tried to wipe away the secretions caused by her anxiety. She looked around the room, hoping that focusing on something around her would give her a chance to calm the river of sadness that wanted to flow freely.

"Yes, that was the plan until I popped up on Aiyden and saw him with another girl." Her head shook at the memory. He promised her forever and couldn't stay faithful for two semesters. "It's crazy that I found out when I did."

She toyed with the round diamond pendant on the necklace Kamaal gifted her on Valentine's Day. The lumps she tried to swallow made her feel like her neck was expanding.

"I went there for an important reason. I received some news that day and needed him to know. I was expecting to give him the news, but when he didn't answer *and* the chick did, I hopped on the highway without a second thought. I just wanted him to know ..."

"Know what, Ty?" Toni coaxed when Tyree didn't continue. Her brows met between her eyes.

Tyree took a deep breath and counted backward from ten. Her painful secret that had only resided at her father's gravesite caused a shiver to snake her spine.

"That I lost our baby."

Toni went still. "Wait, let's back up." Toni put her hand up in the air to silence Tyree. She stood and paced the length of the room. She turned to Tyree. "Baby? Ty, are you telling me you were pregnant with Aiyden's child?"

Tyree nodded. "I was without knowing it. One day, I woke up with the worst cramping and saw that I was bleeding. I figured it was a bad cycle and didn't think much of it until the next day. I was in so much pain that I couldn't walk. My doctor told me I had been about six weeks along." She scratched her jawline when she felt a tickle. Her fingers felt the moisture from the tears she hadn't known clung to her face.

Toni pinched the bridge of her nose and squeezed her eyelids shut. Her head cocked to the side, and her other hand was balled in a fist, resting on her hip. Tyree knew she was processing the news.

"What did Aiyden say?"

"He didn't say anything," Tyree answered as she swiped the tears from her cheeks. She used her hands to fan her face, suddenly feeling hot. "I never told him."

Toni sat back down beside Tyree and took her hand into hers. "You went through all of this by yourself with nobody knowing?" Toni wiped her own tears that fell from her eyes.

Tyree gave a pained smile while she thought about her father. "My dad knew. He was the one who rushed me to the doctor that day. He didn't have to ask me whose baby it was. He'd known that Aiyden and I had been spending a lot of time together."

"What did Uncle Robert say?"

Tyree chuckled. "I was prepared to see my mom again because I just knew he was going to kill my ass. I didn't see my dad reacting any other way. But you know what? He surprised me. He held me and told me everything was going to be all right. I think he saw how much I was suffering, both emotionally and physically, and didn't want to add to it. He did everything he could to make me feel better about things."

"I moved on with my life. The only way I could do that was by removing him completely, which is why I asked that we not talk about him."

Toni took her seat beside Tyree again and pulled her into a hug. Not a church hug you gave across the pews when instructed to give your neighbor some love. She gave Tyree a strong hug, one used to transfer energy and vibes from one party to the next. A mammy hug to help undo four-year-old damage.

"I'm so sorry, Ty. If I had known, I would not have kept the news about Aiyden from you."

She wiped her face again and turned her red, swollen eyes to Toni.

"I know, and I'm sorry for keeping that from you for so long." She took a deep breath, feeling the weight on her chest lighten. "Here I am, out on my ass because my man is a lying, cheating-ass nigga, and the only place I can run to is with the first man who broke my heart. What kind of sad hood tragedy is that?" She laughed because she needed to lighten the mood. She felt exposed, naked now that her secret was out there. *Un-fucking-believable.*

Toni sat quiet for a few minutes. Tyree could see she was processing what she'd just learned.

"Do you think that it would help if you two have a real conversation about what happened?"

She thought for a second before answering.

"I don't know, Toni." She stood and walked over to the window, watching as Aiyden took the rest of her things out of Toni's trunk, still in awe of the demented blast from her past. "It happened years ago, and I've gotten over it. It may be best to leave it in the past. I'm dealing with this mess with Kamaal, and that's all I can handle right now."

Tyree hung the last of her clothes in the walk-in closet then looked around, proud of how quickly she was able to put all her things up.

"Good job," she commended herself.

After Aiyden brought the rest of her bags inside, she eagerly took him up on his offer to ride with Toni to pick up her car. She was thankful for the time alone to sort through her thoughts.

Kamaal and Aiyden.

Her past and her present were like a fierce whirlwind that whipped through her life, destroying the perfect bubble she resided in. Once again, she was left to deal with the damage, and she now had to cope with her harsh realities.

She heard a car door shut outside and looked out the window as Aiyden locked her truck. Her eyes followed him until he crossed over the threshold and disappeared inside the house. She took a deep breath and said a silent prayer to ask for guidance before she left her room to meet him.

In the living room, he stood by the sofa scrolling through his phone. He looked up when she approached and took steps toward her.

"Here you go." He dropped her keys into her palm.

"Thanks. I meant to say this earlier, but thanks for putting me up here. I really appreciate it." His eyes widened briefly. He was surprised. "I know . . . I know. I freaked out, and that's only because Toni hadn't given me a heads up that I'd be seeing you. It was . . . a shock."

"T told me she felt that this was an instance where asking for forgiveness was better than permission, so I get why you were taken aback." His eyes flickered and one side of his lip lifted in a half-grin, exposing his pronounced dimples. "I bet I was the last person you expected to see."

Tyree pursed her lips, annoyed by the amusement he got at her expense. "Yeah, you're right about that."

"Is your room OK?" he asked as his mirth faded.

She rubbed the knot forming in the back of her neck. "Yes, it's great."

His dark brown eyes squinted. "I know it's not what you're used to these days, but I think it'll do."

"What are you talking about?" She frowned. "Your house is perfect."

Aiyden gave her a look that said he didn't believe her. "I'm sure this little 2,000-square-foot cookie cutter has nothing on your boy's."

"Here one day, gone the next," she said with slumped shoulders.

They stood there at a comfortable distance where only their eyes could reach the other. They knew each other, but they didn't *know* each other. She and Aiyden were acquainted strangers. She despised the awkwardness that filled the air around them and wanted to clear it.

"About before, with us . . ." He shifted nervously, trying to rid the uneasiness that came with the topic.

"That's in the past, and we've both moved on from it. No need to bring up bad memories." She waved her hand to dismiss the subject.

After her emotional talk with Toni, she didn't have the stamina for another draining conversation. Bringing up the bad memories would add no value at that time. This was day one, and if they were able to exist peacefully, the talk where they bore it all to each other could wait. Why rehash the bad experiences? *But . . .* they weren't all bad memories. Tyree wondered if he only thought of the lousy moments whenever he thought of them, of her. Did a crash ending outweigh the smooth sailing?

Aiyden watched her. His lips trembled as if he was internally battling what she had said. His face softened, and she could see the acceptance in his expression.

"OK," he acquiesced.

Tyree nodded. She slowly exhaled her relief of his compliance. "Well, I'm pretty worn out from today; I'm going to turn in." A yawn clipped her last words for more believability.

"Goodnight, Tyree."

"Goodnight, Aiyden."

She turned and headed to her room. "Help me through this, Lord," she muttered, with her eyes pointed to the sky.

sixteen

Aiyden's breathing was expertly controlled as his feet stomped on the treadmill inside his garage he'd converted into his personal gym. The machine vibrated with each step; the shakiness beneath him mirrored how he felt all afternoon, uneasy and on unstable ground. Both attributed to the woman resting in the bedroom across from his. Tyree had blossomed over the years. She still possessed a fresh beauty that was more developed than when he'd last seen her up close. He'd snuck looks at her body when they spoke. Her body was curvy and tight; he could tell she worked out. The definition in her limbs showed she took care of herself. Even her hair was longer than he remembered. Her ponytail stopped in the middle of her back. She'd flourished those years apart from him. Confusingly, the thought made him feel impressed and annoyed.

He pressed the buttons on the handle to increase both the speed and incline settings to get the maximum workout. He hoped doing so would help relieve the nervous energy that bubbled inside him. His jitters attempted to wind down, but thinking about everything that happened that day, as well as projections of the future, kept his mind occupied. After a few hours of fighting restlessness, he tied his locs back, threw on some running shorts and his Air Max 95s, and headed to the garage.

Unlike Tyree, Aiyden had known all along she was coming to stay with him. Toni tried withholding her identity, but he'd refused to agree to her request without knowing who it was that needed his help. He wasn't having that shit. When Toni told him she needed him to help Tyree, he kept a straight face and waited to hear the chiming of symbols and a punchline because she had to be joking. He told her as much as he laughed into his phone and stopped when he realized his cousin hadn't joined in. He wanted to know what the hell she'd been thinking and why she would think Tyree would even want to stay with him. Toni responded by asking if he'd been aware of what had been happening with Tyree.

He hated to admit it, but he was aware of the drama that'd gone down surrounding Kamaal and his cheating. One had to literally be living under a boulder to not know. The scandal and the updates that seemed to come every other day kept the blogs busy; he couldn't get through one scroll on any timeline without seeing a post about it, whether it be from a blog site, the news, a fan, or someone amused that a person from the first coast had gone viral. Aiyden tried to ignore the news story, but that quickly proved futile. Days after the news of the affair, the fight, and attack on Tyree, he found himself searching for more developments.

Aiyden had been disappointed in himself at how he'd screwed up and how that led to them ending, but he refused to let it go before he could explain himself. In a last-ditch effort, he got on the highway, determined to see Tyree. When her father stood condescendingly on his porch, not only refusing to let Aiyden see

DELIVER ME FROM DUVAL

her but insisting she didn't want to see him either, he had begun formulating another attempt.

He spent days coming to the realization that things were *really* over between them. He laid in bed, kicking himself for getting caught up with his study partner. She'd thrown hints at him each time they got together to go over notes, but he had ignored it all—until that day. Earlier that day, he received a call from his mother. She wanted to let him know that his father had been in town and they were spending time together. She promised he no longer was abusive and was ready to get his family back. He'd been so angry and questioned his mother's sanity before telling her not to call him for help when he used her as a punching bag before hanging up. He didn't make a habit of disrespecting his mom, but knowing she had once again fallen for his bitch-ass daddy's tricks had him incensed. The inebriation brought on by the three Four Lokos he threw back, along with the advances from his brazen study buddy, had him acting stupid. That one moment of weakness caused him his present and future with Tyree.

The treadmill slowed, whistling a congratulatory tune and signaling the end of his workout. He read the summary while he walked to bring his heartrate back to a normal pace. Five miles in thirty minutes—that was a new record. He mentally patted himself on the back.

Satisfied with the amount of energy and calories burned, he used his towel to wipe his face and arms. He turned off the machine, Bluetooth speaker, and fan, then headed inside. A loud thumping noise sounded on the other side of Tyree's door as Aiyden walked into the hallway. *What was that?*

He paused and waited for another sound when another thump echoed from inside the room. He turned on the hallway light and pressed his ear to the door.

109

"Tyree?" he whispered.

Using his right index finger, he tapped on the door lightly, and it creaked open. The room was dark and quiet. Tyree's even breathing let him know she was asleep. His eyes swept the room in search for what caused the noises he heard. He looked down and found her cellphone and television remote on the floor right beside the bed.

Aiyden shook his head, grinning. "Still a rough sleeper."

Without thinking, he stepped inside. As he bent down to retrieve the items off the floor, Tyree groaned and turned over to face him in her slumber with her arm above her head.

Oh my.

Her shifting caused the comforter to slide and a quick look down caused the air he'd planned to release in an exhale to become lodged in his throat. The first two buttons on Tyree's pajama shirt were undone, and her right breast escaped the top in all its glory. It was fuller than when he last saw it, last experienced it, tasted it. He closed his eyes, and in a second's time, he was transported to another era. He was no longer a man salivating over his ex's nip-slip; instead, he was off Dunn Avenue on his mom's couch as he made out with his then-girlfriend.

He and Tyree kissed; their tongues mated with the same intensity as the hormones swirling around the bottom of his stomach. His hands burned with the need of feeling her skin; he reached beneath the hem of her shirt and inched his way up until he cupped her peaks. Her quick intake of breath startled him; his inexperience mistook her small gasp as a sign of objection. The way she intensified the kiss while his hands were under her shirt, resting on her stomach, told him she was enjoying the moment as much as he was, and maybe him touching her there was OK. He wanted to go in for another feel but didn't want to assume she would welcome it. Not wanting to make their sensual moment awkward, he pulled his lips from hers and asked, "Can I taste them?"

Tyree groaned and shifted again, bringing him back to the present. He hurried out of her room, pulling the door closed until he heard it click. Ever since he foolishly agreed to Toni's favor, he'd been preparing for this, the reunion he'd waited four years for. He told himself that what he agreed to had been no big deal, that a young romance they had on the brink of adulthood was a greater deal back then than it was now. *How could she be even more beautiful than before?*

Tyree dipped a spoon in the pot and tasted her grits. She nodded in satisfaction and placed the lid back on the pan. Being away from the drama of Kamaal's mess proved to be what she needed. With her being thirty miles away from home, she found peace knowing she didn't have to look over her shoulder for pestering paparazzi. She was confident that another pop up from Kamaal was less likely since he had no idea where she was. Both gave her something she hadn't been able to have in weeks: a good night's sleep.

She woke up feeling like a good, home-cooked breakfast could start her and Aiyden off to a day better than yesterday. Happy to find all the ingredients needed to make some of what she remembered as Aiyden's favorite dishes, she went to work making biscuits, grits, and sausages. When she became old enough, she took on the responsibility of cooking for her and her dad. With the long hours he worked, she knew he needed her help. After her fair share of hits and misses, she became comfortable in the kitchen.

Tyree checked the biscuits in the oven and saw they were done.

As she bent over to retrieve the pan, she heard Aiyden clearing his throat behind her. She turned around to find him standing at the entrance to the kitchen.

"Good morning." She smiled as she closed the oven door and placed the pan of biscuits on top of the potholder that sat on the countertop.

"Good morning," he responded. His face was stoic as he walked to the refrigerator and grabbed a bottle of water.

"I made us breakfast. It'll be ready in a few minutes."

Aiyden glanced at the food she cooked and checked his watch.

"I actually gotta get going."

"Oh, OK."

Tyree watched Aiyden's eyes shift around the room. He looked at everything but her.

"I can put it up and you can eat some later if you want."

"Sure, thanks."

He rushed out of the kitchen and out of the house as if he couldn't stand to be around her a second more.

Tyree made herself a plate and sat down at the round table in the nook. She tried to not let Aiyden's abrupt exit deflate the good mood she'd woken up in. Oddly, sleeping under Aiyden's roof wasn't as unsettling as she'd imagined, and that was why she tried to extend an olive branch. Tyree knew his discomfort stemmed from their past and the conversation they needed to have. Until then, Dumbo would just have to chill in the corner. She took a bite of her food.

"Shit is bussin' though."

seventeen

The next weekend started off normal for Aiyden with a trip to the gym. He kept his membership for amenities his home gym didn't include, like group classes, a sauna, and a basketball court. He'd finished a few rounds of intense three-on-three games before calling it a day. His hooping partner and friend, Landen, came over to watch a few of the Saturday college football games.

"I see you got a new whip outside. That Benz is clean, bruh."

Aiyden finished sipping from his Bud Light bottle.

"That is a nice ride, but it's not mine. I have a friend staying here for a little bit."

"Oh, that's what's up."

The men turned back to the television and cheered when a player for the University of Miami recovered the ball that he caused the receiver to fumble.

A few minutes later, Tyree sauntered out of the garage, clearly just having finished her own workout. Her white cut-off top wet from her perspiration stuck to her chest. Her dime-sized nipples protruded beneath the shirt, causing Aiyden's pulse to thump in his neck. She made sweating look sexy. Her black leggings, decorated with mesh material that paneled the sides of her shapely thighs, fit her like a second skin. *Down, boy,* he thought as he shifted in his seat. Aiyden turned to Landen and found him just as entranced by her body as he was.

"I didn't know you had company, Aiyden." Tyree wiped her hands on the towel hanging from her neck and glided to the couch. "Hi, I'm Tyree."

Her smile was bright and genuine as Landen stood to accept her proffered hand. *Fuck is she cheesin' for?* Aiyden all but rolled his eyes when his friend reciprocated her grin with his lurking eyes roaming her figure. He rolled his head and tried to alleviate the heat trailing up his neck.

"Hello, Tyree. My name is Landen. I'm a friend of Aiyden's and hope to be a friend of yours too." He gave a wink, which Tyree responded to by lifting her brow.

"That might not be a bad idea. Maybe you and your girl Robin can come kick it one weekend." Aiyden surprised himself with his suggestion. Where did that come from? He told himself it was to let Tyree know up front what type of dude she was encountering, knowing there was more to it that he didn't care to distinguish. Landen turned to him, his brows lifted, and he tilted his head to the side as if to say, "Nigga!" Aiyden innocently shrugged his shoulders.

"That sounds like fun. You should bring Robin by some time. It would be nice to hang out while catching a few games." Tyree pulled her hand back.

Aiyden didn't miss Landen's lingering fingers as hers retreated. *This nigga here...*

"I'll leave you guys to it. Nice to meet you, Landen."

Aiyden sneered at Landen, who didn't turn from his tactless ogling of Tyree's ass until it was out of sight. He was unashamed and grinned sheepishly when he looked at Aiyden.

"What? With friends like that, what the fuck am I doing over here? I need to go so you can handle that. Ain't nothing hitting better than raw, wet, and sweaty pussy."

Aiyden snorted. "Maybe your ass needs to take Robin for a hike then."

Landen was cool, and they rarely bumped heads, but right now, nothing brought him more pleasure than the thought of showing him the fade where he sat.

Landen caught on to the disapproval in Aiyden's tone and lifted his hands in surrender.

"My bad, Aiy. You hitting that?"

Aiyden gave a subtle shake of his head. He wanted to say he was so his predator of a friend would back off. Him mentioning his old lady, who he lived with along with their daughter, wasn't enough to suck in his wagging tongue, but he couldn't lie on their relationship—or lack thereof.

"Naw, man, it ain't like that with us," Aiyden confessed on a sigh. "But it's not about to be like that with you either, ai'ght?"

Landen nodded. The devious grin on his lips told Aiyden he would be limiting his visits while Tyree was there.

"I hear ya, bruh. Loud and clear."

"Hello?"

Aiyden turned up the volume on his car's Bluetooth so he could hear her better.

"Hi, T, you have a second?" It was Wednesday morning, and he reached out to his cousin while he drove to work.

"Hey, Aiyden. Sure, I just pulled up to the office, but I have a few minutes. How are things over there? I planned on coming to hang with y'all this weekend."

After another night of barely scraping five hours of sleep, Aiyden concluded that his and Tyree's living arrangement wasn't going to work. It was time to bow out.

"I don't think this shit is going to work."

"What isn't going to work?" Toni asked.

He brought his car to a stop at the light and rested his head on the headrest. "Us," he breathed out. "Her living with me," he corrected.

"Has anything happened? You aren't fighting, are you?"

"Nothing happened," he said, as images of Tyree's curvy body flashed in his head. No, nothing happened, but him wanting something to spark had him conflicted. He'd gotten over the nip-slip incident and been able to keep his desire under control. Landen looking at Tyree like a fucking dog sniffing out a bitch in heat caused a bout of jealousy to rear its head, forcing him to experience feelings he preferred to keep suppressed. Having his teenage love under his roof turned him back into a horny boy who could barely keep control of his raging hormones. It had been a few months since he'd been intimate with anyone, and up until yesterday, that had been doable. Tyree being around was driving him crazy.

She hadn't done anything to pull this longing in him; he was sure she was oblivious to it. That's how it was for him before. She could get him to react without even trying. Normally, it was the things she absentmindedly did out of habit that brought about impure thoughts. The way she bit her lower lip when she was in deep thought, how she curled her hair around her fingers as she read, even the body splash she put on after bathing caused him to salivate. He didn't have peace when he was around her. She kept him wired and the crotch of his pants tight. That's why she needed to go.

Toni broke up his thoughts. "You know what she needs right now more than anything?"

He knew she was about to swing from the left but asked anyway. "What's that?"

A few beats passed. "A friend."

"Doesn't she have that with you?" Aiyden asked with a scoff.

With a sigh, Toni answered, "She does, but she may not have the most faith in my character these days."

The deflation in her voice caused his confusion to grow. "What do you mean by that?"

"Nothing," she responded hastily. "Tyree is having a rough time and could really use people in her corner. I don't know the ins and outs of what happened when you guys were together, but I know it began with a friendship—a strong friendship—and I do believe that with a little work, you can build that back up." A few more beats passed. "She may need that today more than anything."

"Why do you say that? What's going on today?"

"It's the anniversary of her dad's passing."

He felt a nudge within. Robert Morris was a kind man who was special to him. He possessed a gentleness that Aiyden never experienced from his sperm donor. Tyree's father showed her that not all fathers were as cynical as his.

"Damn."

"I know, right." She paused. "I don't mean to run, but I need to get inside to get on the teleconference on time."

"No problem, I'll get at ya."

Aiyden rubbed his hand down his face and blew out a frustrated breath. He didn't want to, but he agreed with his cousin. Tyree needed a friend, and no matter their past, he would be that for her.

"Shit, man."

eighteen

Tyree took a deep breath as she sat with her legs tucked under her. She closed her eyes and rubbed out the building tension in her temples. Today was a rough day. Every time she picked up her phone or looked at the bottom corner of her laptop screen, she was reminded of the date. The numbers on display made sure she didn't forget what today was. It was the day she'd lost her father and only relative. Her father grew up in foster care and had no relatives. The day he died she became alone. The people who turned their backs on her mother when she needed them the most were just people who she shared DNA with. They weren't her family. Never were and never would be.

Her recent breakup with Kamaal compounded the hurt that always reared on this day. The pain from his betrayal didn't care that her grief had a standing reservation on this day. She tried to help herself by keeping busy. Not wanting to fall victim to the risks of an idle mind, she used her time to work toward getting back on her feet. She spent most of the day right where she was, in the living room, seated in the recliner with her face in her computer, searching for jobs.

With him, a job hadn't been necessary. Her needs and wants had been met with ease. Instead of concerning herself with a clock to get on, she'd busied herself planning out the empire she wanted to build with the powerful Mr. Duval. Being with him separated her from the normalcy of working-class dealings. Spending the day searching the internet for work told her that easing back into it wouldn't be easy. Aside from two companies that looked promising, Indeed, Monster, and Jobs.com all listed the same opportunities: ride sharing or package delivery.

Deciding she could use a little retail therapy for a pick-me-up, she clicked on the pop-up that previewed an email she'd just received from Nordstrom. The store's pitch of the new collections had her interested, and she opened the message in her browser. She scrolled through the pages, stopping to add pieces to her shopping cart. She gave a last-chance skim over the remaining pages of inventory before beginning the checkout process. The three tops and skirts totaled just under two thousand dollars. The amount was steep for someone of her recent circumstance, but she recalled the cash Kamaal had sent her and decided to treat herself.

When she clicked the payment field, hers and Kamaal's stored cards populated the screen. She hovered over his black card, and knowing there would be no opposition, she clicked. She thought about Blu Cantrell and her instructions in "Hit 'Em Up Style." Maybe it was time to teach Mr. Duval a lesson. Her computer's screen dimmed, warning that the battery was almost dead, before she could complete the purchase. She patted the cushions beside her as she looked for her charger. *Shit, it's in the car.* Not in the mood to put on shoes and go outside, she went into Aiyden's office to borrow the charger she saw in there once before.

She tip-toed into the office as if he was home. Being in this space without him there to give permission felt like she was crossing a boundary. She looked around, hoping to find the charger so she could get out of there quickly. Everything was in its place and well organized, just like Aiyden, an opposite they found attraction over. She smiled at the charging cord neatly tucked beneath the desk as expected. He'd even taken the time to wrap the Velcro strap around the excess slack. *Some things never change.*

She unplugged the charger and began to back out of the room. Something in the corner of her eye caught her attention, and she paused her retreat. The five-tier bookshelf that towered in the corner was crammed full of an eclectic collection of literature. Her eyes danced over the titles of different pieces; some she recognized, a lot she didn't. She made her way to the shelf and immediately took hold of an original she knew well. The colored cardboard spine with black and red polka dots cascading down its length with no particular pattern was designed with intention. It was different enough to stand out slightly, with no intention to catch everyone's eye, just those it was intended for.

She opened that aging album and read the announcement.

To, My Yin. Love, Your Yang

Tyree flipped the pages of the scrapbook she had assembled as a Valentine's Day gift to him. It was her senior year in high school and his freshman year in college. The long distance had begun to wear on them, so for lover's day, she wanted to give him something to reflect on. She was surprised he kept it all this time. And it was right in his office, in a room he visited each day. Right in his reach. She wondered if he looked at it often. Had any of his girlfriends questioned it?

Her eyes bulged at some of the pictures she had forgotten all about. She smiled at the picture of them at the movie theater.

While waiting in line to get inside the auditorium, Aiyden had asked a woman standing behind them to take their picture. He wrapped his arm around her shoulders, and she took his hand and leaned into him. His hands were frisky that night; most of the movie went by in a blur, watched through hooded eyes. She continued to flip through the pages while she cringed, at one point laughing out loud at their fashion choices.

Her eyes landed on the last picture she included in the album. The second half was intentionally left empty, as they were going to fill it up with new memories when they began their life together. The empty pages were a sore reminder of the part of their story that will remain unwritten.

Turning the picture over, she read the message she penned on the back of it. The blue ink had faded somewhat over time, but the words were legible.

To Ayedee, My Boo-Boo

I am so happy with you. You make me believe in fairytales. You lead like Simba, you're strong like Hercules, and as mystical as Aladdin. I can't wait to be there with you.

Love Always, Your Ree

She chuckled at her words. Disney taught her about love, and at that point, she believed all her wishes upon stars had won her Prince Charming. A folded piece of paper stuck out from the back, and Tyree curiously turned to the page to inspect it.

A sob escaped her lips as she stared into the face she missed for the past three years. Robert Morris smiled up at her; the dates below indicated when the sun had risen and set in his life. She remembered that day, the day he retired from the military. After serving his country for two decades, her father retired as a captain. She spent hours going through pictures, and when Tyree saw this one, she knew this was the perfect sendoff for a perfect man. She knew no other would do for his funeral program.

Tyree felt the volume of her emotional grievances near its cap. She took heavy steps into the hall, no longer having the desire to complete another meaningless purchase. Seeing the program forced her to face the sadness she'd been fighting all day. She felt zapped, and she detoured to her room and fell across the bed. Her body rocked as she fell into a soul-stirring sob with the photo album held tight against her chest.

Ding Dong!

Tyree blinked as the chime of the doorbell weaned her from her slumber. She hadn't known she had fallen asleep until she woke up. She rolled over and sat up on the side of her bed when the doorbell rang again.

When Tyree opened the door, Toni was there holding up bags from her favorite seafood restaurant. One of the bags had a few bottles of pink Moscato. She answered Tyree's question before it had been asked.

"I know you could use some company today."

Hakeem sat up straight in the driver's seat of the rented sedan. He'd been on a stake out and followed his subject around all day with hopes of getting a glimpse into their life and routine. He needed to know the ins and outs so his moment of attack would have the most impact.

He watched as the woman got out of her car and stretched her limbs before she proceeded to the check-in desk. After a few moments of waiting, the miniature version of his nemesis walked out of the gym's doors and into her open arms. He knew this was his way in. That was confirmed as he watched the two embrace. He took a pill from the bottle he kept in the center console and swallowed it.

As if the woman could feel his eyes on the back of her head, she turned around and centered right on his car. Instinctively, he ducked, not wanting to break his cover. Moments later, not wanting to risk another slip-up, he pulled off when a Gentlemen's Ice semitruck stopped in front of him, blocking his view from his subjects. A content smirk beamed from his face. This was too easy. His plans were going to work perfectly.

nineteen

"Hey, girl!"

Tyree stood aside as Toni hugged Nique, a friend of hers from work. They'd just arrived at Ray's Place for Throwback Throwdown, a huge party hosted at the lounge that happened once a month from June through September. "Tootsee Roll" could be heard roaring through the speakers when the doors to the club opened.

"Let me see that tootsee roll!" The crowd could be heard outside.

Tyree wasn't a big clubber, but she would humor Toni by going with her a few times a year. She was unusually eager for tonight's visit and looked forward to a good time to help her relieve some stress. With it being the last Thursday in September, tonight was the last throw down of the year.

"I figured it would be easier if I came and got you guys," Nique advised after her and Tyree greeted each other. They now stood adjacent to the large orange T-Rex statue that was a staple for the southside of Jacksonville. "C'mon, it's lit in here tonight. There's even some Jags players inside." She cheesed at the mention of the hometown hunks that were there.

"That's cool," Tyree said, answering the cautious look Toni gave her and hoping her indifference was legible. "I'ma do me tonight," she added. She damn sure wasn't going to let the possibility of being in the same place as Kamaal change her plans. He no longer had that power.

The ladies followed Nique inside the lounge that was packed full of the twenty-one-and-up crowd. The dance floor was over capacity as a sea of people danced to summertime hits they loved from the past. The ladies maneuvered through the building until they reached the VIP area in the back and settled in the booth that included a table and two couches. Tyree leaned back in her seat, glad to be able to finally rest her feet. She smoothed the lines from her black fitted Valentino lace jumpsuit. The outfit was audacious and received second—even third—looks from patrons. She crossed her leg, resting her bent knee across the other. Her pink Christian Louboutin Kate Crystal pump peeked from under her pant leg and matched her YSL lipstick.

A hum of "ohs" filled the space as the instrumental to a down south classic flowed from the speakers. The drums of Trick Daddy's popular song ticked as the party rocked side to side. The buildup increased everyone's excitement as they waited for the famous line.

"Anybody wanna mu'fuckn die?" the crowd shouted.

"Come see I," Toni picked up.

Tyree joined in, "Who, me?"

Everyone in attendance knew every word. It reminded Tyree of the yearly festival Jacksonville used to host. The all-day concert always included a lineup of both local artists and the acts that held the top position on the charts.

The group of ladies danced and laughed over rounds of drinks. Tyree stepped away to go handle some personal business. On the way back to the section, she stopped by the bar and ordered The Mysterious Marijuana. She turned and watched the crowd as she waited. The club was hype as the attendees had their middle fingers in the air, screaming what to say to the other side as "Donk Mode" started playing. The bartender returned with a turquoise barbiturate in a glass, and Tyree thanked her and asked her for a cup of water. She'd been thirsty, and using white liquor to quench her thirst was just asking for trouble. Jacksonville police was perched and ready for some shit to jump off, and she wanted no parts. Tyree bopped to "Naked Hustle" as she walked back to the section.

"Are we grabbing something to eat after this?" Tyree asked before putting the cup of water to her lips and taking a sip. "I'm *hooongry.*" The sip turned into a gulp before she pulled the empty cup from her mouth. She'd graduated from thirsty to parched.

Toni wore her amusement and asked, "You thirsty as hell too. Did you eat today?"

"Now that I think about it, just a smoothie for breakfast." Tyree rested her chin on her fist and thought for a second. "Oh! And that cookie I swiped from your kitchen when I was waiting for you to get ready. Sis, it's time to go grocery shopping."

Toni frowned. "I don't have any cookies in my kitchen."

Tyree smirked. "You don't *now* because I ate it. That was the only snack I could find because, bitch, you need food."

"I know I need to go grocery shopping. I checked the kitchen when I made my list, and that's how I know I don't have any—"

"What?" Tyree asked after Toni didn't say anything else for a few seconds.

"This cookie . . . was it a chocolate chip with sprinkles wrapped in green plastic?"

Tyree smiled coolly. "Why yes, yes it was. It was gooder than a bitch too!"

Toni pursed her lips and rubbed the center of her forehead. "Let's go."

Tyree shook her head. "Go? For what? We haven't even been here that long."

Toni grabbed Tyree's wrist and pulled her forward; her lips spoke directly into her ear. "That wasn't a regular cookie, Ty. That was an edible, and you've been drinking. Any minute now, you'll be feeling it."

"What? Toni, you can't have that stuff just laying around." Tyree shook her head in disbelief. She'd tried weed before and didn't like the dizziness it caused so she stayed away. "It's cool; I'll be all right. Plus, I don't want to miss Supa Chino's performance. I'm ready to toot it out!" She bent over and gave a little twerk while sticking her tongue out.

Toni peered at her. Tyree could see she was studying her eyes.

"Your eyes aren't red yet," she observed. "OK, only if you're good, but you *have* to let me know if that changes. Edibles have a tendency of sneaking up on you. Trust me."

<hr />

"*Edibles have a tendency of sneaking up on you. Trust me.*"

Toni's warning rang in her ears as she waited in the line for what had to have been her fourth trip to the restroom. The effects of the alcohol and edible had her head feeling heavy, and she leaned back on the wall to stabilize herself.

"Hey, brown skin, you a'ight?"

The pungent smell of Hennessey on her inquirer's breath made her turn up her nose. Damn, that shit smelled like cough syrup. Her stomach flipped as her mind traveled to her childhood where Robitussin was the cure-all. Nasty work.

OMG, do you smell that? a voice from inside her asked. She'd been having conversations in her head all evening. *Girl, yes. Tell his ass to step back. Give you fifty feet.* The THC unlocked a part of her consciousness that had her thoughts answering themselves as she was a bystander to the internal exchange. She named them She 1 and She 2.

Just as Toni said, the effects of the cookie snuck up on her. Cotton mouth had her reaching for whatever was in reach to quench her thirst. She gulped down the bottles of water that came with the section. When that was out, she sipped on the Moet Nique selected for them. The Crown Apple straight was a double whammy; it tasted good, and it pulled her deeper into a stupor.

Her eyes grew tight, and it seemed like the party turned into Comic View because everything was funny. No matter how much she tried, she couldn't keep a straight face. Next to nothing would send her into a giggling fit. She owed an apology to Toni and Nique's coworker, Danielle. On her way back to their table, the woman tripped and fell. While she asked Danielle if she was all right, she laughed hysterically. It was uncontrollable, and Toni's scowl did nothing to calm her giggles.

They won't be inviting your ass out anytime soon, She 1 stated between her ears.

"You hear me, gorgeous?"

The man's inquiry brought her back.

"Yeah, I'm good," Tyree politely responded. Her head was off the wall.

"Looks like it's about time to get you out of here and into bed."

Tyree snapped her head to the right of her where he stood and frowned.

"I mean, you look partied out, and it's time for you to get into your bed," he corrected with a chuckle.

She nodded, glad that the man hadn't been a total creep. She blinked and got a better glimpse of him. He was just a few inches taller than her sixty-six inches. His skin was of the deepest black. His crisp white eyes were the perfect contrast to his profound melanin, and he had a mouth full of the shiniest gold. True Florida boy shit.

"Thanks, but I'm straight." She gave a polite grin and made her way into the ladies' room with slow steps, careful not to kiss the ground like Danielle. The thought had her snickering in the stall.

Tyree finished in the restroom and headed back into the hallway, hoping the man from before had gotten the hint and left. She didn't have the energy to once again explain that she didn't need any help getting into bed. Her phone's display read one thirty, thirty minutes until let out. It was time to let Toni know she was ready to leave so they wouldn't get caught in the closing crowd.

She inwardly sighed when she stepped into an empty hall. Her eyes remained ahead as she weaved through the patrons who were making the bar's last call. Once she made it to the dancefloor, there was a tug on her hand. The light reflected off gold caps, announcing the identity of the hallway homeboy.

"What's good, shawty? You ready for me to help you into bed?" He strengthened the grip on her hand and pulled her into him. The heel of her shoe slipped on a spilled drink, causing her to lose her footing and land on the man's chest. "Or I could help you in my bed, all night." He smirked confidently, as if he had said something.

"No, thank you," Tyree declined. She attempted to push off his hard chest and found herself tighter in his grip. "Let me go!" she snarled in his face. He smiled knowingly, like he knew her bark had no bite. Panic swept through her, and the prickling feeling on her neck reminded her of when she'd been slammed against the wall months before. The pit hollowing in her stomach forced its contents up her esophagus and into her throat. Did she have a sticker on her forehead advising she was partial to attacks?

She felt his slimy hand plant itself at the center of her back, right above her ass. His breath was another offense as it fanned her face.

"I don't know why you playin' like you don't want this. I saw you out there. Shaking that—"

His words ceased as he was yanked back. Since Tyree was leaning on him, she lost her balance and stumbled hard before catching herself.

A familiar scent of cedar and citrus filled her nostrils and warmth brushed across her back in response to . . . what? She turned to find Kamaal with the man who grabbed her hemmed up on the wall.

"You don't know how to walk the fuck away when a woman tells you she isn't interested, fuck nigga?" Kamaal barked in the man's face. The base in his voice competed with the 808s vibrating through the club. The man's response was broken and incoherent; Kamaal's fingers were like a pair of vice grips around his neck.

Florida boy hadn't stood a chance when Kamaal dropped him and he stumbled to his feet. He swung without coordination, and Kamaal caught the man's hand in mid-air, keeping his arm raised as he shot jabs to his ribs. The hits caused him to lean over, and Kamaal took advantage of his bent posture and connected a forceful punch to his nose, which leaked all over the True Religion graphic tee he wore.

Two security guards appeared.

"We got it from here, Mack," one of them stated as he and his partner apprehended her harasser. Kamaal's amber squint followed him as they hauled him off. Obviously, security had been privy to the events that had taken place before Kamaal emerged.

"Knuck if you buck!"

The classic beefing song began to play. *How fitting,* Tyree thought. The crowd jumped up and down while hitting one balled fist into the palm of their other hand. It was risky playing this song in Duval County; it bought out the beast in everybody. Tyree had seen too many times what happened in large crowds with that song as a soundtrack.

"You OK?" Kamaal asked as he peered down at her with his warm, golden eyes; his brows met in the center of his forehead as they did when he was bothered or concerned. Tyree knew that both applied in this instance. "Did he hurt you?" he asked through clenched teeth. His six-piece, diamond-encrusted bottom grill gleamed under the club lights.

She subtly shook the shiver that shot through her. Seeing him switch off his aggression to see about her was doing things to her. She 1 and She 2 talked over each other, both calling out things she tried to ignore, like how his smooth umber skin glistened under the lights or how good he smelled. She recognized the K by Dolce and Gabana; it always jump-started her lust.

"Ye-yeah," she stuttered as she watched his eyes darken and his expression turn deadly. "I mean, yes, I'm OK, and no, he did not hurt me," Tyree explained hurriedly. She forced her eyes to widen as she felt them closing into slits. The cannabis-driven haze made it hard to stay alert. Even so, his flawless face was legible through her shrunken gaze.

She could see when the recognition hit him. His eyes widened for a moment before they narrowed.

"Are you high?" he asked.

"I . . ." she stammered, feeling butterflies in her belly. "It was an accident," she pled her case. The furrow of his brow uncovered he was peeved by the realization of her influenced state.

Kamaal snorted and grabbed her arm to lead her outside. She followed him, feeling like a child whose mama was going to rip into her for cutting up in church service as soon as she could get her alone.

twenty

"Hey!" Tyree fussed at Kamaal's back. He ignored her and moved people out of his way, his firm grip holding her wrist. Some of the people he'd pushed turned around ready to confront him, but their scowls turned into amazement when they recognized who he was. Tyree saw people pointing at them and taking a few pictures as they passed. She cringed and could only imagine what the headlines would be tomorrow.

"Stay here," Kamaal ordered. She wanted to tell him he had some nerve telling her what to do, but the look he gave her told her he meant business. Instead, she crossed her arms, leaned on his Rolls parked by the front door of the lounge, and waited as he retrieved his keys from the valet. He returned to her and tugged her arm, pulling her from the car so he could open the passenger door. The warmth sent through her, and she also felt a tug in her chest from the touch. *Don't go there*, she thought.

"What are you doing?"

"I'm taking you home to sober up. What are *you* doing? You

have no control of yourself. Anyone could take advantage of you!"
He stood close to her and spoke in a loud whisper.

Tyree recoiled at his audacity. "What? Nobody has taken advantage of me more than you!" She poked him in his hard chest. "Now you want to swoop in and save the day like Captain Save Tyree when you're the one that broke this shit. Fuck you, Kamaal!" The zeal of her impassioned response sapped her energy, causing her to lean on his car to steady herself. She pressed her fingers onto her temples to still the spinning.

"What's wrong, Ty?" Kamaal's voice was laden with worry, with no hint of offense taken by her disdainful remarks toward him.

Tyree averted her gaze, embarrassed by her outburst. She wanted to appear as if she coped well without him. Tonight exposed how she felt, like she had no control over her life, that she was just out here reacting.

"Nothing's wrong."

Kamaal remained silent as if he were waiting for her to continue. Once she didn't, he shook his head. Tyree took the time to study him in the light. A navy-blue Boglioli wool sport coat stopped in the middle of his robust thighs. A V-neck shirt was tucked into black denim jeans, with high-top Gucci sneakers peeking out underneath them. His thick beard lined his face crisply. She was sure he'd visited, well most likely was visited by, his long-standing barber, Clay.

Why did he have to look so good? His attractiveness made her feel an array of responses she'd tricked herself into believing she'd rid herself of. Him coming to her rescue again provided the comfort of having an ally that was powerful in more ways than one. Him staring down at her with profound possessiveness made her feel . . . sick. No, his handsomeness didn't debilitate her, the barbiturate binging had. She cringed at the sensation of her stomach knotting in addition to the filling of her mouth. She wrestled against the urge to push.

Her body overtook the control her mind tried to exert, and Tyree was left no choice but to relieve it. Kamaal must have read the moment correctly. His face softened, and he asked her if she was all right. Before he could fully get the question out, his black sneakers were covered with her stomach's contents.

———◦◦◦———

"Ty—"

Tyree lifted her hand, cutting off Toni. "No."

Toni snickered. "But, I just—"

"No," Tyree interrupted again.

After her last ounce of dignity evaporated at the sight of Kamaal standing in a puddle of her vomit, Toni appeared, having been looking all over for her. Tyree begged for them to leave; she couldn't stand being at the club or near Kamaal. He attempted to talk her into going home, and Tyree declined, letting him know she refused to step foot in *his* house. After a handful of nos and Toni guaranteeing she was OK to get her and Tyree back home safe, Kamaal conceded, but not without threatening another pop-up if either of them didn't let him know the minute they were back at Toni's.

It was past three in the morning when Tyree finally came down from her high and somewhat recovered from her drunkenness. They needed greasy food and plenty of liquids to flush out the impurities they consumed during their partying. On the way from the club, they stopped to pick up All-Star meals from Waffle House.

They inhaled their drunk delicacies, then passed out. It was now after two in the afternoon, and their minds were clear enough to discuss the events of the night before. Not that Tyree cared to rehash that catastrophe.

Tyree knew her bestie wanted to revisit the details of the night before, aka earlier that morning, but she didn't want a debriefing. She scrolled through her Snapchat posts and had gotten the idea, the embarrassing idea. She was mortified while watching the snippets she posted. Only believing it because she saw it with her own eyes, Tyree almost lost it when she watched herself bust a mean Wu-Tang dance.

"Stop fighting and get it over with," Tyree chastised Toni, who did an awful job controlling her laughter.

"I'm sorry. It's just that you kept walking up to people singing, 'That boy got stretch pants! That boy got stretch pants!'" Toni buckled over in laughter with her arms hugged around her middle. "Ah! My stomach!"

"Fuckin' *Roll Bounce*," Tyree uttered while she shook her head. "No more Bounce TV for me," she huffed. She watched her friend, who for some reason thought her embarrassment was so amusing. "OK, Toni, you can stop laughing now."

"OK, OK." Toni sniffed. "You're right, just let me get this little bit out. I mean, what are the odds? The first time you go to the club all year, you get high out of your mind and rescued by Kamaal. You should play the lotto."

Tyree could feel her cheeks warm at her recollection. If her impromptu dance routine on stage wasn't bad enough, she'd been so lit that she hadn't had the strength to fight off Florida boy, and Kamaal had to swoop in to save the day.

Tyree fell back on the couch in exasperation and lifted the arm that shielded her eyes. "I may get a ticket. I could take the money and disappear."

When the shock wore off, she hadn't wanted to crawl in a hole and die like she had when she watched Kamaal pummel Hakeem in Toni's front yard. The protection she felt from Kamaal's unexpected intervention excited her. He had yoked the old dude with whiplashing speed, then hit him with a one-two combo that would make Mayweather proud, before security escorted the creep away. And how did she thank him? By blessing his shoes with the contents of her stomach. Shit, she wished she would've left when Toni suggested. *Oy vey.*

"Give yourself a break, Ty. That cookie had 700 grams of that good in it. I'm glad you ate it because that was the most fun you've had in a long time. You needed it." Toni smiled. "My homeboy was cooking up a new recipe and wanted me to check it out. Lemme call Jon-Jon and tell him he got that pressure!"

Tyree shot a disapproving squint as Toni's mouth twitched. She sniffed and put on as if she were wiping her nose to hide her laughter.

"My life is ruined, and it's not that funny. I would think my best friend wouldn't find that much enjoyment out of it."

"Tyree, chill. It's not that serious. All you did was get messed up and send a few harmless text messages. Now, ya boy looked like he lost his best friend when you refused to leave with him. I'm glad you told Kamaal your next will be better than your ex." Toni paused, and Tyree watched her as she contemplated her next words. "Now, you blew my mind when you told him you were going to get you some big, black co—"

"No!" Tyree pled. "Don't say it. I don't even know where that came from. I don't even use that word. Ever."

Toni wiped the tears her laughter brought her to. "That is a weird one," Toni agreed. "We don't even say that word. It's *dick*. Who you been hanging around?"

Her phone chimed again, signaling another incoming message. She opened it and saw it was from her friend, Channing. She read the text and jumped up, squealing.

"What is it?" Toni asked.

"Cherise is in labor!" As soon as she said the words, she realized her mistake. Tyree watched the amusement drain from her bestie's face.

"Oh, that's nice." Toni tried with great zest to mask her wound. She sat silently for a moment then stood up. "I'm going to shower up, then I'll get you to Aiyden's."

Tyree watched Toni scurry to the back of her house and knew that her departure had been an excuse to get away. She leaned back on the sectional sofa and slapped both her palms on either cheek.

"I'm never drinking again."

twenty-one

Kamaal parked in front of the small house on Myrtle Avenue, contemplating his next move and knowing there was no going back from there. His opponent had already crossed the line with Tyree, so that meant he could go there too. After doing his own digging, he received the answer he suspected but wanted to avoid. Bitch-ass Hakeem had been sloppy and alluded to another player on the team that he was going to use Tyree for revenge. Now that Kamaal knew the truth, he had no other option. Hakeem bucked first, so he had to buck back.

Rage coursed through him whenever he thought of the bruises he'd tried to kiss away from Tyree's body. The thought of anyone harming her had murderous thoughts swimming behind his eyes. He could've snapped ole boy's neck when he got rough with her at the club three weeks ago. Twice, she'd been taken advantage of by men who leapt over the line. He felt like shit because he knew his offenses against her hurt the most.

He dialed the number to the burner phone his contact used.

When the person answered with "Yeah?" Kamaal advised him that he was outside.

"A'ight."

Instead of his S-560 or Rolls truck, Kamaal waited in his Toyota Camry, careful to move under the radar.

A police cruiser turned down the street, driving slower than the thirty-miles-per-hour speed limit. It was the afternoon, so there wasn't any rumbling in the streets yet, hence why Kamaal chose this time of day to meet. Some areas in Jacksonville transformed when day turned to night, and he decided that hitting the block at night wasn't good for his brand. He had just enough time for this meeting before he was due back to the stadium to review tapes from last week's game against the Jets. He was going to make this quick.

He sat up and killed the engine just before the police cruiser passed by him. The door to the house opened, and a petite woman proceeded down the front porch steps and headed his way. Kamaal unlocked his doors and welcomed her inside.

"Hey, KD." She leaned her back on the inside of the passenger door. "What's up?"

"'Sup, Red, how ya been?" Kamaal held up his fist, which she pounded in return. He eyed the woman. She wore her hair in waist-length braids that were all seven colors of the rainbow with black sprinkled throughout. The playful look went well with her honey-brown skin. Her fitted crop top accentuated her full bosom and showed off the flat stomach she'd had contoured at the same time she got her Brazilian butt lift after giving birth a few years ago. She'd really blossomed from the scrawny, pimple-faced girl he grew up with.

He and Red had been close friends ever since he moved into the projects with his aunt Brenda after his dad got locked up. He held her down and made sure everyone knew she wasn't riding solo in the streets, and she was always willing to dog-walk a bitch for him because he'd been too much of a gentleman to put his hands on a girl himself.

"Shit, I'm good. Same ole' shit, different day."

"For real, for real." Kamaal nodded. He pulled a white envelope from the door pocket and tried to hand it to her. She'd swiftly pushed it back toward him.

"C'mon, Red, stop playing."

"Un-uh, KD. I told you; we're good. You already did enough paying off the house and the car—too much actually. You work too hard to get where you are just to give your money away."

When Kamaal signed his deal with the Jaguars, the first thing he did was keep his promise to his aunt. He moved her out of the hood and took care of her as she did him when he had no one. Getting Aunt Brenda to rely solely on his support hadn't been an easy feat. She refused to depend on someone because people failed her, so she agreed only when she was able to sign on as his housekeeper and Karl's nanny.

Just like Aunt Brenda, Red was opposed to the "handouts" Kamaal extended her way. She'd been a front row witness to people attempting to gain access to his wealth and celebrity. Red never wanted to be mistaken for a leech and did everything she could to separate herself from the likes.

"I know, and this isn't what that is."

Red tilted her head to the side and pushed her lips into a doubtful pucker. "Then what is it?"

"I got a job for y'all."

The guest bathroom door opened, and the soft scents of jasmine and vanilla filled the hallway. Tyree being there was just the addition needed to balance his masculine manor. It was a refreshing change from the usual cedar-heavy fragrances he preferred.

"Hi, Aiyden," Tyree greeted with a soft smile.

It was obvious she had washed her hair after her workout. When he headed out to take care of a few things, he heard her in the garage. He watched her towel-dry her hair. She was dressed in an oversized "Free-*ish*" grey T-shirt and black joggers. He looked down and noticed her small, pretty feet. She looked so comfortable as she moseyed through his house like she was his girl.

Aiyden despised the thought immediately, scolding himself for allowing his mind to wander there. "Hi."

"You just got back in?" Her questioning sounded domesticated. It was familiar.

"Yeah, I like to get all my running around done earlier to beat the large crowds." His right shoulder leaned against the hallway's wall.

"That makes sense. I try to beat the crowds myself. Less stressful that way." She pulled the towel from the crown of her head and rested it on her shoulders. "What?" She noticed him staring with a slight scowl.

He cocked his head to the side. "Your hair."

"My hair?" She tugged at a curl with a cute frown. "What's wrong with it?"

Aiyden shook his head, realizing she misunderstood. "There's nothing wrong; I just never seen it like that. I didn't know you had curly hair."

A proud smile found her pretty mouth. "The fro that I grow, got no perm in it!" she sang. "Yeah, I caught on the natural wave, and I love it. I watched *Good Hair,* and it changed my life. It's so much healthier than when I had all of those chemicals in it."

Aiyden wasn't well versed in hair, but he could agree with that. It looked healthy and beautiful. It was thick, juicy, and had a lot of volume. Her mane was fucking fabulous.

"Then why do you usually keep it straight?"

He didn't miss the flash of pain that flickered across her face when she turned away. He knew the answer had something to do with Kamaal.

"I just like that style." She returned her eyes to his. "What are you washing?" Tyree asked after seeing him step into the laundry room at the end of the hallway.

Recognizing her attempt at changing the subject, Aiyden went along with the new topic. "Some whites."

"Mind if I throw this in?" She held up the white bath towel she used to dry her hair. "I did laundry yesterday and don't have anything else to wash this with."

"That's fine."

Tyree stood beside Aiyden at the washer and placed her towel inside. She watched as he pulled a new bottle of detergent from the shelf.

"What are you doing?"

Aiyden gave her a puzzled expression. "I'm washing."

Tyree smacked her teeth. "We've established that. Why are you opening a new bottle of detergent?"

Aiyden chuckled; he didn't understand her questioning. "Because this one is out." He motioned toward the open bottle that sat on the dryer.

She shook her head. "There's plenty in there for this load, maybe even another."

Aiyden tilted his head to the other direction. "I checked that one; it's not enough, Ree."

"Wanna bet?" Her sly smile cautioned him.

Aiyden quirked a brow. "Depends on the stakes."

Tyree's grin grew. She knew she had him. "Nothing high. How about, if I'm right, you cook enchiladas tonight."

"Still a greedy ass I see." Aiyden shook his head and chuckled lightly. "Ai'ght. What if I'm right?"

"It don't even matter because I'm going to win," she stated with the confidence he remembered and admired. Robert Morris poured into his daughter and made sure her head was big so no one could just come in and diminish her light. "I'll let you decide something."

———◦◦———

Aiyden angled his head and considered her proposition. She watched as ideas played across in his mind. Some he quickly dismissed; she could tell by the subtle shake of his head. Others, he took a few moments to ponder before moving to the next idea. He looked upward while rubbing his beard. His pink lips twitched into a mischievous smirk. Tyree felt a strike of nervousness hit her; that look usually meant trouble. She remembered when they were kicking it at his place alone and she asked him what he wanted to do. Aiyden sent her the same smirk and before she knew it, they were skinny-dipping in the community pool after hours. Her center pulsated at the memory.

Tyree cleared her throat at the thoughts of their salacious past. *Don't go there.* "Are you finished wasting your time?"

Aiyden's pearlies peeked through his smile. "Yeah, I'm finished for now." He reached at the hem of his shirt and pulled it over his head and tossed it into the washer. Tyree's mouth watered.

His skin was smooth and the color resembled nutmeg, just as she remembered. What she didn't recall were the modifications he'd made since she'd seen him last. His strong chest was full of tattoos that extended to right above where both of his biceps began. The collage of art was eclectic, full of illustrations she recognized as his hobbies. Sports and family member names filled his robust pectorals.

Not like Kamaal, whose skin was drowned in ink. Both his arms, most of his torso, and even his legs were covered in art. Beautiful, but it didn't fit every scene and limited his options when he needed to take on another role. She'd seen Aiyden in all kinds of tops and did not know what canvas lay below. Creative and responsible; she admired that.

"A lot of poorly planned decisions I made when I first started college. Peer pressure from the team, I guess," Aiyden offered when he noticed how she observed his skin.

Tyree shook her head fast. "They look great. I'm just surprised I hadn't seen them before now." Her eyes continued to sweep over his chest.

"As intended." He gave her a smirk that poured iced water on her dormant senses, causing them to awaken. His dimpled cheeks looked deep enough to get lost in. She didn't like that.

"So, what is your wager?" Tyree asked.

Aiyden smiled again. "I'll tell you later."

twenty-two

Aiyden swallowed as he watched Tyree taste her first bite of food. He didn't need her to tell him it was good. The way she closed her eyes and moaned as she chewed let him know the recipe he'd dusted off still had it. He shifted in his seat; the way she moaned reminded him of the sounds she used to make when she nibbled on him. He hadn't known that watching a woman eat could be such a turn-on. He filled with pride as he watched her enjoy his food. He'd been just as confident in his culinary skills as she had been gauging detergent liquid.

She had been right. The detergent not only was enough to clean his whites, but his lights as well. Being kept by a baller hadn't taken all her normalcy. There was still a little of the frugal woman she had been with him. For some reason, that pleased him.

"Good as you remember?" Aiyden asked just before he took a bite of his enchilada.

Tyree's eyes fluttered open, and she smiled sheepishly while sweeping her tongue across her bottom lip. "I mean, it's not Chuy's, but it's good," she said with a smirk.

Aiyden laughed. His feelings would have been hurt if she didn't act like his food was as good as sex. "Yeah, a'ight."

She scooped some yellow rice and black beans onto her fork and took a bite. "I'm just joking. It's perfect. Being here may not be good for my waistline." She gave a pointed look before taking another bite. "Oh! I forgot. I picked up some beer when I stopped by Publix earlier. You want one?"

"Sure, thanks."

Tyree pushed back from the table and walked to the refrigerator. Aiyden used the moments alone to think about the time they had while he cooked. Tyree asked if he minded her company in the kitchen while he cooked, and he hadn't had a problem with it; he welcomed it. They talked about their favorite television shows once Tyree brought up seeing one she enjoyed recorded on his DVR. Coincidentally, they both were behind, and she invited him to binge-watch with her. He agreed.

"Here you go."

He looked at the bottle she held up to him.

"Angry Orchard? I thought you said beer."

Tyree rolled her eyes. "This *is* a beer, see." She pointed to the label and read. "Well, it's a cider, and that's close enough." She sat down and took a sip from her bottle.

"Man, this is juice." He shook his head pathetically. *Poor baby.*

Tyree sucked her teeth and stood again with her bottle in tow. "Give it here."

Aiyden ignored her outstretched hand. "No, it's fine. I'll manage."

"I got something that'll help put some hair on that baby chest of yours. Let me see it really quick."

Aiyden indulged his curiosity and passed her his Orchard.

She went to his bar cart and poured some Fireball into his bottle. She shook it up to mix the contents before giving it back to him.

"What is this?"

"Hard cider and cinnamon whiskey. Angry balls." She sat down and took another bite of her dinner.

Aiyden frowned. "Nigga, what? Angry balls?"

Tyree smiled and nodded. "That's what this is called."

Aiyden's face scrunched as he pondered the notion. He sat the bottle down on the table, no longer needing a sip.

"I usually don't prefer balls in my mouth, especially angry ones."

Tyree tilted her head back as laughter built in her gut and erupted from her mouth. Her guffaw was excessive and genuine; he couldn't help but join in.

"You men take your testosterone too seriously."

Dun dun dun. Dun dun dun.

Aiyden recognized the tune coming from Tyree's phone. He was subscribed to the same app.

"ESPN?"

Tyree answered with remnants of laughter in her voice. "Yep. I like to stay updated with the latest on sports. I'm a whole fanatic now."

He opened his mouth to ask another question when her phone sounded again. "Don't tell me your phone goes off with every update."

She shook her head. "Just when it's about my team. I will peruse their site to see what's going on with the league from time to time."

Aiyden checked his phone and saw that he hadn't missed an update. He adjusted his settings to only notify him when it was regarding the Jaguars since that was his team. He was a huge fan just like most of Jacksonville; he even followed Kamaal's career. That he would never tell Tyree.

"What's up with the Jags? I didn't get the update yet."

Tyree's eyes crinkled, and she picked up her fork. She took a bite and Aiyden had to shift in his seat when she swept her tongue across her bottom lip. She took a sip from her bottle and answered, "That wasn't about the Jags."

Aiyden tilted his head to the side. "I thought you said you get notified about Jacksonville."

The amusement in her eyes traveled to her mouth, which now sported a quirky grin. "No, I said I get notified about my team, and that happens to be Dallas."

Aiyden sat back in his seat and studied her canny mien. He was impressed at her having her own mind and not converting to appease her ex.

"Who do you have going to the big game this year? I know it's still early in the—"

"How 'bout dem Cowboys!" Tyree chanted through cupped hands while noticing his disapproving grimace. "What? They have a nice roster. A Jaguar may have had my heart, but I'm a Dallas girl by blood. My dad would not have it any other way."

"So that's why Kamaal kicked you out." Aiyden realized his joke bombed as soon as he said it. His amused grin dissipated at recognizing his words shifted the atmosphere. "Hey, I'm sorry. Horrible joke, I didn't mean anything by it."

Tyree shook her head. Her eyes slanted to the right and stayed there.

"No, but it's true. I mean, I wasn't technically kicked out, but Kamaal's actions forced me out." She sat her fork down on her plate and pushed it aside.

Aiyden's shoulders dropped at the sight. He hated seeing how his slip of the tongue dulled her demeanor. "You should be proud you stood up for yourself and left a situation where you were mistreated. Why can't you see it that way?"

"Because I'm embarrassed, Aiyden!" Tyree answered loudly.

Aiyden's phone began ringing, and he glanced down to see who the caller was. Tyree stopped talking to give him time to answer. She watched as he pressed the volume button to silence it before looking back up with her.

"You were saying?"

"Are you going to answer that?"

Aiyden picked up his fork to get another bite. "No, we're talking, aren't we?"

"Yeah, but it's OK. I can wait."

"They wait. You don't." He made it a point to stare in her eyes when he made his statement. "Now, why are you embarrassed, Ree?"

Tyree didn't resume talking for a few seconds as she got over the shock of him not tending to his phone call. She recently learned that he was in management for a distribution company he worked at while completing his bachelor's in business. The higher-ups had been impressed with his performance and held true to their promise by giving him the opportunity to manage the new St. Augustine location. His job was to get that office to perform as efficiently as the Orlando office where he began his career as an intern. She understood that being in a higher position meant longer work hours, especially with truck drivers who worked all hours of the day. Phone calls at any time, day or night, were expected.

Kamaal being who he was for the Jags, as well as the other deals and ventures he had, kept his phone going off. His trades became too much for one phone, and he had to get a second line to handle the overflow. Tyree was conditioned to Kamaal stopping whatever he'd been doing when the phone rang because that was money calling. When the phone rang or chimed, she knew to press pause on their conversation while he handled business. Before Simone, his phone was the other woman. Aiyden declining the call was a sizable gesture.

"Months ago," she started once she gathered she held his full attention, "I was on top; I had everything. I was a queen."

"You're still a queen," Aiyden interjected without humor.

Tyree pursed her lips. She wasn't ready for his compliments or the fuzzy feeling she felt from it. "Look at me now. I'm here bumming on your couch because I don't have my shit together."

"You're not on my couch, Tyree. You have your own room."

She rolled her eyes. "Same thing!"

He swallowed his laugh. "I'll tell you what. How about you handle dinner tomorrow? That'll be your rent payment."

"Deal." Tyree braced her elbows on the table and rested her head on top of her laced fists. "You know, I haven't seen you watch any of the Jags' games since I've been here. I hope that's not because of me."

His eyes shot to the side, giving her his answer.

"Oh no! You don't have to do that!" She palmed her forehead with her right hand and shook her head in bewilderment. "I'm a big girl. Besides, I'm looking forward to seeing them beating the Steelers. Big Ben has been talking out the side of his neck."

"I thought about going to a sports bar to catch the game." Aiyden was relieved; she could tell by the way he sighed. "All right, and you can cook for the game on Thursday. I just ask you leave lasagna to the professionals."

Tyree gave him a blank stare while his words sank in. The memory caused a smirk at the corner of her lips. "You're going to have to let that go."

He raised his palms and gave a simple shoulder shrug. "I've let it go. I just need you to know it was never on *30-Minute Meals* for a reason, hun."

Tyree's chin dropped to her chest. She giggled softly as she recalled the time she'd been inspired by the Cooking Channel and tried surprising Aiyden and her dad with a lasagna she made using ingredients she had at home. She appreciated her favorite fellas trying to conserve her feelings. It didn't take her long to notice the meager bites they took were far apart. It took her telling them that they had suffered enough for Aiyden and her dad to let her know that the attempt was a miss . . . by a long shot. They ended up eating out that night.

Her laughter faded, and she sat with her eyes trained on Aiyden. He met her gaze with an inquisitive one.

"Penny for your thoughts." He sat back in his chair. His arms were at his sides, and his hands laid in his lap. His head tilted back as he awaited her response. He appeared open, eager to be let in.

"I had a great time with you and my dad that day. I can laugh at the funny moments." She looked away and blew a heavy breath, hoping it lifted the weight she felt in her chest.

"But it still hurts to think about him not being here anymore?"

Tyree found his eyes, surprised at how precisely he articulated her feelings.

"Yes. I try to get over my sadness by thinking about the good times, but how can I *not* miss him in doing so?" She twisted her trembling lips, trying to still the waters that beckoned at her lids.

Aiyden drummed his fingers on the table's wooden edge. His head angled to the side and his dark eyes focused on the area above her head. He was considering his words; she could see his passing thoughts.

"I think that it would be impossible. To think of him and not miss him. They go hand in hand. You wouldn't think of something you didn't long for. I think about you all the time."

Tyree's eyes widened at his admission. His face remained stoic as it searched hers. She didn't know what to say. At the moment, she tried to interpret the sensations pooling in her abdomen. His pensive stare had her anxious. Suddenly, she became self-conscious of her appearance. She grabbed the back of her neck and smoothed the loose curls at her nape; her eyes were fixed on her plate.

"Don't." Her eyes flew up to his, her brow arched in puzzlement. "You're perfect."

She swallowed. She so did not expect his straightforward appraisal and felt bad that she enjoyed it. Her and Kamaal had been broken up a mere month and here she was batting eyes at her ex. But all was fair, right? She balled a fist to her mouth under the guise of clearing her throat to conceal the swiping of her tongue over her teeth to catch any debris from her tasty meal.

"I have another penny."

Tyree chuckled quietly, amused by his cute way of trying to get inside her head again. He'd been full of questions tonight and showed a genuine interest in what she had to say. His occasional nod and interjecting to ask a clarifying question made her feel as if in the moment, nothing mattered more than what she had to say. Her voice echoed loud in significance. She didn't feel muted like she had grown accustomed to being in the glitzy superficial world of the ballers.

Not ready to advertise her true topic of reflection, she finished, "I'm just thinking, you never told me what your wager was."

Aiyden's head tilted; skepticism danced in his orbs and had her running from his stare that felt like it had the ability to laser through her fluff.

"Doesn't matter since I didn't win."

Tyree crossed her arms over her chest. "Right, but I still have a right to know what was at stake had I not won."

"I'll tell you later," Aiyden concluded with a scheming grin, ignoring her pout. "Spoiled ass."

"Are you going to try your drink at least?"

"Nigga, no!"

Tyree threw her head back and laughed.

twenty-three

"Tyree?" Aiyden called while gently knocking on the door. After a few seconds of waiting, he heard her answer.

Her voice was low and distant. "Yes, Aiyden?"

"I just wanted to check on you. If you want, we can talk."

A few more seconds of silence ticked away. "I'm good. I just have a headache so I'm just going to lie here. Thank you."

A sniff sounded every few words, and her sadness touched him in his chest. The news she'd received rocked her. Tyree tried to act as if it wasn't a big deal, that she already expected the worst and this wasn't a surprise. But this one hurt her, and she couldn't hide that fact.

"Sure. Goodnight."

He stepped away from her door and into his room. He picked up his phone and read the text message.

Toni: I can't get a hold of her. Is she OK?

Aiyden: She's OK. Just lying down. You'll probably get her tomorrow.

Toni: I hope so. Shit is crazy.

Aiyden: Yeah

He turned his television on and changed to the local news channel as he did every night. He liked to get a review of the day's events and an idea of the weather for the next day. Florida's weather could have a thirty-degree difference from the morning to the afternoon; the meteorologists stayed busy.

"Good evening, Jacksonville and surrounding areas. Thank you for tuning in to the ten o'clock news as we prepare for a spook-tacular Halloween tomorrow. Tonight, the latest bombshell in the Jacksonville Jaguars drama. It's being reported that Simone Sanders, wife of Hakeem Sanders, is pregnant and alleging that wide receiver Kamaal Duval is the father. More on this story in fifteen minutes."

Aiyden turned the television off. He could just check the weather from the app in the morning. He shook his head. *How is that news anyway? Local news has turned into TMZ.*

The news previewed the same information during a commercial that ran during the postgame coverage. They celebrated the Jags beating the Steelers while he and Tyree were straightening up from dinner. She was in the mood for Italian and cooked seafood alfredo, salad, and garlic toast. The food was great, and they had a pleasant conversation while they ate. Whenever Kamaal showed up on screen or was mentioned by commentators, he snuck a look at her. Each time, she seemed unbothered and really got into the game. Aiyden admired Tyree's strength and hoped it was a sign that she was truly OK. Then, that rug was jerked from beneath her again and sent her flying back into disappointment.

Aiyden walked into the kitchen and noted the clock on the stove; it was just after two in the morning. He grabbed a water bottle from the refrigerator and after quenching his thirst, he walked back to his room. Out of habit, he looked at Tyree's door and noticed it was open and she wasn't inside. He looked down the hall and saw that the bathroom door was also open. He wondered where she was and walked throughout the house in search of her. After checking the den, dining room, and living room, Aiyden still hadn't found her. He looked out of the blinds and saw that her car was still out front, so she wasn't far.

The noises coming from the garage alerted him of her presence. He slowly turned the knob and pushed the door; it hardly made any noise as it crept open. It was late and he didn't want to scare her and, depending on what she was doing in his gym, her being caught off guard could be dangerous.

Dressed in a black Nike sports bra and running shorts, Tyree sprinted on the treadmill. The rapid pace of her steps contrasted with the slow melody and words of Beyoncé's "Pray You Catch Me" that she had playing through his Echo. Her back was to him, and she hadn't realized he was there. *I should turn around*, he thought to himself. *That would be the respectable thing to do.* But he couldn't.

Her hair was thrown up into a messy bun on the top of her head. A few loose strands were stuck to her back. Her arms flexed as they pumped at her sides. He leaned over to get a peek at the monitors on the machine. She had been running for over an hour. Five miles had been traveled. He was impressed. For someone who hated running when they were younger, she accomplished a lot tonight, and he understood why. Like a nurse that pinched your arm hard before sticking you with a needle, she was creating more pain to focus on so she could forget about the other pain that kept her up that night.

He turned to walk away but stopped when he saw her place her hands on the rails and hop from the treadmill's belt. She put a foot on either side of the machine to take a break. Tyree bowed her head, and Aiyden watched her shoulders shake as she succumbed to her emotions. This was the Tyree she tried so hard to keep the world away from, the vulnerable woman who'd lost so much early in life that she kept herself protected and hidden. Aiyden walked further into the garage and stood beside the treadmill. He placed his hand in the center of her back to make her aware of his presence. She jumped slightly and turned to him.

His stomach plunged when he saw her face. Her eyes were red and swollen. All the crying she'd done had aggravated her sinuses, and he could hear the air struggling to flow through her nostrils. Her bottom lip quivered. At that moment, all Aiyden could feel was hatred for Kamaal. He hated the man who broke her. He hated that someone held the power to demolish her. He reached across her and turned off the machine and tugged on her arm. She didn't protest as she stepped down. Tyree stood before him with her head low as if she was ashamed he saw her at her weakest. With his fingertips, he urged her face upward so they were looking at each other.

"Keep your head up. Don't let your crown fall. For anyone."

Tyree nodded, and he watched her eyes fill again. Her sorrow ran down her face. Aiyden pulled his shirt over his head and used it to wipe her face. When he was done, the shirt was full of her sweat, snot, and tears. He didn't care; better there than on her beautiful face.

"That's better."

Tyree lifted one side of her mouth. They peered into each other's eyes, saying nothing. The room went quiet as if time stood still. The heat from him blanketing her was comforting. She was confused. The man whose arms she was in was the first one to disintegrate her heart, and his touch felt forbidden but she was still curious. She stared at him. Her first love and first heartbreak. She knew both sides to him; they'd been introduced years ago. Their history showed her that love was measured on a vast spectrum, ranging from the highest, most fulfilling measure to an agony so tormenting that one felt there was a part of them missing. With Aiyden, she experienced a love that influenced each part of her day. From the moment she opened her eyes at the start of her day to the moment she closed them after talking to him for hours, she felt full. It was young love, but it wasn't dumb. She didn't need more years to know that what they had was real.

Usually, when she thought about the good times with Aiyden, her mind also reminded her of the bad. Her subconscious would never let her only remember the half-truths. It kept her from going too far. But not right now. Now, she could only recall the best moments with him. She only thought about the fun they had, the smiles he caused. She just wanted to smile right now. She wanted to feel something. To feel . . . wanted.

Without thinking, she reached up and wrapped her arms around his neck and brought her body against his. Aiyden's brows dipped in surprise; he wasn't expecting this move. Tyree paused, giving him a chance to step back, to be the sensible one and put a stop to it, but he didn't. She pulled his head down to hers and met her lips with his.

She gasped when Aiyden's arms wrapped around her. He grabbed her wrists and locked her in his embrace as he returned her kiss. Tyree slanted her head and opened her mouth beneath his accepting tongue. His kiss could be used in combat; it could disband the strongest defenses. They could be standing on the first floor of the Titanic as it sank to the bottom of the North Atlantic Ocean, and Tyree would just want more of his kiss. Just like before, nothing else mattered when she was in his embrace. Her nipples hardened and pressed against the material of her bra. Aiyden groaned in response, letting her know he'd felt her budding arousal. Tyree felt him harden against her center and grinded against it. The contact awakened a desire for him she thought she had buried.

Beyoncé's ballad ended, and Sam Smith's "Safe with Me" filled the room. She listened to the pledges of a man who told his love they were safe with him, that he was there when the skies were cloudy and black. Damn, she needed that, and she felt that. The hurt of one heartbreak had her in the arms of the one who originally taught her that lesson. Tyree stepped closer into his embrace and further molded her body into his. Wherever he protruded, she grooved. They fit into each other's physique as if they were two halves of a set created for each other. The feeling of belonging he'd introduced to her before crept into her. He was familiar, and her body responded, letting her know it remembered him, missed him.

She added pressure as she continued to grind against him. The strength of his rod beneath his mesh shorts created moisture between her thighs and caused her to shudder. Her knees went weak, and she slacked against his frame, moaning as she massaged the back of his neck with her fingers, one of the places she knew excited him. Aiyden groaned again. He rubbed his hands up and down her back while their tongues danced and competed to stay on top of the other.

Suddenly, as if a warning sounded in his mind, Aiyden pulled his mouth from her and dropped his hands to his sides. Tyree frowned and confusion danced in her pupils. He reached up and gently pulled her arms from around his neck and stepped back. She felt cold from the loss and the disconnection.

"I'm going to get back to bed," Aiyden announced, abruptly leaving the room.

Tyree dropped her head, embarrassed. She wanted to get away from the pit that the news of Simone's pregnancy sent her back in. Had he realized she was using him to escape her misery? She cringed at the thought.

twenty-four

Tyree scrolled through gossip stories on The Shaderoom as she sat in the waiting area. It always amazed her how much she could miss in one night. Lately, her spare time had been spent replaying the kiss she and Aiyden shared. Him abruptly ending it felt like rejection, but after thinking about it, she was glad he came to his senses. Her emotions had been all over the place as of late, and adding a romance with him was the last thing she needed. She'd been wanting to talk to him about it, but she hadn't been able to catch him. His days at work had been longer, and he seemed to only be around when she was away or asleep. It felt intentional, and she didn't want him to feel like he had to avoid her in his home.

She'd been reading about the latest drama when a thump on her foot caught her attention. She looked up into the face of a blue-eyed little girl who looked no older than three. The girl pointed a stubby finger to the floor beside Tyree's foot where her ball rolled. Tyree leaned over and picked up the bouncy ball.

"Here you go, sweetie." She smiled at the baby while handing her the ball.

"Tank you!" She snatched the ball before running to the other side of the room where her mother sat. The woman thanked her for helping her daughter, to which Tyree smiled and let her know it wasn't a problem.

She couldn't look away from the adorable scene. The toddler tossed the ball to her mother, who sat in the office chair with one hand rubbing her protruding stomach. Tyree watched her dream take place in front of her. That was all she ever wanted. To belong. To be someone else's and for someone to belong to her. Only to her. She thought she'd hit the jackpot with Kamaal. She gained much more than a relationship, just for it all to be plucked away when she hadn't seen it coming. She hated Kamaal for cheating. She hated him for lying. She hated him for the sextape. But getting Simone pregnant? What about her made another man's wife worthy?

Tyree couldn't wait to be a mother; she'd been ready since she was eight years old, the age she was when her mom died in a car accident. She'd been incomplete since that dreaded day. There was nothing that could fill the void in her heart. She felt like a water pitcher that had a leak in it; no matter how much was poured into it, it could never remain full. Counseling, sports, Girl Scouts— none of it made her feel full. Until Zumie came along.

Zumie was Tyree's lifeline. A beautiful black baby doll her father gifted her for her ninth birthday. Tyree was immediately taken with the present; it represented way more than a present given out of obligation. Without realizing it, Tyree became the mother she missed dearly. Zumie was her. Tyree made sure her daughter went with her everywhere; no place was an exception. She couldn't risk letting Zumie out of her sight. When she let her mother go to the farmer's market alone, she lost her. Her teacher tried confiscating the doll one day in class, and Tyree lost it. It took her father meeting with the school's guidance counselor for it to be allowed. Tyree gave Zumie the mothering she was cheated out of. *Maybe it was divine intervention,* her inner pessimist observed. Maybe God wanted to let her down nicely. How could she yearn for something she had minimal experience with? Her immediate example had left early in her apprenticeship. How could she strive to be something she only had distant examples to study from? Did her loss warrant her being gifted with giving life? What made her deserving of such a miracle?

"Morris!" The nurse's call brought her back to the present. Tyree was thankful for the interruption, as her train of thoughts had been sending her spiraling into a fury of self-doubt and panic. That was a dangerous pit she'd frequented recently.

Tyree stood and met the medical assistant, who led her to a separate area and took her vitals. She then provided a clean catch urine sample as instructed before proceeding to the examination room.

"Knock, knock," her gynecologist announced before coming inside the room, followed by her medical assistant.

"Good morning, Ms. Morris. How are you today?" Doctor Elaine Thomas stepped inside the room with a folder in her hand.

Tyree smiled at the young doctor. "I'm great, Dr. Thomas. Thank you for asking."

"It's been about three months since we took out your implant in August. Do we think we're pregnant already?"

Tyree's eyes fell into her lap. When she left here weeks ago, she didn't plan on being back until she had a positive home pregnancy test. She planned on her and Kamaal being here together for the next visit as they began their journey into parenthood for the second time.

"Not quite." She looked up and met her physician's eyes. "I want to go back on birth control."

Dr. Thomas nodded. "Let's see here." She picked up Tyree's chart and pulled her glasses down from the top of her head to her face and read. After a few seconds of silence, she said, "Change in plans?"

Tyree nodded her response. They'd had many in-depth, doctor-patient conversations. Dr. Thomas knew of her plans of wanting to wait for children until she was married. Her last visit wasn't something that just happened. After the consultation where Tyree told her of her wishes, the appointment had been scheduled to remove the contraceptive.

"Yes, I'm no longer in that relationship or planning on having a baby. I just want to get on something more standard, like a pill, to help keep me regular." Another idea came to mind. One that embarrassed her to mention, but it was needed. "I also need an STD test," she asked in a muted voice.

"Certainly," Dr. Thomas agreed as if her request was nothing outside of the norm. She walked to her supply area and pulled a pair of latex gloves from the wall.

"Well, let's get you up here on the exam table so we can get you taken care of."

"All right, Ms. Morris, nothing needed from you today. We'll see you around this time next year," the receptionist advised when Tyree stopped to check out of her appointment. "Whoops. I forgot; we need an updated copy of your insurance card. I meant to ask for that when you first arrived."

"Sure, no problem."

As Tyree retrieved her wallet, she overheard another billing assistant repeating the same spiel she'd gotten. Seeing the gynecologist was usually a once-and-done visit each year unless an egg had been fertilized. Then, it turned into once a month.

"Mrs. Sanders, you are all set today. We don't need to see you until your annual next year, and we'll reach out to you thirty days prior for scheduling."

Sanders. That name was jingling a handbell in her mind. Why did it sound familiar? It was a common name, so it wasn't far-fetched that she'd been around another person who shared it. Tyree dismissed the conspiracy theorist in her, but an inkling in her spine wouldn't let up. The clerk helping her stepped away to make a copy of her insurance card, and Tyree used that moment to inconspicuously investigate the next booth.

Her gaze ran slap into that of the women who Kamaal allowed to come between them. Simone Sanders.

———⟡———

"I already know this story didn't go right because you didn't call me to bail you out." Toni interrupted Tyree's play by play of what happened at the doctor's office when she saw Simone.

Toni and Tyree were getting their hair deep-conditioned. The two made it a habit to catch each other up on the latest tea while sitting under the dryer at their favorite hair salon. Since she had to come into town for her hair, Tyree decided to make the most out of the drive by scheduling her doctor's appointment right before this one. She'd been demoted from balling to budget and had to, once again, be mindful of things like mileage and the price per gallon of gas.

The ladies were greeted with open arms when they entered

the salon. They didn't have to sit in the waiting area as the other clients did; their history, associations, and the generous tips they paid granted them preferential treatment. They were both escorted to the shampoo area. Peachey washed Tyree's hair, while her assistant took care of Toni. She couldn't help but flutter her eyes closed as the balls of Peachey's fingertips massaged her scalp. *Definitely worth the drive,* she thought as she tried to fight sleep. She was that relaxed. The drive was one of the few cons of moving so far from the west side of town. Even before moving to St. Augustine to stay at Aiyden's, Tyree trekked from the beach to the northwest side of Jacksonville to have her hair slayed and laid. Residing with the rich and famous gave her access to prominent people and the best resources. Still, there were things the affluent neighborhood couldn't provide, and a stylist she was comfortable putting her thick, long, 4c hair in their care was one of them.

"No, that hoe isn't worth that." Tyree saw a flash of red when she recognized the wrecker of both their homes, but she didn't succumb to the rage. She was about protecting her peace. She was rocked when the news hit and had her moments to process and react to it. Then, just as she did with Kamaal, Tyree had to let it go before it swallowed her whole.

"Please tell me you slapped the heffa, tripped her, something."

"I did something better than that," Tyree answered.

The response piqued Toni's interest, who lifted her dryer head to lean over toward Tyree. "What did you do? Headbutt her?"

"Nothing, Toni." Tyree shook her head, grinning. "I did nothing. I looked at her. Matta' fact . . . I looked right *through* her to let her know she was a non-factor."

Toni stared at her friend with a look that said she hoped she wasn't finished. "OK, Evelyn Lozada. That's all you did? You're acting like you from the southside. You know how we handle disrespect out west. I can't believe you wasted a perfect opportunity of waxing that ass."

Tyree wouldn't argue with Toni. Where they came from, disrespect was handled by way of a disrespectful ass whooping. In school, when someone told you to meet them behind the portables, you already knew what time it was. No talking.

"I did get something out of seeing her though. I heard that she doesn't have to come back until it's time for her next annual." Tyree waited a few moments to allow her friend time to catch on to what she was saying.

"That doesn't make sense. Why a year? The baby would be . . ." Tyree remained silent as the dots began connecting. "Oh!" Toni shouted, gaining looks from the other ladies who sat under hair dryers. "I guess something good did come from the run today."

"I'm letting the lord fight my battles, friend." Tyree pulled the dryer's hood back down and sat back.

"Oh, before I forget again, you're still coming with me to the classic, right? I hear it's going to be lit this year."

"Yes, I'll be there," Tyree answered as she rested her neck on the dryer's hood, closing her eyes for the remainder of the dry time. Finding out Simone wasn't pregnant felt like a break. She prayed it was a sign that things were turning back around for her. For the first time since the season opener, she felt relief regarding Kamaal.

"I sure hope one of these days you'll let me give you a natural style," Peachey stated while she towel-dried Tyree's hair. After her deep conditioner was set in by the dryer, she went to the shampoo bowl for another wash and was back in the chair for styling. "Your hair is so healthy and thick; it would really look good."

Tyree twisted one of her coils with her finger as she looked in the mirror and admired her natural tresses. She knew something that complemented her coarse hair would look good on her due to its thick texture, but she kept it straight and long because that was what Kamaal liked the best. He liked her hair in its natural, thick, and voluminous state, but he *loved* her hair straight and long. Now, she couldn't care less about what he loved; he hadn't when he rived her heart.

"You know what, Peachey?" Tyree met her hairstylist's eyes in the station's mirror. "No blowout for me today. Let's do a twist-out."

Two and a half hours later, Tyree smacked her lips to evenly spread the coat of Fenty Beauty lip gloss she'd just applied while she admired herself in her rearview mirror. She loved the fresh, natural style and wanted to snap a picture while her press was fresh. She pulled her phone from her leather baby pink Fendi Baguette crossbody and took a few selfies.

It amazed her how getting her hair done improved her spirit. A new do was a good confidence booster. You want to see an office full of black women in a chipper mood? Pay attention every other Monday morning. That day, the office was always filled with new sew-ins, relaxers, and braided styles. The Monday following payday was New Hair Monday. If you stayed still and very quiet, one could hear an orchestra of *"Yasss girl!"*, *"You betta!"* and *"OK, then!"* It was awe inspiring; it was pleasantly contagious. It was black girl magic, and Tyree was pleased with her potion.

The early November air was nice and cool. Tyree decided to roll down her window and open the sunroof as she thought about the other changes she would soon be making for her good.

twenty-five

Aiyden rearranged the letters on his phone screen. He tried different words; he wanted to get the biggest bang for his turn. His opponent couldn't come up with a high-scoring word, and he could sew up his win if he played this round the right way. After arranging the letters and utilizing both a double-letter and triple-word tile with one word, he was satisfied with the sixty points the word totaled and played it.

"Hey, you have a second?"

He looked up from his seat at his desk in the third bedroom he used as his den and home office to find Tyree leaning against the doorframe. He appreciated the way her black, form-fitting midi dress accentuated her womanly curves. The wavy, low ponytail sprang into a bountiful puff of coils from the hair tie at her nape and brought light and attention to her clear, baby face.

"Sure, come in."

Tyree stepped into the office and took a seat in the chair that was on the side of his desk next to an end table.

"Words with Friends?" she asked, motioning to his phone.

Aiyden nodded. "You play?"

She returned his nod. "I used to when it first came out, but I haven't in a long time."

"Same for me, then one day, I saw an ad and downloaded it again. It's cool; they added a lot of different things." He pressed the button on the side of his phone to lock it and gave her his full attention. "What's up?"

He noticed her eyes shift to the right like they did when she was nervous. Another one of her mannerisms he had decoded when they were together. He had Tyree figured out. She wasn't exactly how he remembered; she'd evolved, but who she was at heart remained. He figured he knew what she wanted to talk about. In a moment of weakness, Aiyden had shoved his tongue down her throat. The mishap happened at a time when she was dealing with the hurt of Kamaal's alleged child, and he cringed at the thought. A simple kiss had his imagination wild. As he was pressed into her, his mind could see all the ways he could have taken her in that very room. He could have bent her over the treadmill, or he could've laid back on the weight bench and let her take control. Shit, he even imagined what it would be like if she held on to the bars on the pull-up machine while he dug in and out of her from below.

Groping and grinding on her was not what he set out to do, and he felt humiliated every time he thought about it. He'd maneuvered around Tyree's routine to avoid her over the past few days. After he ended the kiss that night, they had barely spoken and only saw each other in passing.

She laced her fingers. "I think we should talk about the other—" Her words were cut off by the ringing of the doorbell mixed with pounding on the door.

"What the hell?" Aiyden stood from the desk and walked out

of the office with Tyree following closely behind. The ringing and banging took turns, one after the other with no break in between. He snatched the door, frowning, ready to go off on the visitor, only to be staring into his cousin's teary face.

"Toni?"

Toni threw her head back. Her fingers gripped her short hair, and she wailed, "I'm pregnant!"

"Look at this one, T. It can detect hCG earlier than any other test."

Toni took the box Tyree handed her and inspected further. "Shit, for twenty-two dollars, it should tell me a due date and the baby's gender," she fussed while putting the box inside the hand-held shopping basket.

After the dramatic revelation on Aiyden's doorstep, Toni walked inside and explained that she knew she was pregnant. She hadn't taken a pregnancy test, but her period didn't come as expected yesterday and she felt tired. Aiyden eagerly excused himself back into his office and left the ladies to deal with Toni's situation in private. Tyree convinced Toni to go to the store to get a pregnancy test to be sure. She was too distraught to drive or take an Uber, so they rode in Tyree's truck.

"How about we have a GNI? Let's get some snacks and some wine. We'll have a toast before you take your test. It just may be your farewell-to-freedom drink."

Toni grinned, liking the idea of a girls' night in. They used to have one at least once a month. Tyree moving in with Kamaal caused their nights to become more infrequent until they ceased to exist altogether.

"That sounds good. Let's grab some cookies before we leave this aisle."

The women were halfway to the snacks when an older white man turned into the aisle. He walked in their direction, with him and his basket remaining in the center of the space. Toni kept her position in the middle as they approached him. Tyree eased over to the right to move out of his way while Toni hadn't budged.

"Step aside, T," she urged her friend.

Toni, who was now right in front of the elderly shopper, answered Tyree while she kept her eyes on him. "No, we were here first, and I have yet to hear those two magical words."

She heard Tyree sigh, but that didn't move her. She and the man were at a standstill, and she refused to give in. Once the man figured that Toni was not moving, he scoffed and turned his basket around, leaving the aisle.

Toni smiled a grin of victory and turned to Tyree, who stood there and shook her head. "What?"

"What was the point of that?" Tyree pointed her head in the direction of where the man came and went.

"You saw. We were here first, and I don't play that," Toni answered, partially annoyed that she had to explain herself.

Tyree sucked her teeth. "Everything doesn't have to be a fight, Toni."

"And some things shouldn't *have* to be a fight, Tyree," Toni snapped in a voice louder than she intended. She agreed with Tyree to an extent. Knowing how to pick and choose battles was an important skill. A black person in America had so many things stacked against them; their life was at risk on all days that end with Y. Being black meant you were taught you couldn't do things like others. You couldn't play with a BB gun, you couldn't wear a hoodie, you couldn't listen to loud music or jog through your neighborhood. So why try it?

Just like many of her brothers and sisters, Toni had learned to adapt to the times. Whenever another devastating story about a black person being killed broke the news, she would follow the story to get the facts of what led to the loss of a priceless life. She needed to know what caused the situation to escalate. She needed to know what they had done that she shouldn't do if ever placed in the same predicament. So far, she learned not to question a police officer at a traffic stop, not to touch a gun for sale in the gun department of the store, not to dare try running away to save your life.

Call it hormones, call it desensitization, call it whatever. Today, she was fucking tired.

Tyree's expression softened. She nodded and squeezed her friend's hand.

"I hear you."

twenty-six

Aiyden kept his eyes on the woman who sat across from him. He nodded periodically, hoping to appear as if he was listening. He watched her lips; he could see what she was saying, but he hadn't heard a word. His thoughts had shifted to Tyree, and they made themselves comfortable there.

Brandy was a stewardess he'd met on a flight while on his way to a work conference some time ago. Her uniform hadn't left much to the imagination as it was welded to her wide hips. She made her interest known with the sultry tone she used only with him. Aiyden didn't miss the ambiguity of her words when she asked if there was *anything* she could do for him. Her fingers lingered on his hand when she passed him his drink. He looked down and saw the small folded note she slipped him that had her phone number on it.

Him and Brandy had been casual over the past year. He enjoyed her company. She was a cool chick; she wasn't shy about her wants and didn't press him about his life outside of her visits. She was aware of his situation and didn't add any drama to it. She would hit him up when she connected in the city, and they would get together and work each other's bodies out, and he wouldn't hear from her until she was routed his way again. When he lived in Orlando, where he settled after graduation, he would see her a lot. The airline she worked for had a large hub there, so they would hook up at least once every six weeks. When she sent him a message with a screenshot of her itinerary along with the heart-eyed cat and eggplant emojis, it had been six months since they last hooked up and since he'd gotten any.

The waiter stopped by their table and took their entrée order. Aiyden watched Brandy as she ordered her usual: fish and vegetables. She'd adopted a pescatarian diet, and it did wonders for her body—a body he was ready to explore again. That way, he would be able to share a space with Tyree without feeling like he needed to climb the walls. Their kiss the other night got him off balance. He thought about it while he was awake. He dreamed about it as he slept at night. He really needed to get a grip. Brandy's message had been right on time. He planned to treat her to dinner before he treated himself to her at a hotel, but Tyree had texted him to let him know she was staying at Toni's, so he decided to just take her back to his place instead.

"So, what's new with you?" his date asked.

Aiyden watched Brandy nibble on her fish. He enjoyed the show, but he didn't feel the pull in his core like he did when he watched Tyree eat. He wondered why that was. *Maybe it's because she tore my food up without an ounce of shame,* he thought. He tried cooking for Brandy a few times early in their entanglement, and she quickly let him know that anything with more than a certain number of calories or carbohydrates would not be touching her lips. He adjusted his dishes by opting for healthier options. Brown rice, if any, no dark meat, and even those changes weren't satisfactory to his body-conscious bed partner. He eventually gave up and bowed out to her strict regimen.

Brandy checked her lipstick in the makeup compact she pulled from her Chanel clutch. She finger-combed her wavy, shoulder-length hair and tucked a few strands behind her ear.

"Aiyden?" she called after a few beats of silence passed.

"Tyree."

Aiyden inwardly groaned as soon as the name left his lips. He hadn't meant to say it and just blurted out what was on his mind. Feeling bad for not being so attentive when she was speaking, he wanted to make up for it by resuming the conversation. He meant to call her name but mistakenly called the name of the woman who'd he been thinking about. Freud would feel vindicated.

"Tyree? Who's Tyree?" Brandy asked with a confused moue.

Aiyden cleared his throat. "That's what's been going on with me. A friend of mine is in a jam, and I'm helping them out." He hoped she didn't notice his slip-up.

"Helping them out how?" Brandy buttered a piece of bread and placed it on the saucer in front of her.

"By letting Tyree stay with me until she gets back on her feet."

The bread she was about to bite remained in the hand that paused in mid-air. "*She?*"

"Yes, she's my cousin Toni's best friend, and she asked me to help her out." Aiyden knew he was giving way too many details to Brandy, but he was doing damage control.

She paused. A series of reactions paraded her features. Aiyden braced himself, unsure of what to make of the sweet smile she gave. It intensely contrasted the hitch of disapproval in her breathing.

"I think that's commendable of you to help out someone in need, Aiyden. Thank you for sharing that with me." Brandy placed her hand on top of his and rubbed his knuckles.

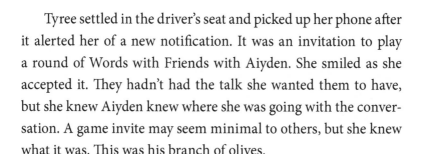

Tyree settled in the driver's seat and picked up her phone after it alerted her of a new notification. It was an invitation to play a round of Words with Friends with Aiyden. She smiled as she accepted it. They hadn't had the talk she wanted them to have, but she knew Aiyden knew where she was going with the conversation. A game invite may seem minimal to others, but she knew what it was. This was his branch of olives.

Toni's phone beeped, and Tyree could see her checking it in her peripheral. "Malcolm wants to meet up."

Tyree had much to say regarding Toni's dealing with him, but she knew now wasn't the moment. They would have that honest conversation at another time, when there would be less distraction from the dramatics of her disorderly life.

"What do you want to do?"

Toni nibbled her bottom lip. "I need to talk to him. No matter what the test says, things between us can't stay like this." She gripped the side of her neck and leaned her head over, using her hand as a headrest. "Could you take me back to Aiyden's? I can catch an Uber back home."

Since the two stopped at the grocery store up the street from Aiyden's, it wouldn't take long to go back to his place.

"No, just take my car. I don't need to go out anymore today, and it doesn't make sense for you to spend that much on another ride." Tyree knew that the fare to get her to her cousin's house over thirty miles away did not come cheap.

Toni agreed. "OK, I'll take your truck. Thanks."

twenty-seven

Aiyden shook his head, aggravated. He'd even surprised himself that night. Brandy had been sending all the signals he anticipated from her impromptu visit. The slow, long fanning of her eyelashes as she blinked. Constantly rubbing her delicate fingers up and down his arm. He gulped when she licked her anxious tongue around the rim of her wine glass. She wanted to fuck. Shit, he did too—at least he thought he did. In untypical fashion, Brandy's advances had the opposite effect as before. Instead of partnering with her in lustful expression, he mentally compared her to Tyree. Round for round, she lost a battle she hadn't known she was contending in.

He chuckled in defeat as he weaned his SS through traffic on 95. He was pining over a piece of ass he couldn't touch. Instead of burying himself into a willing participant, he ended the night right after dinner. *What kind of sprung shit is that?*

Brandy's expression plummeted when he declined her invitation to her room. She thought he was simply playing hard to get and took part in the role play until she realized he was as serious as a baby boomer during a thunderstorm. A string of profanities crossbred with her feelings of regret having wasted an overnight layover on him themed the text message and voicemail she sent to his phone.

He pulled into his empty driveway and cut off the engine when his phone chimed to notify him of a new message. He checked it, and his screen was filled with photos of Brandy clad in a lace negligee. Under the picture were the words, "What you're missing out on." He huffed as he exited his car.

Aiyden could hear bass thumping behind the door as he approached it and figured Tyree had left the television on again. When he walked in, the TV was powered off and the lamp in the corner of the room illuminated the space on its dimmest setting. He followed the sound blaring from his kitchen: a woman singing her request for someone to twerk for them.

Tyree arched her back impressively with her hands on her knees. She ticked her hips left and right in sync with the cadence of the beat. She wore a white, thin-strapped body suit tucked into light denim shorts with a frayed hemline. Her movements had them hiked up, giving him a peek at her smooth cheeks. Her back being to him had her oblivious to the fact she was putting on a show, a very sexy show, for him. Then, the chorus sang through the speaker with a bounce music beat that kicked up the intensity. Tyree straightened and wiggled her thighs, causing her ass cheeks to clap in her denim.

"Sheesh," he hissed. He leaned into the doorway, bracing himself on his shoulder with his crossed arms at his chest. He clapped to express gratitude of her bountiful booty bounce. Tyree's head jerked up and snapped in his direction. Her mouth and eyes expanded to their limits.

"Shieeet!" she shrieked as she clutched her invisible pearls.

She grabbed her phone and turned the volume down. Her chest rose and fell at the rapid pace of her speedy breathing. The layer of sheen on her bosom announced how hard she worked with her twerk.

Aiyden bit back his laugh. "I'm sorry. I didn't mean to scare you. You looked like you were enjoying yourself, and I didn't want to interrupt." He stepped closer to her. She bit her bottom lip and tucked a wayward curl behind her ear. The Jose Cuervo margarita bottle on the counter explained the large, glassy eyes that stared up at him.

She turned around and took a sip from her slim tumbler. "Well, I was before you rudely interrupted." Her playful pout was cute. He watched her eyes sweep him from head to toe. "You're looking jazzy. You comin' from a date or something?"

Aiyden looked down at his powder-blue button-up dress shirt, navy slacks, and cognac plain-toed oxfords, wishing the outfit wasn't revealing of his outing.

"Actually, yes."

Her playful frown deepened into a genuine one. "Oh, that's nice." She took another swig of her drink. "It's barely even nine o'clock. No nightcap?"

He tried to decipher the deflection in her voice. Was there disappointment?

"Naw, just a dinner with a friend passing through." He brushed past her, liking her soft floral scent. With a cup in hand, he turned around to her. "How about I join you for one?"

***

Tyree noticed Aiyden's hair. His edge-up was crisp, and the roots of his locs were twisted neatly. She could tell he'd recently tightened them up. She wondered if he went to a barber or if he sat in between a woman's legs like he did when she would tighten up his wicks when he began his loc journey.

His thick brows raised in question. "If you want to finish your scrub-the-ground session alone, I'll understand."

She blinked, mad that she'd gotten lost in his looks. Tequila made her feel warm and uninhibited, but it also weakened the guards she perfected as a defense mechanism.

"You're good. Here." She twisted the cap from the bottle and poured into his glass.

Aiyden thanked her and pulled open a kitchen drawer. "Wanna play some Tonk?"

She saw the box of cards he held up. "That depends. Do you feel like getting dragged?"

Aiyden laughed, entertained by her trash talk. "Aight. I'll deal first."

"Forty-nine! Automatic win, baby! What's that, three to one?" Tyree boasted. She stood from the dining table and pressed play on her phone, blasting "Twerk 4 Me" from the kitchen.

Aiyden grimaced, not enjoying her gloating. "Man, that's because you keep dropping like we're gambling."

Tyree pushed her bottom lip out dramatically, feigning concern. "Aw, poor thing. We can wager if you want. I could use a bowl of your grandma's famous chili," she offered over her shoulder.

The beat of the chorus dropping activated her like a dime in a jukebox. She assumed the position, with hands on her knees, and popped her ass up and down. The liquor in her system empowered her brazen actions. She was on drink number four, and he was finishing his second. His eyes grew tight with desire. *See, you still got it,* she thought.

Earlier that day, she fell into a trap by looking up Simone's social media profiles. It started with her trying to figure out what about her was so alluring that Kamaal would break her heart. Two hours of self-inflicted torture concluded with her determining she had the package: Amazonian height with curves in the right places and zero body fat in all others, long and wavy natural hair that damn near touched her ass crack. She wiped her tears when it dawned on her why she lost.

Seeing Aiyden enthralled by the sensuous sway of her hips raised her confidence from the ground level it had been on. She accelerated her popping, her movements mimicking those of a jackhammer as if she were on stage; the force of her speed caused her shorts to unbutton. Tyree didn't bother to snap it in place as she liked how the looser fit accentuated her moves.

The feeling of heat on her back prompted her to curiously turn her head, only to find that Aiyden had snuck up on her for the second time that night.

"Damn, I need to put a bell around your neck," she breathed out with a nervous chuckle.

"I like you twerking for me." He didn't join in her humor. His deep eyes slanted. His intense gawking had warmth building in her belly. Her hands rested on his firm chest; she could feel his rapid beating beneath her fingertips. It made her feel powerful, like she hadn't lost it all. In an unexpected move, Aiyden cupped her under her arms and lifted Tyree to sit her on the table.

They stared at each other. Their eyes were loud, showing the other how much they were worked up. The sensations she felt when they kissed before rushed her veins. The heat sailing through her body raising bumps on her skin had nothing to do with the cocktails she indulged in. They hadn't talked about the kiss in the gym. To Tyree, it was understood that it was a one-time occurrence, nothing more but Aiyden comforting her when she'd been distraught about the fake news of Simone's pregnancy. What would be their excuse this time?

Like opposing magnets, Tyree and Aiyden leaned forward, drawing closer to the other. Her blood rushed through her carotid; she could hear it thump just below her skin. The excitement of the moment's potential had her soaring. When Aiyden reached up to hold the back of her neck, she trembled from his touch. His strong hand pulled her forward and she, too, was ready to oblige, to met his lips in a forceful kiss.

Just as before, lightning struck the moment their mouths touched. She parted her lips beneath his, making room for his probing tongue and enjoying its sweet and tart taste of the margaritas. They tangoed in each other's mouth; Tyree was thrilled by their forbidden dance. Each day, she found herself journeying further down a road she told herself she would avoid.

The stiffness behind his zipper caused her to moisten, reminding her of needs she had ignored for weeks. She panted into his mouth, pulling him closer. Her hips rocked against his crotch. His tongue vibrated on hers as he groaned from his throat. She felt him stiffen even more. She was thankful their clothes were a barrier between them because without them, the intensity would've been fierce enough to create a baby.

Baby.

Tyree's eyes flew open. That four-letter word provoked an abrupt termination of their oral embrace. The fog cleared, and she hid behind her hands as she slowed her breathing.

"Hey, you alright?" The concern in his voice threatened the lock with which she secured her emotions.

"Yes, I'm fine," Tyree whispered. Bracing her palms on the table, she stood. Aiyden took a step back, allowing her space. "I'm sorry," she offered as she dashed to her room.

twenty-eight

Tyree pulled her phone closer to her face and tried to focus harder on the e-book she was reading as she laid in bed. She holed herself in her room, unable to face Aiyden after their raunchy encounter on the dining table. Had she not have scared sense into herself, there was no doubt she would have let Aiyden make a meal out of her right there on that table. The thought had her squeezing her thighs together. Needing to keep her mind occupied, she dressed down for bed and resumed her job search. After absentmindedly scrolling over a few pages without reading the job descriptions, she decided to end her search for the night and focus on something lighter.

Pleasure by Eric Jerome Dickey was the wrong choice; it was as light as a cluster of boulders. The descriptive adjectives used painted a picture as clear as the beaches of Exuma, Bahamas. Tyree closed her eyes and could precisely see how Karl, the bad boy twin, pleased Nia Simone Bijou. Him kneeling before her as she stood above him, out in a secluded area of the woods. The chirping of insects mixed with her whimpers and the shutter opening and closing as she snapped pictures of the way he loved her orally created the most sensual tune. *Chicken Soup for the Christian Soul* would've been a better pick for tonight.

She reached into her bedside drawer and pulled out her pink personal wand. *Lord, please turn your head.* She hoped God would oblige her prayer by looking away just for a few minutes; it wasn't going to take her long. She needed to get this out. Between the weeks of unplanned celibacy, an X-rated kiss from Aiyden, and the explicit details of the erotica she read, Tyree was horny. She powered on the vibrator and moved her panties to the side before setting it right on her pearl. She jumped from the intensity of the machine before it putting back on her. She closed her eyes and thought about a nameless, faceless man on top of her seeing that her needs were met. Her free hand cupped her left breast and pinched her nipple.

Tyree held her toy at the right angle and kept her hand steady as it pressed down on the wand. She nipped her top lip with her teeth as she rolled her hips, building the pleasurable burn. She sucked in a quick breath, and her stomach dipped. The buildup was approaching its finale. She pulled her nipple again; the pleasure from her breast and between her legs had her knocking on the door to her climax. The intensity of the vibration lessened, and the humming sound quieted some. Tyree pressed the wand down harder on her essence, trying to prolong the feeling. She was *riiight* there. She just needed a few more seconds and . . .

"Shit!"

She tossed the powerless toy to the other side of the bed, pissed. She was sooo close. Just a few seconds more, and she would've soared the skies. She was wound up . . . tight. This was cruel. It was unfair. Who had she wronged to be the recipient of the most unfortunate luck? She wanted to cry, but her gangster wouldn't allow it.

Her foot shook back and forth as she thought about going across the hall to Aiyden's room. *You bet' not!* Tyree knew Aiyden could put it down; she couldn't forget. Their encounter had her pressed, and she needed an orgasm to see things clearly. She pushed out a frustrated breath and slipped her hand into her sleep shorts.

Her clit was swollen and throbbed under her touch. She pressed down and rotated; the pressure caused a tingling to spark in her center. She closed her eyes again as the faceless man was gone and Kamaal was there in his place. Her eyes flew open. *No!* That was the last person she wanted to think about. She went back to work on herself and willed the nameless man back between her legs. She rocked her hips in a slow rhythm. The variance of pressure fanned her flame, causing it to grow. The figment freak she envisioned went back to work on her. His skill level warranted no instruction. Tyree spread her legs wider as she gave him more access. She pinched her pearl between two of her fingers and rolled it; it slid in her natural juices.

Her lids low, she saw him again. His head bobbed up and down as he continued to feast on her. He had to be a great swimmer; he stayed underwater, not coming up for air one time as his tongue danced in her. His wicks were soft and moist. She wanted to reach down and run her fingers through them.

Wait. When did my mystery man get hair? As if he could hear her silent inquiry, her pleaser peered up at her, his features no longer void. After revealing his identity, Aiyden went back to feasting on her, and she arched her back. Her fingers massaged her swollen sex as it mimicked the ways she envisioned how Aiyden would touch her.

With lips tucked inside her mouth, she hummed. Her arm was locked in position and her fingers rubbed rapidly, sending shockwaves to her center. She knew she was about to come and rode the shivers coursing through her veins. She was taking this episode with her six feet down. Whether or not the Lord obliged when she politely asked that He look away, it wouldn't even get to Him.

Tyree leaned back and stared up into the darkness. She slowed her breathing down to normal as the last of her tremors subsided.

"I'm disgusting," she chastised herself, turning over, ready for the good sleep she knew was on its way.

twenty-nine

Tyree woke the next morning bursting with nervous energy. The events that happened last night had her shaky about where she and Aiyden now stood. *Didn't you say you were never drinking again?* she berated herself. Alcohol wasn't the best choice with her being in such a fragile state. She cringed, thinking about how she paraded in front of Aiyden like she was the third member of the twerk team. He had just come home from a date with another woman, for crying out loud! It was obvious he wanted her; all the signs were there. Being able to extract longing from a handsome man quelled her pessimistic suspicion that she was undesirable. To get lost in the arms of a man who had just left the company of another woman felt like a win against his date.

She busied herself with her Saturday morning ritual of working out and cleaning up. She woke up just after six and hit the treadmill, then went right to the bleach. The Fabuloso brewing in the pot on the stove provided the house with a fresh, floral aroma. The bathroom was cleaned spotless and she moved on to the living room. She was about halfway through vacuuming when the doorbell rang.

"Hi." Tyree opened the door to greet the woman who stood there. A swift head-to-toe sweep let her know she was not a salesperson. She noted the navy-blue belted Gucci jumpsuit from the current collection that paired well with her black satin pumps and matching clutch. The woman could dress. Her warm ivory skin tone glowed without blemish. The curly bob that ended on her shoulder bounced in the breeze. She reminded her of Jurnee Smollett.

"Oh, hi," the woman answered with a scowl that did not conceal her displeasure. "I was hoping to find Aiyden. Is he here?" she asked as she craned her neck to see into the house.

Tyree shifted to the side to block her view. *Thirsty much?* "He's actually not home right now."

She was just about to ask to take a message because she was not about to let a stranger into Aiyden's house, when she saw a white Camaro pull into the driveway. The woman followed her line of vision and turned around.

"Oh, here he is," she perked with a smile.

Tyree remained in the doorway as Aiyden walked up. He had a peculiar look on his face that told he was not expecting the visitor.

"Hi, Brandy." He approached cautiously. "Hey, Tyree," Aiyden greeted.

Brandy's eyes lit in recognition. "Oh, *you're* Tyree. Over dinner, Aiyden told me all about how you have nowhere to go and that he's helping you. At first, I thought he was trying to run a game on me, but after seeing you . . ." she paused dramatically and eyed Tyree up and down. "I understand completely."

Tyree raised an eyebrow and glanced at Aiyden, who stood

with his hands in his pockets, looking everywhere to avoid looking at her. *Mhmmm.*

Tyree looked down at herself and took in her baggy tee stained by the bleach that splashed when she made the mop water, loose-fitting joggers, and Nike slides. She looked up and met Brandy's eyes. She wanted to knock that smug look right off her tight face. *Wouldn't be so confident if you knew he had his tongue down my throat after said dinner.* She bit the inside of her cheek, surprised by her possessive thought. A slip-up fueled by slight intoxication did not translate to any rights to Aiyden. Their time had passed.

"I'll get out of your way," Tyree spoke to Aiyden. She didn't respond to Brandy but turned around as they followed her into the house.

"She's pretty, dresses nice, and she's model thin. I guess that's what's in these days," Tyree held the phone's mic close to her mouth and talked to Toni in a hushed tone. She laid across her bed, having just left Aiyden and Brandy to have their conversation in private.

She heard Toni kiss her teeth. "No, it's not. You do know the average woman is size eighteen to twenty? You're at least five sizes below that, so you are considered thin when you think about it."

Tyree balanced her phone on her shoulder and leaned her head to hold it in place so she could fold her laundry. "The rules don't apply in the world I was in. A size eight is equivalent to a sixteen. Maybe that's why Kamaal went for Simone."

Toni scoffed. "No, ma'am! You stop that shit right now, Ty."

"I hear you," Tyree sighed. "I don't mind my size. I just know I won't ever make the cut for the Victoria's Secret Angel fashion show."

"Well, isn't that what caused it to be cancelled anyway?"

Tyree nodded into her phone. "Among other things."

"Exactly," Toni agreed. "Besides, Vicky's Secrets can't even hold all we have down there anyway. Savage Fenty for the win!" The two laughed, and Toni continued after they sobered. "Kamaal messed with Simone because she was willing and he was stupid. That's not on you. You *are* enough."

Tyree reciprocated her encouragement. "So are you, Toni." She hoped her friend truly heard her. She wanted Toni to want more for herself than settling to be a mistress. They didn't talk about her affair with Malcolm, but all the signs of its continuance were there. The way she would hide her phone's screen so Tyree couldn't see who she was in contact with. The disappearing to have secret conversations. Her evasiveness. She needed to realize love wasn't supposed to be a secret. When a man loved a woman, he should be proud, even boastful. She was worth so much more.

Two soft raps on her door caught her attention. "I'll call you back, T." Tyree ended the call and opened her door.

The co-star of her fantasy stood in her doorway in a black tank top and black jogger pants that hung on his waist. The band on the waist of his Calvin Klein boxer briefs was visible, as his pants sagged slightly. Images of her salacious, orgasm-inspiring fantasy flashed behind her eyes. The junction between her thighs flexed in an involuntary kegel. *Be still, petunia!*

"Hey." His greeting was timid. He looked unsure as his eyes searched hers, trying to gauge her temperament.

"Hey," Tyree answered tightly. She'd been bothered by his visitor and her remark about Aiyden disclosing her predicament. Why had she been a topic of discussion? She could only imagine what else had been said. Did they talk about Kamaal? Did they laugh at her pain while discussing Hakeem's interview? The sex tape? Her confidence plummeted from its elevation, brought on by Aiyden's blatant wanting of her last night.

"Where's your friend?"

Aiyden glanced away for a second. When he returned his eyes to her face, Tyree read their disappointment. "She left to report for duty at the airport."

She nodded. "She's a flight attendant?" He gave an affirmative dip of his head. "That's nice." She didn't know what else to say.

Aiyden's small shrug told her she had been a reason for this cutty friend's departure. She hoped God didn't judge the sliver of satisfaction she got from that. Envy green didn't look good on her.

"Don't worry about it. I hope you weren't uncomfortable with that." He slipped his hands inside his pant pockets.

"It's fine, Aiyden. Really, it is." The smile she gave was more authentic than she'd been able to muster all morning. She worked to keep it from fading as he walked up until he stood before her. "You don't have to worry about you and me. It was just a kiss, nothing more."

Aiyden's eyes stretched at her forwardness. "Friends?" he said, with an outstretched hand.

She looked down and studied his hand. A truce wasn't needed. He really hadn't done anything wrong. Wanting to get past this moment so it could be stored in her mental vault, never to be talked of again, Tyree accepted his hand and shook.

"Friends," she repeated while she tried to ignore the flutters she felt from his touch.

Yes, it was time for her to move out and move on.

thirty

Tyree smiled at the spitting image of her friend. Cherise's twin sister, Channing, opened the door and pulled her into a friendly hug. Channing and Cherise were closer than close. A lot of the time Tyree spent building a friendship with Cherise included Channing because they were usually together. Thus, Tyree gained a bonus friend. They were a bundle deal that could not be separated.

"Hey, girl!" Channing stepped aside. "It's good to see you."

"It's good to see you too," Tyree replied as she walked inside.

"Where's Toni?"

The question made Tyree choke; she cleared her throat to play it off. "She's getting over a cold and didn't want to bring her germs."

"Aw, that's too bad. Tell her that I hope she feels better, and we missed her today."

"I will be sure to pass that along," she said, knowing she would do no such thing. Being in Cherise's face knowing the dirt about Toni and Malcolm had been awkward enough. She felt it was best to leave that topic untouched until she was able to get ahold of her own problems.

Tyree admired the changes that had been made to the house since she last saw it. Cherise had redecorated most of the house when she got urges during her nesting period. The cool theme had been switched in favor of warm, bright colors.

The two walked in the direction of voices and laughter until they met the crowd in the great room. She waved and said hello to the group at once.

"Hey, Ty," Cherise greeted from her seat on the sofa. An older version of Cherise sat beside her, cooing at the infant she held. Tyree walked over to Cherise and the two hugged.

"I want you to meet my mom, Candace. She's visiting from Miami and will be staying with us for a few months to help with Malcolm Jr."

"That's awesome. Nice to meet you." She smiled at the woman, who smiled back and repeated the sentiment. Tyree turned back to Cherise and handed her a baby-blue gift bag. "This is for you."

"A bottle for the baby and a bottle for mommy too." Cherise read the card that was tucked in the bag on top of the decorative tissue paper. She first pulled out a Tommee Tippee baby bottle. "Awww."

"Google said it is designed to mimic the shape of a woman's breast to make it easier for babies to take it even though they're breastfed."

"I did read that in a blog," Cherise's mom confirmed. "That's a good one."

"Thank you, Tyree." Cherise placed the bottle down on the glass table in front of her and reached back inside the gift bag. "Ooweee!" She squealed as she pulled out a bottle of Ace of Spades Champagne.

Tyree laughed. "Just a little something to make the best of your quiet moments, whenever you get to have them."

"I'll take that off your hands." Malcolm appeared behind Cherise and took the bottle of champagne from her. "You will not be getting my son drunk."

"It's called pump and dump. Now, give me my bottle!" Cherise reached for the bottle that Malcolm pulled away from her.

Malcolm playfully swatted her hand away and held the golden bottle up in the air. His wife was no match for the reach that came with his six-and-a-half-foot stature. The people in the room snickered at the playful bickering between the two. They looked like a couple in a love so strong that nothing could penetrate it.

"Hi, Tyree."

"Hello, Malcolm. Congratulations on MJ. He's precious." Tyree's words were sincere, but the smile on her face was fabricated. *Lying, cheating ass.*

"Thank you; we're truly blessed." He placed his arm around Cherise's shoulders and drew her to him. He placed a kiss on her temple. Tyree got his message. He was showing her the happiness she had the power to destroy with what she knew about him, but the message wasn't needed. She cared about Cherise too much to deliver the news to her right now.

"I'm glad you know it. A lot of men tend to forget about what they have at home." Tyree gave him a pointed look. The others in the room hushed, and everyone looked at her. She knew they all thought she was talking about Kamaal, and that was fine. Malcolm knew those words were for him. He slowly nodded with a somber expression on his face. The doorbell rang, and he excused himself to go answer it.

Saved by the bell, she thought.

Cherise grabbed the infant from her mother and kissed him tenderly on his cheek. "Go wash your hands so you can hold him."

After returninig from the powder room, Tyree eagerly held her arms out for the bundle of joy. She settled him in the crook of her arm and fell in love the moment she gazed down into his face. His smooth skin resembled the color of caramel, and he smelled like a mixture of baby lotion and milk.

"Hey, precious. You're going to be a little heartbreaker, aren't you?" Tyree cooed. As if he understood her words, Malcolm Jr. laughed in his sleep, and she fell more in love. One day, she would know what it felt like to cuddle a child that came from her, and she couldn't wait.

"Another one of MJ's uncles is here," Malcolm announced, walking back in the great room.

Tyree looked up, and her gaze instantly crashed with Kamaal's. Her eyes widened for a second, and she recovered quickly, replacing her look of shock with one of indifference. The room remained silent. The bystanders looked back and forth between the two as if they were opponents fighting for the first-place trophy at the US Open.

Just as when she'd bumped into Kamaal—*or when his fists repeatedly bumped into the nose of a pestering admirer*—Tyree knew there was a possibility of her seeing him there. He and Malcolm were good friends, just as she was with Cherise. They had many double dates and even went on a few bae-cations together. She didn't expect for Kamaal to stay away from his friend just because they had dissipated. While she got dressed this morning, she tried to mentally prepare herself just in case. She unintentionally spent twice the amount of time it usually took to do her hair and makeup. Just in case she ran into Kamaal, she wanted him to see she was doing just fine without him. She wasn't prepared to see him looking as if he was fine without her also. He had a fresh hair-cut. Instead of the hair on the top of his head being a little longer than the sides, he now sported a low fade. His trimmed sideburns seamlessly flowed into his thick beard and goatee. It wasn't fair for him to look that good.

"Ty-Ty!" Karl appeared from behind his dad and ran over to her. Tyree leaned over to the side and hugged Karl, careful not to wake the baby that was now sleeping in her arms.

She smiled at him. "Hey, sweetie!" She missed him so much. It was hard being away from Karl, as he'd become a big part of her life. Her breaking up with Kamaal meant she had to sever those ties with his son. That was a part of their split that Tyree hadn't thought about when she reacted to the devastation of Kamaal's betrayal. She had pulled the trigger and shot at their relationship, sending bullets flying in all directions to ensure it didn't make it. She didn't consider the others who were caught in the crossfire. Pulling the trigger on Kamaal and Tyree also took away Aunt Brenda and little Karl. She lost a mother and a son. There were days she cried at the thought alone. She woke up having it all one morning, and by nightfall, it all was taken from her—all because he broke her trust and reintroduced her to heartbreak. Talk about déjà vu.

"Come and meet your nephew, man." Malcolm headed toward the couch. Kamaal waited a few seconds and reluctantly followed.

Tyree's palms moistened with each step. She wasn't ready for this. She should've sat this Sip and See out, but she knew she couldn't do her girl like that. Now that she was facing her ex before she was ready, she regretted not sending that 'I'm sorry, but . . .' text. She shifted Malcolm Jr. so his father could pick him up, but he declined.

"No, I don't want to bother him while he sleeps. We can just look from here." He and Kamaal stood above her and watched the little guy sleeping. They looked on as they made observations and debated which parent he favored more. Malcolm Jr. began to squirm in her lap, making it known it was feeding time, and a very attentive Cherise speedily whisked him away to nurse him. Malcolm and Kamaal went to talk football in the den, and Tyree relaxed at the distance between them.

Karl came in from the backyard where he played with the other children and walked up to Tyree.

"Ty-Ty, I'm thirsty. Can you give me something to drink?" he asked, panting.

Tyree excused herself from the conversation she was having and walked with him to the nook area where refreshments were set up. She poured punch into a clear plastic cup for him and put a few finger foods on a plate when she noticed his hands were filthy and took him to the bathroom to wash them.

"Make sure you scrub good and get under those fingernails," Tyree instructed from above him.

Karl sped up his scrubbing in response. His exaggerated washing sent soap flying everywhere.

"Hey now!" she playfully barked while she wiped the bubbles from her chin. Karl giggled an apology and rinsed his hands.

"Are you still mad at us?" he casually asked.

Tyree handed him a napkin to dry his hands. "Mad at who, sweetie?"

"Me and my dad."

"You?" Tyree frowned. "Why do you think I'm mad at you?"

Karl averted his eyes. "Because you left us." Somberness overtook his expression.

Her heart tore. What could she say? He was right. She didn't leave him when her and Kamaal separated, but that is what happened. Like Cherise and Channing, Karl and Kamaal were a deal. They belonged together; they were inseparable.

"It seems that way, and I am sorry I haven't been around. I didn't want to leave you. There are grown-up things that your dad and I are dealing with, and I need to be away." She wanted to add "for a while" but knew it would only make matters worse to give false hope. She leaned forward until their gazes were level with each other.

"I'm not staying there with you, but that doesn't mean I am not always thinking about you. Do you think about me too?" Karl nodded. "Good, that means we are together in our thoughts. I am always here for you. You know that, right?"

Karl tucked his chin and nodded. She knew that meant he didn't like what he was being told, but he understood it.

"We can't do stuff together anymore?"

She glowered with regret. "Not really, sweetheart. I'm sorry." Her lips clamped closed. They had to be or else she would end up promising things she shouldn't. The Band-Aid needed to come off—slowly, but it had to go. She loved him too much to give false hopes. Things were different, and he needed to hear that from her.

"What about my game? You said you were always going to be my number one fan for my Jaguars game." Karl sniffed his disappointment.

He was right. The Jaguars held a special game where the children of the players and staff played at the stadium. The event was closed to the public; only family and friends could attend. Ever since Karl became old enough to play, Tyree cheered him on the sidelines, going all out and above what she did for Kamaal's games.

"I'll be there." Tyree figured his game was neutral enough grounds for her to be able to still offer her support. Karl's face broke into an abounding smile, and he wrapped his arms around her, hugging her. She cherished the thought of meaning so much to one of her Duval men. "Let me take you to your dad on my way out."

"You didn't have to walk me out."

Kamaal looked down at Tyree. When she brought Karl downstairs to the man cave to leave him there, he insisted he see her out to her car.

She peered down the street, while Kamaal unashamedly admired her. He watched the small beauty mark on the right side of her jaw twitch by the way she chewed the inside of her cheek. Her hair was in its coarse, coiled state and was pulled up into a full puff on the top of her head. The swirly pattern she laid her edges in gave a youthful vibrance to her young face. A layer of shiny gloss adorned her thick lips. He pressed against his zipper as he remembered how deadly those soft pillows could be.

"I wanted to speak to you for a moment." He stepped forward, and she stepped back, instantly widening the gap he just shortened. He cleared his throat to hide his hurt from her rejection. Her needing to keep space between them pierced him. He took two slugs in the chest. "I know Karl talked to you about his game. I just wanted you to know you don't have to go if you don't want to."

He watched her spine stiffen. With a serious eye roll, she answered, "I know that, but I want to be there for my guy." Kamaal peered at her; he kept his expression nonchalant. "That's unless . . . you have a problem with me coming to Karl's game."

He felt like he was walking into a trap but took timid steps anyway. "Why would I have a problem with you coming to his game?"

He'd taken the bait. She rolled her almond-shaped eyes up to him. "I don't know. Maybe Simone wants to cheer him on." Her mouth twitched in irritation by the mere mention of her name. "I hear congratulations are in order," she added, appeasing the devil in Prada pumps swinging from her left shoulder.

His face hardened at the mention. The name reminded him of his transgression, one he had no excuse for. Her name was powerful. It could halt his agenda by just being spoken. It was the trump card. When it was thrown on the table, there was no tallying necessary. Its rank was instantly recognized. He sucked his teeth loudly.

"That shit isn't true. It's just Hakeem fucking with me. But you just wait."

Her interest was piqued by the menacing tone of his voice. "What? Wait for what, Kamaal?"

"Nothing." He shook his head and focused his gaze down on her, his emerald scrutiny full of fury. "I don't have a problem with you coming," he resigned. He slipped his hands into his back pockets. The movement caused his shirt's material to thin as it extended across his burly pectorals.

"Great, then that settles it." Tyree pulled her phone from her purse and began typing away at the screen. She needed the distraction. Desire needled her skin and reminded her that this had been the longest she'd gone without sex. She didn't even send Kamaal a glance as she walked away. She continued to type as if she were lost in her phone, totally forgetting he was there. He felt disregarded, forgettable. He'd been kicked out of the club and was dying to find a way back in.

Kamaal spent most of his time in Malcolm's den, pretending to pay attention to what his teammate and friend talked about. He'd been busy replaying the moment he walked into the great room and saw Tyree on the couch with the newborn in her arms. Her smile had been bright and showed the deep dimples in her mocha-colored cheeks. His stomach had dropped at the sight. An image he dreamed about many times was before him. He pictured it just like that; it was all he wanted. A knot formed in his throat when he remembered he wouldn't get it. He'd been so close to scoring the baby he desperately wanted but lost his grip and fumbled the ball in a moment of vulnerability. What he wouldn't give for a flag to be thrown on the play; he just needed one do-over.

A buzzing in his pocket drew his attention to his waist. He pulled the phone from his pocket and read.

U really messed up... u'll find out

Kamaal frowned; the message was sent from an unknown number. He wondered if it was truly a message intended for him. Without thinking much of it, he deleted it and went back inside. He was ready to go home.

thirty-one

Tyree tried to mitigate her nerves as she swallowed to push down the lump in her throat. She glanced at the clock on the stark-white wall for the umpteenth time. *What's taking him so long?* She'd been on edge ever since the detective called and asked that she come to the sheriff's office for an update on her case.

"Hey, it's going to be OK." Aiyden placed his large, strong hand on top of hers.

She stopped the absentminded tapping of her fingers on the table. "Thank you, I hope so." She was glad Aiyden had been home when she received the call. As if he could detect her fear, he offered to drive her to the sheriff's office. The week after the dinner he prepared as payment for his lost bet had been refreshing. Their talk, even his candid remarks, were like an ice pick to the superficiality of their interactions. Conversation turned organic as their comfort level with the other improved.

"Sorry to keep you waiting." The door to the interview room opened and an olive-complexioned, medium-built man with salt-and-pepper hair walked into the room. "Thank you for getting with me so soon, Ms. Morris," he greeted Tyree while shaking her hand.

Aiyden stood and shook the man's hand. "Hello, I'm Aiyden Hughes, a friend of Tyree's. Nice to meet you."

"Nice to meet you as well, Mr. Hughes. I'm Detective Jack Abrams, and I am working Ms. Morris's case." The detective took off his charcoal-gray suit jacket and hung it on the back of the metal chair before taking a seat. "I called you here today to give you an update on your case. We were able to get surveillance footage from the hotel and wanted your opinion."

Tyree nodded as she folded her hands in her lap. "OK."

"Great," Detective Abrams responded. "If it's all right with you, I'd like to show you that footage."

Tyree pursed her lips as she considered his suggestion. She wasn't sure what good it would do if she were to see the tape. She was there, and as much as she wanted to, she couldn't forget a single moment of the assault. Knowing that the detective would not have suggested it if he didn't feel it was necessary, she agreed.

"Yes, it's OK."

Detective Abrams opened the laptop that had been sitting on the table and pulled up the video player. The three of them watched as he pressed play and the video began.

The images of her walking down the hotel hallway before she was ambushed by a tall man that hemmed her up on the wall disturbed her to her core. Seeing the video heightened her senses and catapulted her back to that day. She could feel the weight of him on her back and the warmth of his breath on her neck. She jumped when she felt Aiyden's hand encase hers in her lap.

"You have to breathe, Ree," he coached. Tyree released the breath she unknowingly held and turned her attention back to the computer's screen. She watched as the husband and wife, along with their two children, walked up and scared the man away. Tyree turned away from the video when the screen displayed her sliding down the wall to the floor.

"I know that is hard to see, Ms. Morris, and I want you to know we are doing everything we can to solve this case. However, I do need to be honest with you." He sat up and placed his elbows on the table. "Other footage shows that the assaulter had been watching you while you were by the pool. He waited in the shadows and hid in the hallway while others passed until you went inside."

"It sounds like she was targeted," Aiyden observed. His voice was tight, and Tyree noticed the flex of his jaw.

Detective Abrams nodded. "That's what I believe as well. We ran the plates of the car, and not surprisingly, the car was stolen. Now, we are working on getting with the vehicle's owner to see if we can determine who stole the car. If it is the same man who assaulted you, we will be that much closer to solving this case."

Tyree took in his words. She wasn't feeling any better about the situation than she'd been when they arrived at the precinct. Hearing and seeing how she'd been sought out by the attacker had unnerved her. What had she done to deserve that?

"Me and you can give them both a taste of their own medicine." Those words haunted her. Some days, she couldn't get them out of her head. Those thirteen words played on a continuous loop like a song you couldn't stop thinking about. A broken record. Tyree wished the case would be solved soon, and she hated feeling that it grew colder with each day that passed with it being unsolved.

"Until we can confirm you weren't sought out and targeted, it's best that you continue to remain off the grid. Try to deviate from your normal routines and utilize the buddy system as much as possible."

Tyree sighed. She hated feeling like she had to hide but would do what she needed until that crazy person was locked up. Hearing the detective's suggestions made her glad that she stuck to her decision to not stay with Toni. She would never forgive herself if she were to put her friend in danger.

"I will make sure she does, Detective," Aiyden answered before she had a chance to speak.

Aiyden watched Tyree as she settled in his passenger's seat. She'd worn that synthetic smile during most of the meeting with the detective, but he could see through it. She struggled with the news she received, and seeing the video made it worse. It took everything in him not to flip the table when he saw how that motherfucker pushed her against the wall. He knew flipping out wasn't going to help Tyree, and he held on to that notion to keep his control.

He told himself that his anger was due to him caring for Tyree as a friend. That seeing any woman being attacked would piss him off. That thought sounded good, but he had to be honest with himself. He kept thinking about how devastated he would be if the family hadn't walked up and scared the harasser off. A chill slithered down his spine when he imagined what could have happened.

Aiyden knew there were deeper reasons to explain his response to the video, but he decided it best that he didn't delve into them. He refused to. He and Tyree were hot and heavy when they were kids, and that was that. All they could be now were friends.

"There's a game coming on in a bit, how about we put something together and watch it at home?"

Tyree turned her attention to him and grinned. "I would like that a lot."

thirty-two

"*Hi, Ty-Ty. It's me, Karl. Remember, my game is this Saturday, November 12, and you said that you were going to be there. K, love you, bye.*"

Tyree stared up at the stadium through her windshield as she sat in the parking lot. She replayed Karl's voicemail message the entire drive over. His reminder pushed her to stay en route to the venue when her nerves nearly succeeded in making her turn around. *Lord, please be a headache in that boy's daddy's head so only Aunt Brenda will bring him.* Even if God answered her petty prayer, Tyree knew it wouldn't be enough for Kamaal to miss his son's game. Kamaal could total his car and break his leg on the way to the game, and he would hop all the way there with a smile on his face. With him being the only present parent in Karl's life, Kamaal worked harder to give him everything so his miniature version would be so occupied with all he had, he wouldn't notice what he was missing. Man, he reminded her so much of her father.

It was twenty minutes before kickoff, and she needed to head inside. A quick glance in her visor mirror confirmed that her no-makeup look was still fresh and not in need of retouching. She placed the Jaguars dad cap on her head and pulled it down on her straightened hair that was parted down the middle before stepping out of the car to check her full reflection in the shiny paint of her truck. The teal midriff top, Balmain distressed high-waist skinny jeans, and Balenciaga sneakers seemed suitable for today when she assembled the outfit a month ago, but now it seemed inappropriate. On Kamaal's arm, she was comfortable with taking more risks, being daring. There wasn't a ring on her left hand but having a burly Adonis on her arm had the same effect. Now that she was a single woman, she found herself covering up more. She would rather go without the attention, and the thought of getting it from Kamaal or anyone else made her palms secrete. Everything about this day made her nervous. She wished Toni could've made it, but she cancelled at the last minute, claiming cramps had her stuck in bed with a heating pad. Tyree found that odd since they normally caught their cycles at the same time and hers wasn't due for another two weeks.

She saw Kamaal briefly when she stopped by Malcolm and Cherise's to see their baby, but this sighting was different: it was public. The buzz surrounding their love quartet had died down, but she knew curious eyes and cameras would be on her today. This would be her first time being around Kamaal with spectators around, and she needed to remember that a picture was worth a thousand words, and it didn't take much for people to draw the wildest conclusions from the least amount of context.

Her head straight, eyes forward, and back tall, Tyree strutted through the stadium like she was working for tens across the board at the ball. The confidence she exuded was potent and opposite of how she truly felt. The uneasiness flowing throughout her body reminded her of the jitters she felt the first time she'd come to the stadium as Kamaal's guest. Tyree was a firm believer in never letting people see her sweat, so she'd be damned if she even glistened. Even though she had lost her happy home and acquired family, it looked like she still possessed everything. And right now, that meant everything.

"Tyree!"

She stopped walking and turned toward where she heard her name being called. It was Lisa, Jeremiah Cunning's girlfriend, waving her over from her seat near the field. She put on a smile and walked over to Lisa and the other families that came to support the young players.

She stood in front of their row and greeted Lisa and the other WAGs.

"I was hoping I saw you today; we've been thinking about you. How have you been?"

Tyree looked at the bothered looks on the women's faces and felt that a part of them was genuinely concerned for her. But she knew their nosey asses were just trying to get in their business; it's what they did for entertainment. Besides, she'd seen them at Cherise's a few weeks ago.

"That means a lot. Thank you." Tyree placed her hand across her chest, acting as if she'd been moved. "I've been great." She smiled.

"I haven't seen you around the neighborhood. Did you move?" Amanda, wife of defensive back Daniel Knowles, asked.

Tyree looked at the woman who sat at the end of the row. "Yes, I did move. Kamaal and I think it's best to live separately while we work things out." She regretted the words as soon as she said them. The women's faces lit up, letting her know she'd thrown them the bone they were searching for.

"It's wonderful to hear you guys are working things out, Tyree.

I admire you for going after what you want no matter how embarrassing it may be."

Tyree was certain she heard a record scratching. Kamaal's mistress's friend, Keisha, sat back in her seat with a smug expression on her face. She'd been a close friend of Simone's ever since their men played together in Dallas. Tyree understood the woman's need to shoot darts at her in defense of her bestie. She almost expected it. She knew it wasn't easy over in Simone's camp seeing that most blamed her for the discord within the team. In those weak moments when Tyree fell to temptation and perused gossip sites, any comment about "homie hopper" or "Jag jumper" included a snake emoji. Yeah, commenters would go in on Kamaal for his involvement, but Simone was a woman and with this society, it was *she* in the equation who was faulted the most.

"I appreciate that, Keisha, it means the most coming from you because I know nothing could be as embarrassing as that thing that happened with Cortez and your sister, but look at you all today. Ain't God good?"

A voice came over the speaker and announced that the game was going to start in five minutes.

"I'm going to take a seat over there, so I can get good pictures. It was good seeing you all again." Without waiting for them to respond, Tyree walked to the next section, leaving Keisha to pick her face up from the bleacher as the others discussed the encounter in true messy fashion. *Fake ass Sunbeams,* she thought, causing her to chuckle.

Hopefully, she learned a valuable lesson concerning herself with the dust bunnies at her front porch. "Bitch."

Tyree settled in her seat and took a few pictures of the stadium. The event was open only to the families of the children who were playing, which allowed her to take advantage of the things she couldn't see when she sat above.

Now that she'd gotten that awkward encounter out of the way, she could focus on why she was there: to support Karl. She'd just posted a few pictures to her IG story when the air around her seemed to thicken. Strands of hair on her neck stood erect as a sense of familiarity overcame her. Her pulse quickened and all the saliva in her mouth evaporated, which only meant one thing.

She sensed Kamaal the moment he approached her row. Their connection allowed her to pick up on his presence before he had the chance to make it known. Their separation hadn't severed that line.

"Hi, Ty," he greeted her while taking the seat beside her. "You look beautiful."

She closed her lids and rolled her eyes.

"Thanks," she answered without looking up. The scent of his Versace Pour Homme cologne infiltrated her nostrils, sending vibrations through her. *Nigga think he slick. He knows what that cologne does to me.*

She had immediately thought of Kamaal when she tested the fragrance while shopping at the town center one afternoon and bought it for him. The cedar and musk notes complemented his natural smell, combining to make the perfect concoction that caused instant panty wetness. Before, the scent brought about carnal thoughts of coitus. Now, it turned her stomach.

Her cheeks puffed with the deep breath she took before easing it through her parted lips. She deliberately chose her seat so she could minimize interacting with others. In separating herself from the larger group, she made it easy for Kamaal to have a moment alone with her. Just like her moving in with Aiyden, her decision pushed her closer to an ex she wanted space from.

Her eyes remained on her phone as she opened her Gmail application. Now seemed like the perfect time to clean out her inbox.

"How have you been?"

Tyree sighed. He was really going to do this. After everything that happened, he was going to sit there and engage in small talk as if they were two pals catching up. He conversed as if he hadn't yanked her heart out of her chest.

"I've been really great." *Without you.* She resumed reading the promotional email she received from Sephora.

"That's good," Kamaal replied. He didn't wait for her to ask him how he'd been because he knew it wasn't coming. "I've been worr—"

"Woo-hoo!" Tyree jumped from her seat and clapped while she watched the young players run out onto the field. *Perfect timing,* she thought. The group of girls and boys waved at the crowd; their eyes searched for their loved ones in the bleachers.

***

Kamaal sat back. He wouldn't try to force the conversation. He knew Tyree was using the game as a reason not to talk to him, and he would leave it there. She hadn't run in the opposite direction when he sat beside her, so he celebrated the small victory.

Karl found Tyree in the stands and rushed over to where she sat. Since they were in the front row, they could talk to each other with nothing but the protective railing between them.

"You made it, Ty-Ty!" Karl said with twinkling eyes.

"Of course I did, mister man! I told you I would, right?" Karl answered by nodding his head. "What time is it?" she asked with a raised voice.

"It's game time!" Karl yelled. He balled his hands into fists and flexed his biceps. Tyree opened her phone's camera and took a few pictures of him.

"Make me proud!" She blew him kisses as he retreated to the other side of the field where his team huddled.

"Let's go offense!" Tyree yelled through cupped hands as if they were a megaphone. At first, Kamaal thought she was over-exaggerating her interest in the game so he wouldn't try talking to her, but now he knew it was sincere. He watched her as she watched his son. Her eyes stayed glued to the field; she didn't miss a single play from Karl. She even made a poster-sized sign that she waved in the air. Kamaal had stifled a few laughs during the game when she didn't agree with the referee's call and made it known. To her, Karl couldn't do wrong. She encouraged him with a genuine gaiety; it wasn't forced. She was a mama bear who supported his cub like he was hers. She'd been there when he lost his first tooth and on his first day of school. She even managed the concession stand during the season for his Pop Warner football team. Tyree was in her element when she was in her mama role. She didn't have children, but her nurturing couldn't be taught; it was innate. How could a woman who bore no children be better at being a mother than the woman who carried and birthed his child? How was it that Tyree had perfected putting Karl before everything, and Marie chose to put everything, including her son, second to drugs?

He read the back of her shirt. Duval. 99. The kids wore their dad's number on their jersey for the junior game, so technically, Tyree was wearing Karl's name and his number, but he knew his son didn't mind sharing. Both looked good on her. The name should've been hers; she had earned it. Why couldn't he realize that before it was too late? He knew hindsight was 20/20, but a present, clear-eyed view would've saved a lot of heartache for multiple people.

⊰⊱

The game ended with Karl's team winning. Tyree and Kamaal rushed the field, along with others who wanted to congratulate their champions. Karl spotted them heading his way and broke out into a full sprint, meeting his father halfway. Kamaal thrusted Karl upward before catching him and holding him close to him.

"You did it, fella!" he cheered, his forehead touching his mini's.

Tyree smiled; her cheeks pushed her eyes tight as her face washed over in glee. "Great job, mister man!" She looked up into the young boy's beautiful face.

"Did I make you proud, Ty-Ty?"

"The proudest, sweetie." She leaned up and brushed a quick kiss on his cheek. Karl looked around as if he hoped his teammates hadn't seen the kiss.

"Daddy, everybody is going to the hibachi place. Can we go?" Karl asked Kamaal as his dad eased him to his feet.

"Yes, we can go," Kamaal answered as he sat Karl down on the ground.

"Ty-Ty, can you come to eat with us? Please?" He jumped up and down with praying hands clasped in front of his face. "It'll be fun. We haven't ate together in a long time."

She checked the David Yurman on her left wrist; the game ended a little earlier than expected and the restaurant wasn't far from the stadium.

"Sure, I'll come."

A celebration lunch was innocent. Besides, it was tradition, and she knew Karl really wanted her there.

"You can leave your car here and ride with me," Kamaal offered.

"No, thank you. I'll drive that way. I can head home from the restaurant."

Kamaal nodded.

"Can I ride with you?"

Tyree looked down at Kamaal's twin. His eyes that inherited both the same color and influence as his dad's disabled her defense. She didn't envy the mothers of the little girls who would be tested by his charm. *Sorry to those moms.*

"If Daddy says so."

Tyree saw Kamaal's eyes instantly flicker at her remark. She knew where his mind went without him speaking it. He became a father when Karl Duval entered the world six years ago, but to her, he was also Daddy in the bedroom. She wondered if Simone called him Daddy too.

"Yes, Daddy doesn't mind." He kept his eyes on her as he responded. She pushed away what her body began to feel.

"Yes! Let's go, Ty-Ty!" Karl grabbed Tyree's hand and led her off the field. She was glad for the chance to get away from Kamaal.

Kamaal stood in the same spot, his eyes on Tyree and Karl until they were inside. He couldn't hear what his son was talking about, but he knew it was a lot about a variety of topics. Karl had some making up to do. He missed Tyree, that much he told his dad. Kamaal hadn't realized how much until he noticed the improvement in his son's attitude after they ran into her at Malcolm's. Her agreeing to come to his game was just what he needed to brighten his mood, and Kamaal held his breath until he'd seen her sitting by herself. He knew he didn't deserve anything from her, and he was grateful his child didn't reap his transgressions.

He bruised when Tyree said she would drive home after dinner because right now, her home wasn't with him. He didn't even know where home for her was. He knew using his position to bribe hotel workers for information was a bit much, or a lot, but he'd been so desperate to see her to plead his case that he didn't consider how abrasive it was. Another move of his he wished he could take back. His obsession pushed her farther away from him, and now, he didn't even know where she laid her head.

"That's back on?" Kamaal's teammate and friend, Jeremiah Canning, walked up with his son beside him, his small hand tucked inside his father's.

Kamaal looked back in the direction were his ex and son went. "No, but it will be," he answered with a determination that stirred in his pit.

He had to get that old thing back. He had her, his son had her, and there was no being without her. He knew his work was cut out for him. The battle was uphill; it was steep, of Himalayan proportions, and he was ready to climb.

thirty-three

Aiyden looked at the picture on his phone for what had to be the hundredth time. He told himself it wasn't the picture itself that bothered him, only Tyree's lateness. She told him she would be home in time for dinner, and the photo confirmed why she reneged on her word.

When Tyree told him about going to Karl's game today, he believed her when she said it was only to support him like she promised she would. He wasn't her man and was not owed an explanation, but he'd been glad to hear it.

"John Redcorn" was on repeat. He listened as SiR sang about the struggles of being the man who hadn't been chosen. He felt him when he said that he hated he gave a fuck. Caring made you vulnerable. It would be easier to give both middle fingers and move on. If only it was that simple.

The picture that was posted online was one that was taken without them knowing. Someone captured a tender moment of Kamaal, his son, and Tyree in a celebration. Karl showed all teeth, minus the two front ones that had been whisked away by the Tooth Fairy, while he beamed in his dad's arms. Tyree and Kamaal, who were standing rather closely, shared in the young boy's joy, with their eyes squinted in glee. Karl looked like their child. They looked like they belonged to each other. All three of them.

He'd known for a while that he'd once again fallen for Tyree. Being here with her reignited feelings he tucked away. She wasn't the same impressionable young girl who he planned a lifetime with. She had grown into a beautiful, strong woman. Experiencing the grown-ass version of Tyree refurbished his feelings for her, but he knew that would lead down a path of regrets. He was the moth to her flame.

Aiyden heard a key slide into the front door lock, and he clicked away from the picture. He stopped the song.

"Hey," she greeted.

Wanting to appear nonchalant, he gave a slight head nod.

"Hey." His eyes remained on the TV until she walked past him. "Nice outfit."

His tone caused her to stop.

"Um, thanks," she answered cautiously.

His faced remained straight as his eyes followed her movement.

"How was the game?"

Tyree regarded him for a moment. "It was good." With a warm smile, she added, "Karl's team won."

Aiyden nodded. "Did it go into overtime?" Tyree raised an eyebrow as if she hadn't followed his question. "You said you would be back by dinnertime; it's midnight snack time." He scolded her for arriving back home after ten that night.

Tyree ignored his question and proceeded further into the house.

"I'm sure Karl appreciated you getting your hair done for his game. For you to not be working and staying with me, spending money on a new do can't be as minimal as what you've grown used to. That should mean a lot to him."

With tight eyes, compressed lips, and tense shoulders, Tyree unzipped her crossbody and pulled out some bills. Stomping over to Aiyden, she counted them. "Twenty-five, twenty-six . . . eighty-three and—" She flipped her purse over and shook it, dropping the change into her palm. "Sixty-two. This should be enough for the weeks I've been here and next month."

Aiyden glanced at the money she slammed on top of his coffee table.

"I didn't ask you for money. But I'm sure your baller boyfriend has taught you well."

Tyree scoffed. "No, you didn't ask, but you condemned me for treating myself, which I think is worse. I want to compensate you for your generosity, Aiyden. I don't want any drama."

Aiyden laughed as if she delivered the most impressive punchline. "Drama comes with being around you, Tyree. My cousin is still raking up letters from her yard every day. If you want to play this back-and-forth game with your rich jock as if you aren't in danger, then you need to do it somewhere else. I don't need your shit showing up here at my door. I'm already risking enough having you here."

She recoiled; guilt surfaced on her beautiful features. He knew he stung her with his reminder of the shitshow that was her life as of late.

Tyree averted her eyes from his as if she hadn't wanted him to see how much his words injured her. She stepped past him and walked into the kitchen, and that's when she noticed what he'd done. He'd cooked the chili she begged him for, even when he said he wouldn't. He watched her eyes soften and knew that his gesture caused some of her anger to subside.

She sighed. "Look, Aiyden. I went out to a Hibachi spot with the team to celebrate the game, and I lost track of time. Had I known I was going to be so late, I would've let you know. I'm sorry."

"Don't apologize for doing what you want, Tyree. Your pictures are everywhere; you had a good time with Karl *and* Kamaal."

His hair cascaded on his shoulders as he shook his head. "I know everyone has their price; I just thought yours would be higher than yum-yum sauce."

She jerked her head to the side. "Wow, and you're the one to talk to when you have bitches burning through employee benefit perks to get dicked down by you. What was the Betty bitch's price? Lobster bisque?"

Hands on her hips, her neck craned as it rolled a complete rotation. He wondered if she realized that she complimented his lovemaking skills; his mouth twitched in amusement.

Tyree continued. "I know I don't top the list of people you want living under your roof, and as I've told you, I appreciate the fuck out of you for it. I'm really trying to get my shit together while keeping it as least awkward as possible, but it seems like you are going out of your way to make it hard. What is the problem? Why do you care what I wear and what time I get home so much?"

His eyes tightened. He didn't have an immediate answer for her valid question. Him helping her didn't negate that she was a grown woman who had the right to be with whoever she pleased. He even tried his hand at averting his attention to someone else. He had planned on staying out of her way; instead, he criticized her clothes, waited up with one eye on the door and one eye on the clock, and acted like a concerned parent waiting on their teenage child who missed curfew. He'd acted like a jealous husband, and he wasn't even her boyfriend. They were still trying their hand at being friends.

But still . . .

His hands lifted on their own accord and gently squeezed her arms. "Because I still care about you." He put his head down like the confession defeated him. Tyree jerked her head back and snapped her lips together. Aiyden sighed. "I still love you, and it's hard to see you falling back into a trap of a man who broke you.

"I didn't sleep with Brandy. I thought I wanted to—I even tried to—but I couldn't because here I am, still stuck on a woman who walked out of my life when she meant the most to me." He snatched his hands from her arms, moving as if him touching her burned his skin. He stared in her face, searching for a reaction. All he saw was shock. He stepped back. "I'm going to take a ride."

In what felt like one second, the door slammed behind Aiyden. Tyree remained stuck in her spot, eyes wide and mouth shut while her mind hit rewind then play.

"But you broke me first," she said to no one, finally finding her voice. The realization of what she needed to do sent a jolt through her, relieving her of her frozen state. She ran to her room and immediately began packing.

"Reservations line. How may I help you?"

"Yes, I would like a room for tonight," Tyree answered as she merged onto the highway. After she got over the shock of Aiyden's confession, Tyree went into her room and packed a bag of essential needs. She felt that both her and Aiyden needed some space and decided to stay at a hotel. She would go back and get the rest of her things later.

"We're just about booked up for the night, but we do have a king bedroom suite available. Would that work for you?" the associate asked.

"Yes, that will work."

Tyree read off the card number to the reservation specialist. She memorized her card number but couldn't remember the sequence at the moment. Her mind was too occupied replaying Aiyden's words to her, and she couldn't focus enough to call out the sixteen digits from memory.

"Thank you, and the security code on the back?" the woman asked.

"Yes, eight one zero." Tyree glanced down as she slid her credit card back into its previous slot in her wallet. She looked up at the road at the same time a loud horn came her way. She stared into oncoming headlights a moment too late and was unable to correct the wheel and get out of the way. She heard a scream and a crash and braced herself for impact.

Tyree closed her eyes and willed her thoughts to a happier place, a defense mechanism she developed from her early traumas. Instead of spiraling in her truck that spun uncontrollably, she laid on the beach as her parents buried her in sand—one of the memories she held on to dearly.

"How is Mommy's little sand mummy?"

Tyree squealed in delight as her mother packed more sand onto her. Her parents surprised her with a trip to the beach to show how proud they'd been of her being in the county-wide spelling bee. She only made it to the semi-finals, but to them, she took home first prize.

The sun warmed her skin comfortably. The weather on that Saturday in March was perfect. The temperature nestled in a sweet spot between not too hot and not too cold.

"You ready to get up, Chunk?"

Tyree smiled at the sound of the nickname that only her mother called her. She told her she had the cutest, chunkiest cheeks as a baby. Shanie avoided using the common name Chunky Monkey; she hated that her people were referenced as such and refused to call her daughter a monkey. So, she settled for Chunk, and Tyree loved it. It was their thing.

"Nooo." She tossed her head from side to side. Her braided pigtails flung sand as they swung.

"I guess that means you'll stay here while Mommy and I go get ice cream," her father teased. "Let's go, Mommy!"

Robert Morris jumped up, tugging his wife along with him and acting as if they were walking away.

"No, don't leave me!" Tyree fussed as she wiggled from under the mountain of soft sand.

"Last one there is a rotten egg!" Shanie took off on a slow jog, giving her baby girl an opportunity to catch up.

"Ma'am, can you hear me?"

Tyree blinked as she tried to focus on the man's voice. She wanted to call out to her hero; she wanted to thank them, but fear still gripped her throat. She couldn't move; she couldn't speak. She felt herself being pulled up from the concrete. She didn't know if someone pulled her from her car or if she'd been thrown during the accident. Her glazed-over eyes watched the man's mouth move, but she couldn't make out the words. She couldn't hear them.

She knew that the other senses strengthened when others weakened, but why had her vision worsened? Her sense of sight followed suit and faded with her hearing and speaking. The man shook her to try to get her to snap out of her shock, but that drove her further away from consciousness.

She wasn't sure what came next. All she knew was what came after included no words, no light, and no sounds. Only darkness.

thirty-four

Tyree felt stuck. On her back, she couldn't move. Without the energy to adjust her position, she tried opening her eyes. Her lids were heavy and proved unyielding when she tried to lift them.

"Tyree, can you hear me?"

A warm breeze accompanied by the aroma of Cheetos fanned her face. Yes, she could hear him. Instead of words, she groaned her response.

"See, Dad, I told you she's waking up!"

"Yes, you're right, little man. "You stay with her, and I'll go get her doctor," a familiar voice responded.

Kamaal!

With a renewed determination, Tyree forced her eyelids upward, and they were immediately met with two young, innocent amber ones.

"Ty-Ty! You're up!" Karl excitedly jumped up and down.

A groggy rumble sounded instead of the words she tried to speak. She cleared her throat.

"Yes, Karl, I'm up," she struggled, her words coming out as a raspy whisper. She glanced around the hospital room and took in her surroundings. She had to squint to read the name that was above the informational dry erase board that hung close to the door. Baptist Medical Center South.

"Hold on, baby boy, be careful."

Tyree looked toward the door and saw Kamaal standing with both concern and relief in his handsome features. The worry around his eyes couldn't diminish the fact that he was still in the clothes he'd worn to the game earlier.

"He's OK, Kamaal." She grabbed her throat; it burned with each word she spoke.

Kamaal rushed to her side and grabbed a cup that sat on the tray beside her. "Here, drink some of this." He held the cup to her lips, and she took a sip. The cool water relieved some of the discomfort as it traveled down her body.

"Thank you," she uttered softly. She wanted to hate him, but she preferred to not be alone at this moment.

The room's door opened, and Aiyden rushed in. He took in the moment taking place. Tyree in the hospital bed while Kamaal consoled her and Karl watched. He paused, only for a second, and stepped to the bed, and Tyree frowned. For a moment, she didn't understand why he was there. Then, she remembered something.

She turned to Kamaal. "How did you know I was here?"

He placed her cup of water on the tray. "The hospital called me. You were by yourself, and they found my number in your emergency contacts."

Tyree completed the list of whom to call in the event anything happened to her. It wasn't a long lineup—just Kamaal, Toni, and Brenda. She'd forgotten all about it. Her limited list was even shorter these days. Toni was it.

"*He* called you?" Tyree asked Aiyden, gesturing to Kamaal.

"No." Aiyden frowned. "The hospital called Toni after *he* didn't pick up." He tilted his head in Kamaal's direction. "I was able to reach her, and she let me know what happened. She's on her way now."

The two men stared at each other. The pointed glares they gave each other made Tyree uncomfortable. She cleared her throat to get their attention.

"Kamaal, this is Aiyden, Toni's cousin and a friend I know from high school. Aiyden, this is my ex, Kamaal, and his son, Karl."

Tyree introduced the two men out of obligation. She preferred they hadn't met and hoped that the precise introduction would be the means of an uneventful meeting.

Kamaal pushed the right sleeve of his heather-grey hoodie up before extending his hand to Aiyden.

Friend? he thought. He knew all Tyree's friends, and this one hadn't been around in two years. She hadn't mentioned him. *Can't be that close of a friend.*

He tilted his arm, which placed his ink on full display. Each letter of Tyree's name was saturated and flawless in all their two inches of glory as they traveled down his skin. He was branded. The permanent body modification embroidered on his epidermis broadcasted who he belonged to and who belonged to him.

"Nice to meet you."

Aiyden looked down at Kamaal's arm and smirked before accepting the hand and giving it a tight squeeze and firm shake.

"You also."

Tyree's attending physician entered the room at the perfect time to provide an update. While she, Aiyden, and Kamaal listened intently, the doctor explained that her MRI and X-rays came back normal, except for a sprained ankle that would clear up in a week or so. And since she did suffer a mild concussion from hitting her head on the steering wheel, she felt it was best to keep her for one night for observation. If that checked out, Tyree would be discharged the next day.

"That's great news, Ty. You're just a little banged up, but you'll be good as new in a few days. I can arrange for my physical therapist to work with you this week to get you back better than ever." Kamaal was relieved to hear that all she suffered was minor bumps and bruises compared to what could have happened. So many thoughts ran through his mind when he got the message from her nurse.

Kamaal had a serious heart to heart with the Lord as he drove to the hospital. Him and God were familiar with each other. Kamaal was sure to give thanks to Him whenever he woke up from and went to bed, and he took the time to bless all his meals. Today, he hadn't driven by with his usual routine of "Hi," "thank you," and "Bye." He offered everything he owned, even a few things he had yet to attain in exchange for Tyree to be spared. His aunt and son were the only things he hadn't offered. There was no way he could lose her.

"I'll get started on the claim for your truck as soon as I leave here. In the meantime, I'll bring one of my cars for you to use. You like driving Carrera; how about I bring that one?"

"That's a great idea. I could even help pick it up once I get you home," Aiyden spoke and reclaimed her attention.

Home. Kamaal went still. Not a house, not *your* place, not *her* place . . . but home. He'd been dusting his shoulders off, mentioning his physical therapist and her truck as if the bystander should take notice of his place in her life. He was using her means of transportation as a pawn on the chessboard, while Aiyden had been sitting back making his move on his queen until it was time to reveal himself. Checkmate. He wanted to pop that smug look off of Homie the Clown's face but decided to play it cool—for now.

Knowing he'd lost this battle, Kamaal conceded. "I need to get Karl home; we just wanted to check you out." Kamaal patted the side of her bed twice and stepped away. "Come on, Karl. We'll leave Tyree with her . . . friend."

"Hey! I'm her friend too!" A fault line appeared in his heart. How was he supposed to comprehend their breakup if they kept popping up in each other's lives? The calls and visits were enjoyable and meant as a means to aid in dealing with the changes, but now, he questioned if they were fair to his son.

"You are, but she has other friends too, and we have to share," he comforted his pouting son and placed a nurturing hand on his shoulder. He looked at Aiyden before opening the door. "A'ight, it was nice meeting you, Quavo." And he was out of the door.

───────⌒◇⌒───────

"Woah, he's in the Migos?" Aiyden heard Karl ask out in the hallway and rolled aggravated eyes to Tyree.

The blatant disrespect caused her bottom jaw to hit her chest. "I'm sorry about that."

Aiyden shook off the tactless remark. He rocked back on his heels as he looked at her, unsure what to say. The silence in the room left his thoughts loud, screaming at him to do something, say something. He'd professed feelings for her then stormed out of his home because he couldn't take the apprehension he saw when she stared back at him. He cracked and showed his hand and ran away when she folded hers, and now he regretted the way he acted. He'd almost slammed in the back of the car in front of him when Toni called him to tell him about the accident. She was so hysterical, he couldn't even hear what she was saying at first. He had to coach her to get her to stop crying long enough for him to make out her words

"Tyree . . . accident . . . hospital."

Aiyden decided he would pump the brakes on the romance. Tyree wasn't ready for it. Her lying in this hospital bed was a clear indication of that. Remembering his cousin's words, he resigned to only being what he knew she needed . . . a friend.

thirty-five

Toni waited in line for her turn at the check-in desk. She was at the hotel in downtown Jacksonville as instructed. She was surprised to receive a text message from Malcolm asking that she meet him but decided to give into her curiosity and see what he wanted. As she waited for the customer in front of her to finish up, she pulled out her phone and reviewed the messages that summoned her there.

Malcolm: I've been thinking about you. Can I see you?

Toni: I don't think that's a good idea

Malcolm: Please, I really need to talk to you.

Toni: I think we've said everything that was needed and should leave it there. Thankfully, I'm not pregnant, and it's best to stop b4 things get worse.

Toni hadn't received a quick response from that message and believed he believed her. It was two hours later when her phone advised her of a new text.

Malcolm: I don't like how things ended and just want one conversation. Please say you will come.

That had been enough for Toni to agree to one last meeting with him. She was happy to hear that he wasn't happy with their last conversation. After dropping Tyree back home, she sent Malcolm a message asking him to come see her whenever he could get away. He'd shown up to her house just before one the next morning with sex on the brain.

Toni shut down his agenda as soon as he got inside. She told him that they needed to talk, and just like that, his temperature cooled. Malcolm seemed disinterested in what she had to say. Once he recognized he wasn't getting in her pants, everything about him switched off. She barely held his attention until she said the word "pregnant" and he jumped off the couch as if it had been on fire. Before she could finish her story, Toni had been called all types of careless and opportunist. One word changed Dr. Jekyll to Mr. Hyde. She was grateful to see "Not Pregnant" on the test result window.

Malcolm eagerly agreed to them ending their affair after Toni assured him that she was not pregnant. Once he had been assured that Toni didn't want anything from him and would not be telling his wife about his extramarital activities, he'd been out the door. Toni stuck her chest out, keeping her pride intact until he left her house and life.

"I can take you right here, ma'am."

She stepped forward to the desk. On the way there, she sent a text to let Malcolm know she was picking up the room key. She wasn't sure why she would need one for this meeting but went ahead with it. If this is what it took to get the apology she deserved, then so be it.

Malcolm texted back instantly letting her know he was waiting for her. Toni tried to ignore the contradicting emotions she felt. One side of her felt irritated that she was even there. He'd showed her how things were with them on multiple occasions. Even if she missed earlier signs, there was no chance of missing or mistaking his reaction to the possibility of her being pregnant. The other side felt the excitement she usually did when she knew she was going to see him. She could feel the increased thump of her heartbeat below her ear and the flapping wings in her stomach that she tried to will away as she leaned on the elevator wall.

She rubbed the slickness from her palms as she trekked down the tenth floor hallway. She took a deep breath as she reached Malcolm's door. "Let's get this over with."

Toni opened the door to the suite. "Malcolm," she called out into the room as she walked further inside.

Because the blackout curtains were closed, the room was completely dark. The only sliver of light in the room came from the crack beneath the bathroom door.

"Malc?" she called out again on her way into the bathroom.

Candles had been lit, creating the soft glow she was able to see under the door. She was taken aback by the romantic scene. Rose petals formed a path from the door to a standalone soaker tub that was full of bubbles and a six-and-a-half-foot-tall quarterback.

Malcolm rested in the tub looking like a prized delicacy. His sandy dreadlocks were pulled up into a messy man bun, and his latte skin glistened as the light from the low flame added dimension to his face.

"What is this?" Toni didn't know what to make of his presentation. It was a far cry from the words that he parted with when she informed him of her pregnancy scare weeks ago.

"It's exactly what I said, T. I know we can't go on like this forever, and I understood you." He sat up in the tub, and the water swooshed with his movement, causing the bubbles to move. Toni couldn't help but peek into the water and see how happy he'd been to see her. "I don't want you to think you were just a body for me, and I hated how I reacted when we last spoke."

Toni nibbled on her bottom lip. He'd been saying all the things she wanted to hear, but she hadn't anticipated it being wrapped in a smooth, muscular, ten-inch package.

"I appreciate that, Malcolm. If you'd like, we could continue the conversation out here." Toni gestured toward the suite's sitting area.

"That sounds great, but let's soak first. I can tell that you're tense; let me rub that out for you."

His words sent a shiver up Toni's spine. Her mind went back to the many times Malcolm's skilled hands brought her ultimate satisfaction without even nearing her erotic areas. His touch rivaled that of those who'd spent months in school perfecting the craft of massage therapy.

"I'm not asking for much, just a proper goodbye."

Toni pondered his offer. She meant what she said when she told Tyree that her affair with Malcolm needed to end, and that was not a decision contingent on the display window of a pregnancy test. The scare was enough for her to realize that the life of a mistress was not what she wanted to be a part of. It had been hard separating from Malcolm, but each day got a little easier. She feared undoing her moving on by indulging in this final rendezvous. Withdrawal from consistent loving had been brutal. She found herself aching deep within her, where her fingers couldn't reach. How much harm could one last time be?

"Oh, right there, baby." Toni bit her bottom lip. Familiar tingles shot up her spine, signaling her nearing explosion as Malcolm dug into her from behind. Toni gripped the soft sheets beneath her.

As promised, Malcolm's godly hands rubbed all the stress from her shoulders. His touch, the warmth of the sudsy water, and the chilled Rosé ushered her into a tranquil zone. She would've said yes to anything Malcolm asked of her and hadn't hesitated when he suggested they finish up in the bed.

Malcolm pushed the curve of her back, causing her ass to arch further. His calloused hands took hold of her hips, slamming her back to meet his powerful thrusts.

"Yessss!" Her eyes squeezed shut as she took off into a wave of immense satisfaction. Her moans and the slapping of skin were the only noises heard in the room.

Suddenly, the television turned on. Toni assumed that one of them must've bumped the remote in the bed and didn't break her rocking.

"You like that, don't you?" Malcolm's voice asked, lower than his usual tone.

"Mhmm," Toni groaned. Her inner muscles flexed on his stiff staff.

"Oh yesss, oh my god!" Toni heard her voice shout from behind her.

"What the hell is this?" Malcolm stopped, pulling Toni out of her euphoric ascension. She turned around and saw what had stolen her lover's attention.

Toni and Malcolm watched a slideshow play on the large screen. She was mortified as pictures and videos documenting the coitus interactions they shared with each other flashed across the display.

"Why did you cut that on?" Toni shuffled upright in bed. Malcolm's erection slipped from her folds but remained at attention. The visuals that took turns on the screen seemed to keep him excited.

"Me? I didn't put that on." Malcolm got out of the bed and walked to the television stand in search of the remote. He ran his fingers around the edge of the television, looking for buttons since the remote was nowhere to be found. "How do I turn this shit off?"

"You should try using the remote, dear."

Toni almost jumped out of her skin when Malcolm's wife, Cherise, appeared in the doorway to the adjoining suite with a television remote in her hand. How long had she been there?

"Cherise? What are you doing here?" Malcolm turned two shades lighter as he scurried to put his pants on.

"Wow." Cherise shook her head disappointedly. "My husband is here fucking another bitch, and *I* get asked why I'm here." She chuckled. Toni was amazed at how she found humor in that moment.

"Baby, it's not like that—"

"It would behoove you not to patronize me right now, Malcolm Kinard." Cherise stepped into their room, the light from the TV screen revealed her ensemble: a black fishnet catsuit with nothing underneath. Her feet were clad in platformed sandals. The red of her toes matched the rouge on her lips. Both her and Malcolm showed up with sex on the brain.

Feeling like she was intruding on a moment meant for the Mr. and Mrs., Toni slid from the bed and tiptoed to her pile of clothes that were thrown on the bedside chair.

"Where are you going?" Cherise asked Toni, who stopped in her tracks. Cherise raised her arm, brandishing a Beretta that Toni hadn't noticed before.

"Please, don't hurt me," Toni pleaded. "Just let me leave, and you can have him."

Toni's words incensed Cherise, and fury flashed in her pupils.

"I already have him, bitch!" she howled. "That's what's wrong with women like you. You think throwing a nigga a little ass gives you notoriety, that you have rights to claim. You ain't claiming

shit. Just like the others, once he's had enough of you, he's returning to sender and coming home with me."

Toni kept her hands up, her eyes focused on Cherise's index
finger resting on the pistol's trigger guard. *Please don't let her put
her finger on the trigger,* she prayed silently.

"You're right, Cherise. I have no right, and I am sorry. I promise this won't happen again." Toni clenched her thighs to keep
her bladder from spilling down her legs. She pursed her lips to
control their quivering. She again prayed that she be spared. Her
hands trembled on either side of her head. The hairs on the back
of her neck stood erect. Moments of her life zipped between her
ears. She saw her biggest accomplishments as of date. Graduating
high school and college with honors, her recent promotion at
work, memories with her family that she cherished. Toni also
thought about the things she hadn't accomplished. She was only
twenty-two and couldn't believe that she had to beg for her life.
All over borrowed dick.

"That's good to hear," Cherise answered with a satisfied smile
on her face. "You can go."

Toni snatched her clothes and put them on and was fully
dressed in a jiffy. She picked up her purse and turned toward the
door when Cherise called after her. Not wanting to further upset
a betrayed wife that had been armed, she turned around.

"You can go after we're done."

Cherise laid across the unkempt bed and spread her legs, giving both Toni and Malcolm a clear view of her femininity.

"You." She pointed the gun at her husband. "I want you to fuck
me like you fucked her."

Malcom's jaw dropped in bewilderment. He glanced at Toni
with guilt swimming in his orbs. He rubbed his large hands down
his face and sighed exasperatedly.

"Babe, c'mon. Let Toni leave so we can talk about this."

Cherise responded by cocking the gun; the sound of a bullet sliding into the chamber sent eerie chills down Toni's spine.

"Get over here, *now.*"

Malcolm moped to the bed. His shoulders were slumped and his head was low. He didn't resemble the confident tempter who persuaded her into having one last romp between the sheets. Cherise positioned herself on her knees with her head at the foot of the bed. She braced herself on her elbows, arching her back and tooting her ass high in the air, all while keeping her weapon pointed at Toni.

Malcolm disrobed and kneeled behind Cherise, his shaft full of life. With his hand wrapped around the base of his penis, he slid his phallus, still coated in Toni's juices, into his wife.

Cherise's eyes fluttered closed, and she hissed through her teeth. Toni looked up and watched Malcolm as he watched his member disappear and reappear with each plunge. He bit his lip and tilted his head back in satisfaction. He was in his zone. She recognized it. His grunts were authentic; they told her his sexual release was nearing. How could he make love to her like she wasn't in the room? Had they done this before?

"Eyes on me!"

Toni jumped and looked down at Cherise who stared at her. The rage in her gaze battled with the pleasure her husband created behind her. She moaned, and with her free hand, reached between her legs and rotated her clit. Cherise's cries grew louder and bounced off the walls in the room. Her cries of pleasure competed with Toni's that came from the television, which still premiered a slideshow of their extramarital encounters. Toni cried silently as she was imprisoned by the sadly salacious interaction.

Toni couldn't control the tears that flowed from her eyes as she rushed through the parking garage. She had never felt so low, degraded, and minute. To be forced to watch her lover, ex-lover, fuck his wife for hours was cruel and unusual as fuck. There was a thin line between passionate and deranged, and Cherise played hopscotch with that motherfucker.

The lesson had been learned. Never will she ever get involved with a married, engaged, or involved man in any way. She could do bad all by herself. She sat in her driver's seat and took a moment to compose herself. Once her tears dried, she picked her chin up and drove away from that chapter in her life. "No Problem" by Tokyo Jetz blasted the entire way. Just like the song, Toni didn't need the problems of a man who belonged to another woman.

thirty-six

Tyree shifted from her side to lie on her back in search of a comfortable position to soothe the subtle throb at the base of her neck. Tired of lying in bed, where she'd been confined for five days, she decided to venture to the couch. The Monday after the accident came too soon. When she was discharged on Sunday, she acted as if she was all good and capable of being alone the next day. She obviously gave a less than stellar performance because Aiyden stayed home to make sure she was OK. He told her that he knew she was full of it and needed his help. He was able to deduce what she needed but was too prideful to say. That's how it was with him before.

It wasn't long until the subtle throb grew into forceful pounding in her temporal lobes, a side effect of the mild concussion her doctor warned her about. The light in the room intensified the ache. She pulled the pillow over her eyes and held it down with her arm to shield them. In a few short minutes, sleep took over.

"Ree, are you good?"

Tyree came to, feeling a soft squeeze on her arm. She opened her eyes and removed the pillow from her face. Immediately, the throb returned with a vengeance. She looked up into Aiyden's concerned eyes.

"Your leg is hanging off the couch, and it looks swollen. You need to elevate it," he urged as he took her foot in his hand and gently placed it on the sofa. "Are you having another headache?"

Tyree sat up; she grunted in discomfort.

"Wait, let me help you." Aiyden rushed to help her until she was upright. "Are you sure you're good? You look like you're going through it."

Tyree waved him off. "I'm fine; it's time for my medicine. I'll be good once it kicks in." She leaned forward to get up and was stopped by Aiyden's hand on her thigh. His warm hand in that spot sent a flash of satisfying sensations through her veins. She trembled from his touch.

Aiyden's forehead wrinkled as he looked her over. "Are you cold? You're trembling." He grabbed the throw blanket from the arm of the recliner adjacent from the couch and covered her with it.

Oh no, she cringed inwardly. "I just had a chill. I'm fine." Aiyden continued to spread the blanket. His hand accidentally brushed her breast, and she sucked in a quick breath. Aiyden's hands stilled, and he looked at her with knowing eyes. She could see him trying to hold back a grin. Tyree could feel the warmth spread through her cheeks.

"Hold up, I'm going to take care of that for you." His voice was husky. The sexual rasps in his cords had her imagination wild with a multitude of ways he could take care of her. None of them had to do with a swollen ankle or an aching head. "I'll be right back."

Tyree tossed her head back on the arm of the sofa and sighed as she looked heavenward.

"Get it together, girl," she said under her breath.

The light in the room turned off, and a pleasant smell infiltrated her senses. She looked to the left and saw a lighted diffuser on the console table emitting a mist.

"Here, take this," Aiyden instructed. He held a glass of water and her prescription pain pill. She thanked him while accepting. After she took the medicine, he took her glass and set it on the table.

Aiyden walked to his state-of-the-art entertainment center and powered on the soundbar; moments later, the sound of rain softly hitting the ground filled the room. He walked up to her and ordered her to sit up. Tyree wasn't sure where he was going with this but obliged him. He sat down on the end seat and told her to lie back. She looked down at his lap and back up to his face with a questioning mug.

"Just trust me." His grin knocked on her libido. She wasn't sure she could handle this and was about to decline when a sharp sting shot from temple to temple. "Come on, girl. Stop being so damn stubborn," he fussed at her, nudging her shoulder until she complied.

Aiyden positioned his hand at the base of her skull, and with his middle finger and thumb, he pressed on her skin firmly about an inch apart. His fingers applied pressure there for about ten seconds before he removed them then repeated the move. She felt the tension ease and her muscles relaxed, setting her deeper into his lap.

"Does that feel good?" he said just above a whisper. Tyree nodded.

He continued his technique for about twenty minutes. Her meds kicked in and all pain had been alleviated. She knew she should tell him he could stop, but she relished in the way he made her feel and decided to take advantage of it for a little longer. She thought about where she was, and that if anyone had told her they would be there together, she would've laughed.

"I want to laugh too," Aiyden said after a chuckle slipped through her lips.

Tyree felt so good in the moment, she decided to be honest.

"I was just thinking about how crazy life is. I would have never thought I would see you again after everything that happened, but here we are."

Aiyden pressed up on her neck again and rotated. Tyree groaned, and it was his turn to chuckle.

"Life has a way of surprising us indeed."

Tyree was silent as she considered his words. His fingers moved up, and with both hands, he began to massage her scalp. That, coupled with the soothing rain sound effects and pleasing aroma, transported her into a euphoric state. When he began to lightly scratch his nails on her scalp, she was a goner. Her eyes involuntarily rolled backward and her lips parted, allowing a few moans to slip through, though she didn't care that he heard.

The love he confessed radiated through his touch. He had been so gentle, doting, and patient. He hadn't repeated those three words since the night of the accident, but she could feel them. Tyree knew they would eventually need to revisit what had led to her leaving before her wreck. That she would see to once she had fully recovered. Until then, Dumbo had a sidekick in the room.

———◇———

"He just knew we were going to always be together," Tyree offered.

Aiyden looked down at her. She had been silent for the past ten minutes, and he assumed she'd gone back to sleep.

"Who?"

"My dad."

Aiyden skipped a beat. Her announcement was a sore reminder of how he disappointed not only the one he loved most but also her father, who was a male role model he cherished. Robert Morris had been someone he looked up to. His stomach plummeted as he recalled the look in his eyes when he showed up to beg Tyree for forgiveness. He continued his scalp massage and waited for her to continue.

"I'm sorry," she whispered. Her big round eyes peered up at him. She nibbled on her bottom lip, a sign of her uneasiness. But why?

"What are you sorry for?"

She glanced away and met his gaze again. She stared at him. The rise and fall of her chest was the only movement she made. He watched her eyes fill and his throat thumped with anxiousness. What could she possibly be sorry for?

"For not telling you about his funeral."

Gut punch.

She laced her fingers and squeezed them. "I know you were close, and I should have." A tear slipped from her lid. "I didn't know where you were in life or who you were with or even if you were willing to speak to me. I psyched myself out of doing it. That is something I regret."

"I was there," Aiyden whispered. He watched Tyree's glare fill with puzzlement. She topped fidgeting with her fingers.

She sat up and turned to face him. "You were there?" Aiyden nodded. "But . . . but how?" she inquired on a rushed breath. He could see the questions flash across her face.

"Toni told me about it, and I wanted to pay my respects. I saw you there. You wore an all-white pant suit. Your hair was straight, and you wore a hat with a lace veil. You looked like an angel."

Tyree blinked repeatedly. Her brows hiked and her breathing sped. "But . . . but I didn't see you."

"I know," he sighed. "We didn't end on good terms, and I didn't want to chance upsetting you, so I stayed to the back and left as soon as the service ended. I didn't want you to feel disrespected. Especially on that day."

Tyree looked ahead and stared into space as she processed the information. Aiyden remained silent. He didn't know if she would feel slighted by him showing up to her father's service uninvited and was too nervous to ask. He would wait until she revealed how she felt about it.

"That explains the program." She looked at him. Her expression softened. "I saw it in the photo album."

Before he could see it coming, Tyree lunged onto Aiyden and wrapped her arms around his neck. She buried her face in his shoulder, and in another unexpected move, she sobbed loudly. Her body jerked as she released her cries. Aiyden would have thought she was upset, but the embrace told him she was OK with learning he was there. His shoulders felt light as a ton of weight lifted from them when he heard her whisper, "Thank you."

————

Kamaal clenched and unclenched his fists as he tried to ease the anger building inside. He wanted to keep calm and act rationally, but that shit teetered on the line of impossibility. He was Bruce Banner, fighting the monster that lived inside, clawing at the opportunity to make an appearance. He'd successfully maintained the monster when he met that clown Tyree was staying with. Now, this shit just about pushed him to the brink of losing control.

He laid his head back on the headrest, inhaled, and pushed the breath out with force, trying to woosah. He knew his son was inside eagerly waiting for him to pick him up for karate, and he wanted to get his attitude under control.

His son. He didn't belong to anyone else in that way. Karl had a mother who relinquished that title when she chose opiates over her family. That breeder pushed him and Karl to the side to catch a high, a high she claimed he and his son blew. Something as minuscule as a pill had been powerful enough to destroy their family.

It was hard accepting that he and Karl were no longer a priority in Marie's life, but he had to step into his big boy cleats and put their son first. He loved Marie enough to let her go and take over her role as mother. Drug addiction was a disease; he understood that. Even after she went her way, he would do whatever he could to try to help her whenever she found her way back home. She would prey on his vulnerability and his dream of them being a unit to weasel back into his home until she got what she came for, which was usually money to feed her habit. After losing thousands of dollars on wasted rehab attempts and however much she stole from him, he made the decision to protect his son and his peace. Obtaining full custody of Karl had been easy. Marie didn't bother to show up to most of the court dates, and the times she did go to mediation, she was beamed up like Pooky. That sealed the deal.

Kamaal severed ties with Marie, and unfortunately, that rolled over to her parents, who yearned for a relationship with their only grandchild. They tried to sue for grandparents' rights, but their dog wasn't a match for his beast in the fight. By then, Kamaal had risen to superstardom and his resources trampled his competition's. It was like a teacup Yorkie trying to beat a pit bull terrier.

Kamaal looked down at his lap and stared at the words. He wished he would have listened to Ms. Wadsmith back in the day when she would scold him for not paying attention in class because they would help him here. Maybe he could get the help from a tutor on this one because he couldn't comprehend. The words on the legal document made no sense.

Petition for Custody

The matter of the phone call he'd just ended had him reeling. His attorney shocked him silent when he said that Marie may actually have a case this time. The documents presented from her counsel supported her rehabilitation, and family court usually tries to find a median with both parents for the sake of the child. Who the fuck did they think they were?

The news that Marie was coming for custody overwhelmed the unpleasant meeting he just got out of with the team disciplinary board. The shit with Hakeem still needed to be answered for. The team took their morality clause seriously, and he barely skated by with just a warning. He needed to tread lightly before he messed up the church's money.

His phone's buzzing grabbed his attention. Kamaal grabbed it from the cupholder and checked the message.

Photoshoot has been moved up. Your flight for Atlanta leaves at 08:00

Kamaal sighed at William's message. He was still adjusting to someone needing to be close to him most times, but the relief he'd gotten from William's help trumped the annoyance of his nuisance. After a few scheduling mishaps, he'd broken down and solicited an assistant. Tyree told him he needed one, and he would always wave off the idea, stating he had been fine handling his affairs and that he had her to help him, which she did.

When he and Tyree began dating, Kamaal's career was just

beginning to skyrocket. He had been on the list of players to watch for when he was drafted in the third round and had a buzz about him when he entered the league, but he knew his professional career would begin with him shadowing the man he would soon replace. It was a bittersweet victory when an injury to his mentor's shoulder sent him into early retirement. Knowing it was now or never, Kamaal gave his all. He left everything on the field every time he graced it, and that translated well. He quickly became a league favorite.

It seemed that his agent contacted him regarding a new endorsement deal every other day. Now, he was always a part of the conversation about the movers and shakers in the league as he continued breaking records and filling seats. He was the face of many brands and even a partner of many prosperous ventures. As of the last quarterly review, he was a fifty-million-dollar man. He had enough money to buy whatever he desired in life, yet the things he wanted most in the world were fading away one by one.

Kamaal stuffed the letter back in the envelope and slid it in between his seat and the center console. He would work out a plan with his legal team next week. Now, he had somewhere to be with *his* son. Especially now that his travel plans had moved up.

thirty-seven

"You remembered," Tyree observed as she and Aiyden passed the sign announcing their arrival to Jacksonville Beach.

Aiyden glanced at her for a moment and turned his attention back on the road.

"Yes, there are some things you can't forget."

Tyree looked out of the window and tried to hide the blush in her cheeks. The beach was always her place of refuge growing up. The best memories she had with her parents were made at the beach. The two small ocean waves she had tattooed on the inside of her left wrist were a tribute to her parents and the time they'd shared together.

She sucked in her lips. She was hit with two emotions simultaneously: the grief of the greatest loves she lost and the wonderment of Aiyden's thoughtfulness.

Tyree had been reminded of this thoughtfulness countless times over the past week. He kept true to his word and took care of her as she recovered from the accident. Aiyden saw to it that she ate all her meals while propped comfortably. He cooked most meals and had them delivered whenever he wasn't available at home. Even when he went overboard with his nursing, Tyree hadn't gotten annoyed by it. When she lost people who had been her only resemblance of a family, she hated the loneliness that accompanied it. She was happy to have him around.

"Here, one second." Aiyden rounded the car and helped Tyree stand. Her sprain was recovering nicely, and Tyree was happy to be able to put weight on it. Her crutches were uncomfortable, and she couldn't get the hang of it. Most times, she had resorted to hopping around on one leg to spare her armpits. Now, she was fine if she didn't overdo it.

They decided on a spot to set up their area. Tyree sat in the beach lounger, while Aiyden dug a hole and perched the large umbrella. He opted to lie on his beach towel on the sand.

"OK, I got a good one. One must go. *Life, Coming to America, Nutty Professor,* or *Dreamgirls?*"

Aiyden snorted. "Too easy, *Dreamgirls.*"

"Jail for you!" Tyree scrunched her button nose, disgusted by his choice. "Beyoncé was in that. There's no way it could go."

"Yeah, I know you and your fellow Beyhive members feel that way, but there are way better Eddie Murphy movies. I'll pass on the sing-along."

"Man, watch out. *Dreamgirls* got hits! Jimmy got, Jimmy got, Jimmy got soul!" Tyree sang obnoxiously. The shoulder shimmy she added tickled Aiyden, who threw his head back in laughter.

His phone went off, and a few seconds later, Aiyden announced that he needed to grab something out of the car. After a few minutes, he returned, announcing that he had a special delivery.

"Ty-Ty!" Karl ran from behind Aiyden. His bright, checkered smile illuminated his warm face.

Tyree gasped. "My guy!" she squealed while sitting up just in time for him to jump into her lap.

"Be careful, baby. Tyree is still getting better," Kamaal's aunt Brenda warned. Tyree's lips flattened as she held back her emotion. "He's OK, Auntie." Tyree squeezed Kamaal's mini man, loving the smell of Cheetos on his breath. She never knew how much she could miss the aroma of cheddar-dusted corn chips. "I missed you!"

"I missed you too, Ty-Ty. Thank you for inviting us, Mr. Aiyden."

"No problem, little man. Tyree could use some extra love today. Can you help with that?" Aiyden held his hand out, which Karl took and shook securely.

He bobbed his head up and down at lightning speed. "Yes, sir. Could I still give her some extra love while I'm playing in the water?"

"I'll take you out to the water in a little bit. We're here to check on Tyree, remember?" Aunt Brenda reminded Karl of the reason for their visit as she settled in Aiyden's beach chair. Tyree wondered why he would bring it and set it up just to lie on the towel in the sand. Now she understood that everything about today had been premeditated. That warmed her inside.

"I don't mind taking him out there while you and Ree catch up, if that's OK with you, Ms. Brenda?"

"Please?" Karl begged as he jumped excitedly.

Brenda conceded. Emerald eyes won again. "That's fine. You make sure you listen to Mr. Aiyden or you'll sit here next to me until it's time to go."

"Bet you can't catch me!" Karl yelled and raced off without warning. Aiyden waited a few moments before pursuing him to the shore. The innocence of a child was so pure and uplifting to watch.

"I was so happy to hear you made it out of the accident OK. Gave me quite a scare there."

Tyree flinched as she remembered the visual of the oncoming headlights right before everything went dark.

"It was pretty scary."

She thought that when she opened her eyes again, she would be staring at God to receive her verdict of life or the lake. Kamaal held to his word and had a new version of her truck delivered days after the accident. She was sure the insurance claim was still pending, but he hadn't let that stop him from making sure she had transportation. Why hadn't he thought about her and her needs like this when he was on top of Hakeem's wife?

"How are your headaches?"

Aunt Brenda's question snapped Tyree from her thoughts. "How did you know about those?"

Brenda answered with a head nudge toward the shore.

"He told you that when he invited you to the beach?"

Aunt Brenda shook her head as she bent to pick up a seashell from the sand and dust it off with her hand. "No, he told me that when he called to give me an update on your recovery."

Tyree frowned; she was taken aback. Why hadn't Aiyden mentioned this to her?

"When did you call him?"

"He called me the day you got home. He knew I would want to know what's going on with you. He's called me every day since."

Tyree became quiet as she got lost in the revelation that not only did Aiyden take care of her, but he also made sure to include her loved ones. Even after he confessed to loving her—another concept she had yet to grasp—he still took care of her. How many other ways could he express his love?

"The ocean is beautiful, isn't it?"

"Yeah, it is beautiful," Tyree agreed wistfully.

Brenda followed Tyree's line of vision, and it landed on Aiyden, who horse-played with Karl where the shore and waves met. Tyree inwardly chuckled at how Kamaal would react to the scene that captured her full attention.

"Jon Kabat-Zinn said it best: 'You can't stop the waves, but you can learn to surf.'"

Tyree's eyes stayed forward. She fixed her gaze on the horizon line while interpreting the famous quote.

"I've been trying to learn, but it seems like I keep falling. Sometimes it feels like I'm drowning," she choked out.

Aunt Brenda nodded knowingly. "Life vests and floaties were created for a reason, ya know. They can be a little obnoxious, and it could show what others may perceive as a weakness, but they keep you from sinking and let others around you know they should keep an eye out for you.

"Look out there. You have some kids with floating devices around their arms and waists and some that swim circles around people twice their age. And look at that." Tyree looked to the area Aunt Brenda pointed to and saw a large burly man buckled in a swim vest that fit snug on his torso.

"We all need a little help sometimes," Tyree observed as she got the message.

"Come on with it." Aunt Brenda was glad Tyree caught her drift. "Man, I miss my father in Christ. Right now, he'll be singing, 'I wish I had somebody!'" It was Aunt Brenda's time to speak wistfully.

"Yes, right before telling the congregation to tell their neighbor that the pastor wished that he had someone," Tyree added with a chuckle. She hadn't been a member of the megachurch but had visited enough to know to be familiar with his adages.

"Tyree, in life, you have to let go of what causes you to sink and hold on to what helps keep you from drowning. And if that doesn't include my nephew, then that's just what it is."

Tyree whipped her head in Brenda's direction. "You wouldn't be mad at me about that?"

"Why would I be? He messed up. I saw that video. Lord knows I wish I hadn't. I saw parts I haven't seen since he was in Pop Warner." She frowned. "Nobody wants community dick."

Tyree gasped. "Aunt Brenda!"

Brenda scoffed. "What, child?"

She frowned at the fact that Brenda had to ask. She'd never been this candid before. "W.W.J.D.?"

Aunt Brenda waved her off. "What would Jesus do? He would tell the truth and shame the devil."

Tyree shook her head, amused by Brenda's motherlike levity.

"You know I love you like you're my niece and not an in-law, so I'm going to tell you the truth." Brenda placed a hand on Tyree's shoulder. "You are a baby and still figuring this thing called life out. I know that in your twenty-two years, you've been through things people twice your age haven't experienced. People will always show you the good parts, and most will keep the bad parts tucked away, and that can pressure you into feeling like you're not where you need to be in life. It's OK to pace yourself, get to know yourself. And you can take all the time you need. Take care of *you*, baby. And I'm not saying that is something you have to do alone, but be sure to keep yourself at the top of the list."

Tyree pressed the corner of her eyes to stop the wetness from leaking. Brenda's hand rubbed circles on her back. She didn't speak. She had nothing to say as she took in the woman's advice.

"These days, everyone is only concerned with three people: me, myself, and I. I don't know if it's a greed thing, an issue of vanity, or a means of self-preservation, but it closes others out and can cause a lot of pain. What I've learned is that finding someone that puts your wants and needs before their own is something you shouldn't take lightly. Let me see your phone for a second."

Tyree obliged without a second thought. Brenda clicked a few buttons then gave it back to her. "I added a little something to this pocket computer. A little reminder to peek at during the day. Never know when you'll need your sword."

Tyree and Brenda caught up with each other before switching gears and swapping their thoughts on the dramas they indulged in every week on the Oprah Winfrey Network. They had just finished discussing the latest findings of *Greenleaf* when Brenda announced it was time for Karl to head back home to meet Kamaal for karate practice. Tyree had to fight to keep her emotions at bay as she hugged Brenda and Karl. She couldn't explain what brought on the despair. It felt like the goodbye she hadn't gotten when she walked away from Kamaal.

Once Tyree was settled in her seat, her phone buzzed in her lap. She swiped to open her screen. The Bible application Brenda downloaded sent her the daily scripture.

"John, chapter fourteen, verse one. 'Do not let your hearts be troubled. You believe in God; believe also in me,'" Tyree read aloud while Aiyden put their beach equipment in his trunk.

thirty-eight

Aiyden forced a breath through his pressed lips as he pushed himself past his normal stopping point. His normal regimen didn't possess enough intensity for him to work through the anxiousness he'd felt since he and Tyree got back home. She had been reserved during the forty-five-minute drive back home. The questions she bothered answering were all done with not more than a few words. What had happened?

He replayed the day in his mind in hopes of shedding light on where he'd transgressed. Each time, he came up empty. Not wanting to guess, Aiyden outright asked Tyree what, if anything, had been going on and if it was something he did. Each query was quickly shot down with a comment that advised everything was fine. He wished that were true, but he could not ignore the taciturn demeanor she developed ever since they came from the beach.

She's probably missing ole' boy after seeing his aunt and kid. He hated the pessimism his insecurities constructed. What else could it be? He thought he was helping Tyree by inviting Kamaal's aunt and son to the beach. A gesture he hoped would lift her mood and earn him brownie points pushed her further in a funk and away from him. It was a tale of when keeping it real goes wrong.

———⌁———

Tyree's pulse quickened. The sight before her transmitted heat through her body, beginning in her middle. Aiyden was laid back on the workout bench. He blew strong breaths as he pushed the bench press bar upward. The weights clanked as they hit each other with each thrust. Tyree had done quick math and counted 250 pounds, not counting the bar.

Aiyden growled as he pushed himself; he was in beast mode. His perspiration coated his skin. Tyree salivated at the view; she would love to lick it. She would welcome the salted secretion that came with his hard work.

"What I've learned is that finding someone that puts your wants and needs before their own is something you shouldn't take lightly."

Brenda's parting words played in her head nonstop since they left the beach. They were continuous, without break, as if it were a track on a record set on a loop. No matter what Aiyden said or did to pull her from the trenches in her mind, the needle wouldn't move. She hadn't meant to be cold toward Aiyden. He'd been nothing but the best and deserved better. She just had a hard time sorting through her feelings. She felt it was best to put some distance between them until she resolved her dilemma.

Then why was she standing at the door like a creeper?

"You need to get a grip," she muttered under her breath.

Aiyden finished his set of presses and stretched up to replace the bar on the pegs. The move caused his muscles to flex. Tyree's sex twitched, mimicking the reflexes. She needed to go before she did something she'd regret. Tyree turned and quietly walked away.

Hours later, Tyree stared up at the ceiling. She thought about all she'd been through these past months. Aiyden's reappearance in her life was right on time as if it had been destined that way. The one who introduced her to the highs and lows of love became the one to pick up the pieces that Kamaal left. Aiyden opened his home to her when she had nowhere else to go, he was attentive to her needs, and he nursed her after her accident. The way he included Brenda and Karl earlier today spoke volumes. He'd constantly put her needs before his own. When she thought of his deceit, it didn't have nearly as much bite as it once had. Could she get over it? Had she gotten over it? It felt like her body had.

Tyree snatched the comforter from her. Her body's temperature had risen a few degrees higher than normal and stayed there. Her creep session of watching Aiyden's workout had done a number on her. She licked her lips in the same way she wanted to lick his tight skin. Tight. Just as her abdomen felt as her core twisted in need, a need that needed to be satisfied expeditiously. A chargeable wand just wouldn't do. She hadn't worn her usual pajamas tonight and opted for something looser, less restricting. Yet she was still on fire. The sheer camisole slip she wore could barely be considered a layer and taking anything else off would leave her naked. *Then again . . .*

Tyree shook the path her thoughts traveled down and picked up her phone, hoping to find something to occupy her until she dozed off. She did her normal scrolling through social media, giving a like here and leaving a comment there. She then switched over to YouTube and checked her recommendations page. A video to a new song she was feeling caught her eye, and she decided to watch it. The love song began a rotation of similar songs, each consisting of emotional and physical satisfaction.

Ro James's "Permission" video began playing, and Tyree stood up from her bed and walked across the hall. She knew what she wanted, more so needed, tonight, and she was going to get it. And unlike Mr. James playing on her phone, she wasn't asking for permission.

Aiyden laid in bed, his back flat and eyes closed as he got lost in his thoughts.

The door creaked, then slowly swung open. He lifted his head and found Tyree standing in the doorway with her eyes fixed on him. She crossed his room's threshold, and he could hear a familiar melody playing from the phone she held at her side.

"What are you doing?"

She stood motionless and said nothing as she let the melodic inquisition be her mouthpiece. Her head tilted to the side. He could tell she was thinking, contemplating.

Tyree continued to move toward him, not acknowledging his question. Pressing a knee into his mattress, she leaned and threw her other leg over his body and straddled him. She bent her body and brought her head down; her lips found his neck. He didn't think it was possible to read more into the situation but still couldn't chance it. He was near combustion and wouldn't survive a letdown. His hands remained at his sides as he refused to make a move until Tyree made her request known.

She took his hands and placed them on her ass; he spread his fingers to get as much of her in his grip as possible. The softness of her cheeks fit perfectly in his firm grip. He rotated his hands and pulled them in opposite directions, spreading them apart. She kissed his neck and trailed down to his chest. The movement pulled her shirt up, revealing her smooth, creamy chocolate thighs.

He closed his eyes and enjoyed Tyree's sampling of his chest. He moved his hands upward and felt her bare cheeks. He hardened even more below her and groaned in his throat. *Precious.*

"You."

All Aiyden's control snapped inside of him with her admission. Just like the song requested, she had given him that green light and allowed him free rein to what they both wanted: each other. He liked that Tyree didn't shy away from taking control in the bedroom and looked forward to that ride another time. Right now, he had to take control; he needed to. He braced himself on his palms, sat upward, and twisted until he was on top with her underneath him.

In a flash, Tyree's cami was whisked over her head and thrown to the floor. Aiyden admired her naked body that had matured so much since they were last together. Her size C breasts were perky and firm. Her cocoa-colored nipples pebbled under his fierce gaze. He leaned down and sampled one breast then the other while Tyree squirmed beneath his mouth. He wanted to taste her between her thighs but knew he couldn't wait any longer; he had to get inside of her.

He slid two fingers past her lips and found her dripping wet. He hurriedly snatched his basketball shorts off and grabbed a condom from his nightstand before he slid it on with a skilled quickness. He looked down at Tyree, who watched his every move with her bottom lip tucked under her teeth. The desire in her eyes told him she was just as eager as he was. They'd both waited long enough, and Aiyden was ready to put them out of their misery.

He grabbed his long rod and positioned it right in front of her slit. He rubbed his dick up and down the length of its opening. Tyree hissed out and spread her thighs further apart before

Aiyden tapped on the doorway to her essence twice. He was asking for permission to enter. *Knock knock.*

thirty-nine

Tyree paused. Here they were, venturing back down a path that had led to nothing but pain and life lessons before. So why was she here now? Beneath him? Aiyden didn't just plow through her gates. He went ninety and left the last ten in her control. This was her "Speak now or forever hold your peace" moment. Would she come to her senses and leave? Her eyes stared at the manicured mane on his head and descended his hard body until they landed on his thickness that proudly jutted from a full patch of curls. The slight hook to the right just as she remembered. The head of it was a shade lighter than the rest of him. His two-toned toe curler. Her mouth watered at the sight, and she knew her answer. Hell naw she was not leaving, not by the little hairs on her chinny-chin-chin.

She reached up and pulled his head down to hers, keeping her gaze trained on his. She raised her head and met his lips as he braced his weight on his knee that he planted in his pillow top. Aiyden settled between her gapped thighs to thrust inside of her.

He didn't move, as if he was seized by the pleasure that crept up her body. Tyree's eyes rolled as she threw her head backward. Her body stretched to accommodate his width. She thought he'd reached his potential when they were lovers before, but she could feel that he'd had more growing to do. Then, Aiyden began to move in and out; it took no time for him to establish his rhythm.

Tyree bucked as heat began to form in the pit of her stomach. She pressed her lips together and fought a scream. She lifted her body and continued to meet his thrusts with the same intensity he delivered.

Tyree didn't protest as she began to lift from the bed. Fighting it proved futile while her body began to ascend higher. Aiyden pushed into her over and over, his grunts matching her groans. Her head rocked from side to side. She was delirious and didn't know what to do but enjoy his strokes. Aiyden pulled back until almost all of him was out of her and plummeted back inside until the head of him met her hilt.

Without warning, Tyree exploded. Her eyes closed, and she saw stars behind her lids. Her words were foreign as Aiyden didn't let up. He fucked her like he was making up for lost time. He was a decent lover when they were younger, but now, he was a grown-ass man who knew what he was doing. She continued to ride her wave as as he continued to ride her. When the intense tremors subsided, Tyree began her descent. Her hands covered her eyes as she braced herself for landing.

Aiyden's breath and paced picked up, and Tyree knew he was coming in at a close second. He pumped a few more times then plunged into her with a greater force. His grip on her hips tightened, and Tyree could feel him filling the condom.

A sigh of relief escaped her throat as she slowed her breathing.

"Wow," she uttered as she drifted into a fulfilled sleep.

Hours later, Tyree fought to keep still. Aiyden's hands had been busy as he stroked between her legs from behind. It took everything she had to keep up with her pretending.

"Hmmm," Tyree groaned as if she was annoyed. She wasn't. She had awakened when she felt him leave the bed for the restroom and kept her eyes closed when he returned. He seemed to have the same idea she had. It was time for round two.

"You gonna keep faking sleep?" Aiyden reached out and pulled Tyree into his chest. He inhaled her hair as he nuzzled the back of her neck.

"I'm not faking, thank you very much," Tyree mumbled.

"Yes, you are. I'm sure of it."

Tyree pushed out of his embrace and turned to face him. She wiped the sleep from her eyes.

"What makes you so sure?" she asked with a squint.

Aiyden peered down at her. The sleep in his face gave him a rugged, sexy look. She pulsed between her thighs.

The slick gleam in his eye had her interest piqued.

"What? Tell me!"

"I don't know if you are aware of this . . ." he began. He pinched his chin between his left index finger and thumb.

". . . yes?" she waved her arms to hurry him along.

"Baby, you snore."

Tyree gasped. "I do not!" she shrieked in horror. She sat up in the bed and held the sheet against her bare breast. "You're lying." She poked him in his strong chest. His muscles didn't budge.

Aiyden laughed. "You were calling Piglet, Wilbur, all the hogs."

Tyree hit him in his chest, horrified by his observation. She only snored when she'd been sleep-deprived or if she exhausted all her energy—so she'd been told. How embarrassing.

"It's OK. Nothing to be ashamed of," he comforted. He rubbed the pec she'd just jabbed. "Shit, you pack a mean punch." He winced. "It's almost as strong as the scent of your arousal."

Tyree jerked her neck back. "Unt-uh, you can't smell me."

"Yes-huh," he replied in the same mocking tone she used. "Women let out a certain smell when they are aroused, and your pheromones have been driving me crazy for about twenty minutes now. You know what I like better than your smell?"

Tyree had an idea where this was headed and decided to play along. "No, tell me."

Aiyden nudged her shoulder, pushing her back to the bed, and eased over her before scooting downward until he was eye level with her apex. He looked up at her with a heated gaze.

"Your taste."

"I want to laugh too." Aiyden watched Tyree from the end of the dining table with a glint in his eyes.

Aiyden cooked them omelets and French toast, which they enjoyed in silence as they reflected on the night before. Tyree's thoughts were all over the place. They started at how good Aiyden had been last night. They then skipped over to understanding sexual frustration now that he had relieved her of it. She felt buoyant with a renewed energy. Her thoughts pulled over and dissected how familiar they were, how their bodies were.

"It's kind of embarrassing."

She tried to console her laughter by biting on her lip. The innocent gesture sped up Aiyden's pulse. Tyree was undoubtedly the sexiest woman he had seen. Not because of her beauty and curvy body but her confidence. When she came to him last night, she was sure of herself and what she wanted. She didn't shy away when he asked what she was doing. She pointedly told him of her need for his body, and to him, there was nothing sexier.

"C'mon, try me. No judgement," he coaxed with twinkling eyes.

She laughed and patted her head with an open fist. "It's nothing major. I was just thinking about how crazy life is. Up until a few months ago, I just knew I would never see you again, and here we are, back with our firsts like we never left." Tyree kept her eyes on her plate as she explained. "Well, my first anyway."

Aiyden smirked. He understood where she was coming from. He felt the same way.

"You were my first too."

Tyree almost lost her grip of her loaded fork at his admission.

"Whaaa . . . no way," she stammered. At his nod, she added, "What about Valencia?"

Aiyden shook his head at the mention of a girl who he kicked it with before he and Tyree became involved.

"We fooled around during some heavy kissing sessions where I felt around a little, but that's all."

"Yeah, but . . . you guys were in your room . . . alone . . . with the door closed that day we skipped at your house. Toni and I just assumed you were sleeping together."

Aiyden gave a simple shrug. "Well, that's what you get for assuming." Tyree's amused expression faded into a serious one, and Aiyden hoped he hadn't fucked up trying to be funny again. Determining her mood was tough. Flashes of her inner thoughts had her face blasted with their variety.

"I have another penny."

She blinked and focused on him. Her face hiked, and Aiyden

knew she was contemplating the level of transparency she would answer with.

"I just always thought I was the only one soaring new heights when we became intimate." She used her fork to push a piece of egg around her plate. "Knowing that we gave our virginity to each other makes it feel . . ." She rolled her eyes upward, and he watched her search for the right word for her translation. "Special."

Aiyden sat his fork down and reached across the table. "Baby, it should feel special because it was. You are."

forty

" just love that beautiful little man. The things I would do if I had the chance," Toni sighed wistfully, no doubt rolodexing through her myriad of lascivious ideas. She sat on the floor in front of the couch as Tyree took out her plaits. *Love Jones* was their entertainment to help get through the grueling task.

Tyree chuckled. "Lorenz Tate? That man is old enough to be your dad. Handsome for sure, but the height-challenged uncle status?"

Toni angled her head to peer up at Tyree, who sat over her on the edge of the sofa. Her eyes tightened in offense to the criticism of her fabricated lover.

Tyree playfully sucked her teeth. "You better turn around or you'll be taking these braids down yourself." Toni pivoted back to a forward-facing position. She readjusted the two pillows she used as a buffer between her bottom and the wood floor. "I don't know why you play with your time and money on these styles you only keep in for two, three weeks tops."

"I like to keep it spicy," Toni replied with mirth. She rocked her hips to the side to get more comfortable and unintentionally changed the channel. "My bad, sometimes I don't know what to do being this thick!"

Tyree threw her head back and hollered in laughter. Toni was a clown, always had been. She made it clear that she wished her petite frame possessed more curves. She always joked about being too thick when that clearly wasn't the case.

"You're a mess. Please put the movie back on, thickness."

Toni aimed the remote to the television when a news reporting caught Tyree's ear. She'd grown sensitive to the murmurs regarding the Jags since being with Kamaal. Her ears perked when they heard the anchor mention Hakeem Sanders.

"Wait, turn that up for a second." Tyree pulled a few braids from the messy pony they were thrown into, and with the scissors, she cut them about three inches from Toni's scalp. *Thank goodness for her short cut.*

"Good evening, first coast. As we broke a few minutes ago, Hakeem Sanders was just rushed to the emergency room where he is allegedly undergoing surgery. Sources say he was attacked and has serious injuries. Foul play is suspected." An eerie chill shot up her spine until it towered above her head as a cloud of fret. Her body responded to the news before her mind could register her reaction's culprit.

It's just Hakeem fucking with me. But you just wait. She thought about Kamaal's rebuttal to her meddling by way of mentioning Simone's "pregnancy" that had been touring the rumor mill. She questioned what he meant the moment he said it, and Kamaal brushed her off, not offering any explanation. "He couldn't have . . ."

"He couldn't have what?" Toni tilted back with a wrinkled nose. "Can I turn it back to my bae?"

Tyree picked up the rat tail comb and resumed unweaving the braid sections. "Yeah, go ahead."

Tyree drifted into her thoughts while Toni remained absorbed with her five-foot-seven-inch crush. She hoped she was overthinking it. Kamaal couldn't possibly have anything to do with Hakeem being injured. *But I was the one who told him about my suspicions regarding him and my attack!* What if?

She'd been so caught up in her potential discovery that she hadn't noticed Aiyden walking through the front door. Tyree was unaware of him bending in front of her until he breached her personal space. The cool mint of his breath snapped her out of her mental recesses.

"Earth to Ree! You good in there?" Aiyden snapped his fingers as if he were a trained hypnotist fetching his subject from his manufactured trance.

Tyree jumped. "Hey, I'm good. How are you?"

His chocolate eyes bounced between hers, searching for clues that her mouth hadn't uttered. Tyree could swear she heard him murmur "mhm" under his breath. He leaned forward and brushed his lips across hers.

"I'm great now," he returned with his lips pressed to hers.

"Oh, this what we're doing now?" Toni acted as if she was insulted. She demanded answers while she unashamedly gaped at their intimate moment that Tyree wished she and Aiyden had the luxury of privacy for. The slight upward curve of her mouth blew her cover.

"Yes, my inquisitive cousin, this is what we're doing now." Aiyden held Tyree in his regard while he answered. He observed Tyree's task by way of fondling with Toni's braids to measure how much were left. "You plan on staying the night? This looks like it's going to take a while."

"Why?" An amused brow hiked. She crossed her arms over her chest and rolled her neck with her words. "You ready to get me out of here?"

Aiyden stood straight and returned Toni's smirk. "Maybe I am. The rain is supposed to come down hard out there tonight."

Toni shook her head, letting him know she hadn't believed him. "I'm sure that's not the only thing coming down hard tonight. Right, Ty?"

Tyree palmed her forehead, not wanting to be a part of this conversation. This was the reason she misled her about her sex life when they were younger.

"Look, could we not?"

"Fine by me." Aiyden clapped his hands. "I'm going to hit some weights. Toodles!" He failed at hiding his laughter as he pivoted and headed to the garage.

Toni cocked her head to the side with her tightened gaze pinned on Tyree, who shifted on the seat.

"Ty-ree," Toni sang. She stretched the two syllables, and the melody reminded her of the famous words, "You got some 'splainin to do."

"OK, Ricky Ricardo." Her resigned sigh sounded as if it were forced through her nostrils. "We're trying this again—us."

Toni's eyes stretched. "What?!" she squealed. "How did this happen? When did this happen?"

Tyree put the comb down. She knew Toni would not sit still until she got her answers.

"Just a few weeks. The attraction has always been there, and we tried to fight it, but it won against our efforts. Now, we're just taking things steady."

"Have you told him?" Toni whispered.

Tyree didn't need clarification. She knew Toni was asking if she told him about the baby. She looked away.

"No."

"Ty!"

Tyree held up her hands. "I know," she sighed. "I will. I know I have to, just not right now. This is still new, and I don't want to overcomplicate it."

Toni stood from the floor and sat next to her. "Can I be honest?"

Tyree nodded, knowing she would be whether she liked it or not.

"This was not what I intended for you when I suggested that you stay here. I just wanted you to get some distance from Kamaal while you figured things out, and I don't want you to run head on in this thing with Aiy only because you're running from the hurt that Kamaal caused."

Tyree recoiled. She wasn't expecting that. She swallowed and looked down into her lap. Was that what she was doing? Leaving one hurt for one that stung less? Four years ago, she felt the walls caving on her, but she didn't feel that way anymore. Time held true to its reputation and healed that wound. The loss of their child still haunted her at times. Random things would remind her of how close she'd come to what she wanted the most since she lost her mother. Tyree had forgiven Aiyden for that part years ago.

"I hear you, T. Now, sit back down before you end up leaving here with half of your head still in braids," Tyree fussed. She needed to move away from the conversation. Time alone would grant her the opportunity to consider her friend's words and determine just what the hell she was doing.

forty-one

Carl Thomas's sultry voice filled the room one late Saturday morning. The words of love and longing and how the two were reminiscent of a summer rain were the perfect forecast for the lovers as they loved each other's bodies that morning.

It was just after nine in the morning, later than when they would normally start the day, thanks to an eventful night that went into the wee hours. They'd made love so long that late had become early. It wasn't possible to make up for the lost time; however, that didn't stop their efforts. When they first started sleeping together again two weeks ago, their love was made with an urgency, a yearning that had them aching at the core. There wasn't time to move slow and give a test run of the skills they'd acquired while separated.

They had been snuggled in Tyree's bed with Tyree's back spooned into his front. She wanted to get more comfortable and shifted slightly. The small move made a huge impact when she felt Aiyden begin to stiffen behind her. Never wanting to miss the heat of the smolder that accompanied her with the morning wood, she pounced on the opportunity.

The words to "Summer Rain" detailed the prognosis perfectly. They couldn't think of a better way to spend a wet and rainy November day. As the local meteorologist predicted, today was a home day. Thunderstorms were scattered throughout the day, and rain was going to be constant. Instead of doing work in the yard as she had planned, Tyree went to work on Aiyden's stick instead. Just like Carl, neither minded the rain. She danced on his pole like a skilled dancer who picked him out of the crowd because he was known to be a big tipper. *Speaking of tip.*

"Ohhh," she moaned as she grinded on his lap. She loved this position. Her being on top gave her control of both of their bodies. Western civilization, as well as many across the world, pinned the man at the top of the chain. The man led the household, controlled the finances, and was expected to lead in the bedroom. When a woman made love to a man—on top of him—she took the reins. Hierarchy didn't matter. The feeling, the moment, all of it was under her control.

Aiyden was deep-seated within her walls, and the tip of his shaft stroked her sensitive pleasure point. The friction was too deliciously painful. It became too much, and she lost the rhythm of her dips.

Aiyden seemingly recognized that she was near her brink. He used his hand to nudge Tyree back slightly, his fingers dug into her hips, and his grip kept her glued to his pelvis. He lifted his hips, and Tyree leaned back and braced herself on outstretched palms. Her recline caused her to come off his steel somewhat. She was positioned perfectly.

He dug his heels into the mattress and elevated his hips and hammered upward, sure not to miss her spot—not even once.

Tyree gulped for air; this shit was intense. There wasn't anything for her to do but sit back—well, bend back—and enjoy. His thrusts strengthened, causing his grip on her hips to loosen a tad. Aiyden took only a moment to rock his hips before he resumed jabbing into her.

Tyree brought her chest down so she could see Aiyden's face. The unadulterated pleasure flowing through his features intensified the slow burning in her core. His jaw slacked and his brows furrowed, a testament of the sensations he was experiencing. She whimpered at the intense desire staring back at her, sending heat up her spine. Her breaths became more frequent and shallow as a new tingle settled in her middle. She couldn't run from this feeling; Aiyden's hands made sure she stayed put. She bit her lip, trying to get control.

"Unt-uh, let it out," Aiyden coached. He strengthened his thrusts, and Tyree saw stars. "Don't hold that shit."

"Aiydeeeeeeen!" was all she could manage as pleasure erupted through every part of her being. All her nerves detonated, and the control she relished faded. Her soul shifted beneath her dermis. This felt more than physical. The meeting of bodies bringing a release that transported her to the cosmos was divine. A gift from the heavens. She was thankful. Tyree threw her head back and cried out silently as she felt warmth ooze from her as her release puddled all over them. She trembled when he didn't relent. He pushed as if her excessive wetness motivated him.

Their groans blended until he sent one last powerful thrust before slamming her down on him. A stream of vulgarities left his mouth as Tyree's muscles clenched him, pulling everything he had to offer. He laid back onto the bed, bringing Tyree down on top of him.

"I need a cigarette," Tyree breathed the words into Aiyden's chest. He chuckled, and she smiled at the way his chest bounced beneath her head.

"You smoke now?" Aiyden asked. Tyree shook her head no, pulling a laugh from them both. The laughter faded as Tyree felt Aiyden's erection come back to life inside of her. She sighed at the pleasure of him filling her. Her back arched, and she began to wind her hips, sending shocks through them both.

Ding Dong.

The doorbell chimed, and the video doorbell announced there was a visitor. Tyree didn't miss a beat as she continued to gyrate. They were busy. Aiyden was on the same time as she. He was so into their lovemaking that Tyree wasn't even sure he'd heard the bell. Nothing indicated that he was aware of anything else but this. But her.

Tyree paused her riding and reached over to pick up Aiyden's phone from the nightstand. She opened the Ring app and advised the FedEx driver that he could leave the package at the door.

"This is certified, and the sender requested a return receipt."

"Shit. OK, one second." He lifted Tyree off of *him* and his lap and set her on the bed. He reached down to the floor and pulled his basketball shorts up before heading to the door to retrieve the package. He signed for the delivery and headed back to Tyree's room.

Aiyden read the addressee field on the package.

"It's actually for you."

Curiosity had him wanting to read the sender's information, but he wouldn't pry. Their sexcapade may have been one for the books, but it hadn't granted him that right.

Tyree accepted the box from him with a confused frown.

"For me? I didn't send anything here." She wasn't expecting

a package and hadn't given Aiyden's address to anyone. Plus, her mail was still being forwarded to Toni's house.

She read the name printed on the sticker at the top left corner of the package. "Omari D." She looked up at Aiyden and wondered if he deciphered Kamaal's middle name and last initial. The move was bold and tactless, neither unusual characteristics for her Hulk. Not wanting to appear suspicious, she opened the package, and her heart dropped.

Kamaal had done it. He'd given her the only requirement for them to start a family. Tyree fell in love. The solitaire that had to be at least four carats was housed in a shiny impressive yellow gold, a quality so pure, she could see right through it. Kamaal had been listening. When she talked about the type of ring she liked, she would become frustrated with his disinterest, but he was listening all along. Her eyes welled up, and she sniffed, quickly hoping Aiyden hadn't noticed.

She read the order receipt that was included in the box, and her stomach hollowed. The slip indicated that he purchased the ring months ago. Since it was a custom order, it had taken longer to fulfill. While she'd been thinking that Kamaal was never going to accede with giving her the proposal. She'd been thinking that her conceding in taking out her birth control was her caving, that she was giving into the big, bad, sexy baller when all along, he was meeting her in the middle.

"You good?"

Tyree snatched her head up. How could she forget he was in the room with her? She cringed at the sight of his uncertainty.

"Yes, I'm good."

She gave the best smile she could muster. Not wanting to take any more away from their moment, she turned and placed the ring inside her nightstand drawer. "So, where were we?"

Aiyden's steps to the bed were slow, doubtful. His stare was pensive as if he was trying to gauge her.

Tyree stood from the bed and took sultry steps toward him, obviously no longer shaken by the ring. When she reached him, she leaned up and pressed her lips against his. Aiyden didn't return the kiss until she forced her tongue past his lips. She kissed him with a hunger that matched her fever when they made love the other night. She took a deep breath as she broke the kiss and began trailing her lips down his body.

"Tyree," Aiyden breathed out. She liked hearing him say her name with such need. She knew exactly how to take care of that.

Tyree smooched down Aiyden's torso until she settled on her knees before him. She snatched his shorts down with force; his hardened staff sprung out and met her eye for eye. Tyree pursed her lips and looked at Aiyden with mischief. She turned her attention to his strong member and licked her lips.

"I love you too."

Aiyden wasn't given the chance to react to her admission. She cupped the base of him with her hand and pulled him into her mouth. Aiyden's eyes rolled upward, and he tilted her head back thinking about nothing but what was going on.

Shit. What package?

forty-two

A sigh of contentment escaped Tyree's lips as she leaned into the soft seats in Aiyden's Camaro. The old-school R&B radio station sent her into a relaxed mood while traveling down memory lane.

Aiyden looked over at the gem in his passenger seat. He used moments like these to study her without her knowing. If anyone told him he would be back here with his first love, he would've laughed then cussed them out. But damn it, here he was. He'd fallen even harder than he had before. Age hadn't been a buffer. He'd just hope she would catch him this time and not let him crash to the ground like before, but he couldn't dismiss the notion that they were losing control of the wheel. He would ask Jesus to take it, but he would rather wreck full speed, head on. He could take it.

They'd been good. Ever since they'd became intimate again, it felt that all endeavors were working toward the same goal—them together and happy. They'd eased down the yellow brick road to complete restoration, and Tyree's untimely package posed a severe delay. Just like rush hour traffic on the Buckman bridge, their progress was postponed by the interruption.

Tyree put great effort into impersonating apathy, but it was one thing he knew she hadn't counted on. He *knew* her. While she thought that her saying the ring was no big deal and that she was over that situation was what he used to gauge her innervation, it was the nonverbal responses he was keen on. He wanted to wholeheartedly believe her when she said she was unbothered and would be sending the ring back to Kamaal, but his gut wouldn't let it go. When she'd been soaking in a tub after a impulsive romp session, Aiyden gave into his intrusiveness and looked inside her nightstand drawer. His heart beat rapidly in his chest as he stared at the velvet box that he was promised had been gone.

But she had told him she loved him too. She hadn't said it since that day right before giving him the best fellatio he'd ever had. Aiyden thoroughly enjoyed it, but he also had a hard time dealing with it because he knew that performance with that much skill only came with experience, experience that she'd gotten during their time apart. He needed to switch gears before he crashed in the back of someone.

"I was thinking, how about you and I catch a movie later next week?"

Tyree, who had been scrolling through her phone, kept her eyes on the screen as she replied. "That sounds nice. When?"

"Um, how about this coming Thursday? We could catch a couple of matinees," he asked, feigning nonchalance, as if the date he chose was a random one when it was anything but. One night while he was asleep, the buzzing of his phone on his nightstand woke him up. With eyes squinted until they were almost closed, he scrolled down the top bar and read a message that indicated that Thursday worked for their schedule. That's when he noticed that the message was from Kamaal and he picked up Tyree's phone by mistake. A jealous pang shot through his core, and he desperately wanted to ask her about it but didn't want to risk her being mad at his snooping.

"Thursday is fine," Tyree agreed absentmindedly while locking her cell phone. She turned her attention to their surroundings as they rode down Edgewood Avenue. She looked out the window and studied the mural that adorned the side of a building: an abstract colorful of the O.G. ghostbuster Bill Murray indicating the Murray Hill neighborhood.

"Wait, no. Thursday isn't good for me. How about Friday?"

"You have plans?" Aiyden asked, hoping he seemed innocent enough.

"Yeah, an appointment that may run over. Let's try for Friday just to be safe."

Thursday

"Here we are, mimosa with a splash of pineapple juice."

Tyree thanked the waiter who placed her breakfast-appropriate cocktail on the table in front of her.

"And for you, sir, your sparkling water." The waiter placed his drink in front of him before walking off to attend to other guests.

Tyree took a sip of her cocktail and closed her eyes for a second to appreciate the flavors. It was just like she liked it. "Thank you ordering my drink. It's perfect."

"No problem," Kamaal answered. He sat for a few minutes and studied her.

Tyree took him in. Sitting there dressed in a matching

Valentino jogging suit, he had his hood on his head and tried to look as inconspicuous as a man of his stature could be. Knowing most of his fans could only identify him with his helmet and jersey on, he felt secure enough that they could dine without interruption. She took another sip of her drink and felt that some of the orange juice pulp had gotten lodged in her gum. She dug inside her clutch and inspected herself in her makeup compact.

"I received your package. How did you know where I was?"

Kamaal sat back in his seat. His pensive stare beckoned her undoing. She set her jaw in a firm line, determined not to crack.

"I always know where you are, Ty."

Her brows hiked. He stated that so matter-of-factly as if he still owned that right.

You can do this, she encouraged herself internally.

"Too close." Kamaal uttered the words lowly, barely making them audible. His eyes were trained on his glass.

"What does that mean?"

"You have a tendency of second-guessing yourself. It's one of the things, if not the only thing, that I don't like about you."

Tyree flinched at his candor. Had he invited her there to insult her over brunch? Give her one last dig before he left her life for good?

"You're too close to the mirror. When you look at yourself, you see the bad. You pick yourself apart. You bring attention to the most minuscule flaws." He used air quotes to express that the term was debatable. "I think that being in my world, being surrounded by superficiality and unrealistic expectations, ruined you."

Tyree recoiled. "Ruined me?"

Kamaal grimaced. "Not ruined, I didn't say that right." He took a deep breath. "Do you remember the night we met?"

Tyree nodded. Of course she remembered. How could she not?

"Yes, I remember."

"I don't think I've ever been more scared in my life. Karl and I were having a good time at the fair. One second, we were laughing over turkey legs, and the next, he was gone. I ran around the fairgrounds, tearing all that shit up because there was no way I was leaving that bitch without my son."

Kamaal had been so grateful for Tyree making sure his son Karl was safe. He repeatedly thanked her for looking out for his child and offered a wad of cash from his pocket.

"Absolutely not!" She pushed Kamaal's hand away. "You're going to mess up the good karma I'm putting in the world. I'm just honored to help a young prince get back to his king." She smiled while rubbing the young boy's head.

Her words paused Kamaal. Did she realize the weight of them? They lived in a time where the life of a dog was more valuable than that of a black man, that has been proven. They lived in a time when an innocent black man could be killed by the police on camera, and the cop would still walk away without consequence. A time where discrimination was technically illegal and sometimes frowned upon, but that didn't mean that shit didn't happen.

Kamaal couldn't ignore the curious glances whenever he was in the presence of the prestigious, the additional questions he received just to make sure he was in the right place. It was hard to feel like a king when, every day, there was a reminder you were viewed as worthless. He felt like Joseph the Dreamer, a king by birth but whose rightful place in royalty was delayed by the scheming of his jealous brothers. They looked down on Joseph because they were threatened by him. The constant berating and mistreatment were used as ammunition to shoot down his power and dismantle his esteem. There was no way they would bow down to the likes of Joseph, like they wouldn't support a black president. And what did the brothers do to stop him and silence him? They sold him into slavery. Talk about full circle.

Tyree reached across the table and took his harsh hand into hers.

"In a moment where I felt hopeless, God decided to sprinkle a little mercy on me and I not only found Karl, but I found you. His blessings must've been buy one get one free, 'cause my ass felt like I hit the jackpot!

"Aside from me finding . . . well, you finding Karl and me finding you was what you said when I tried to offer you money. You remember?"

Tyree smiled at the memory. "I said I was just happy to help a prince get back to you, his king."

Kamaal nodded. "It may not have meant much to you, but it meant everything to me. Who I am causes me to be surrounded by people who always want something from me. Before, I damn near had to require NDAs just to try to get to know a woman. You wouldn't believe some of things people have tried to get money from me. Then, I meet you on some off chance at the county fair, and I'm begging your ass to take my money."

They both laughed at that one. Once the laughter subsided, Kamaal continued.

"I honestly believe I fell in love with you then. That's why it bothered me when you would complain about your weight because you were fine the way you were. You were fucking perfect, Ty. That was all I wanted; you were enough. You've always been."

Tyree quickly swiped away the tear she couldn't fight. She'd struggled with her self-esteem in the beginning of their relationship. Kamaal always told her he loved how she looked and her size-twelve frame was perfect, but that was hard for her to accept when she'd been the only player's companion in double-digit sizes. How could he sit there and pour his heart out about her body-shaming ways when as soon as shit got tough, he ran into the arms of the type of woman who she strived to work toward?

"My being with Simone was nothing more than a stupid-ass decision I made during a moment of weakness. You not making the visit with my dad made me feel like I was losing you, and I fucked up."

His voice cracked, something she wasn't expecting. Ever since the ordeal at the first game, Kamaal expressed more emotion than ever during their entire relationship. She grieved the parts of him she never experienced and wouldn't get the chance to.

"We had a great run, Kamaal. You, Karl, and Brenda mean so much to me. I hope one day, with time, we can be friends. I'm always going to love you guys."

Kamaal jerked back as if her words caused him physical pain. "It's because of him, isn't it?" he uttered, not wanting to speak the name of the man who had taken his love. "He can't do what I can for you. I know I paved the way for him because I messed up, but he can't take care of you like I can. Not financially, mentally, and he damn sure can't take care of you physically. No one can."

Tyree shook her head gently, knowing that he truly believed what he was saying. "It's because of you, Kamaal." She patted his hand and stood to leave. She wished him a good day and turned to leave.

"I love you, Tyree Michelle."

Tyree paused. His admission kept her feet glued to the floor. He said the words low, as if saying them any louder would lead to expressions that neither wanted to display publicly. The four words she would always reciprocate flashed in her mind. They weren't an acute thought . . . but a reflex.

Kamaal's hands fisted on top of the wood table. The fingertips of his right hand pressed into his skin, while the tips of his other hand were hindered by an object he wasn't aware settled in his hold. He looked down at the ring box he'd sent first class to Tyree's *friend's* house. It stung knowing that the friend was of a beneficial nature.

"Fuck!" he yelled, not caring that the dining room was full of patrons. For the first time, he really felt that he and Tyree were over, and that shit crushed him.

Tyree watched Aiyden as she was engulfed in a wave of possibilities. All the dreams she had for them when they ventured into a relationship back then rushed her. She felt giddy, excited at the once-in-a-lifetime opportunity at a second chance with her first love. She bit her lip to conceal her titter. *Damn, this feels good.*

After she left brunch with Kamaal, Tyree rushed home. The relief she'd gotten once she'd received the closure she so needed from Kamaal ignited a spark low in her belly. On the way to the restaurant, Tyree had been anxious and unsettled. The thought of being around Kamaal had her on edge for days. She hadn't liked the fact that she kept the meeting from Aiyden, but she felt it was necessary. Their rekindling was still fresh, and she didn't want to disrupt it with any uncertainties regarding the sit-down she had to have with Kamaal. Now that it was over, she could close the door on that chapter and look forward to the future. For the first time in a long time, she felt free, and that both scared and excited her. This feeling even topped the high she'd gotten when she unknowingly ingested marijuana. It was more potent than the purest indica.

Tyree had rushed inside the house in search for Aiyden and found him lathering in the shower. Not wanting to interrupt the exquisite display, Tyree stood at the door watching quietly.

"You keep standing there looking at me and we won't get anything done today." The smooth bass in Aiyden's voice pulled her back to the present.

Tyree chuckled. "Oh yeah?" she asked as she stepped inside the bathroom. The warmth of the heated ceramic tiles felt heavenly under her feet. She held Aiyden's gaze as she took slow, measured steps. Being in a playful mood, Tyree decided to have a little fun with her spectator. "You promise?"

She stepped out of her shoes, leaving them at the door, and proceeded into the ensuite. While staring at him, Tyree slowly worked her pants and lace red panties down her hips. Her soft fingertips glided over her skin, mimicking Aiyden's touches. Her shirt came off next, and she reached behind her to unclasp the hooks of her matching bra. The garment fell to the floor, revealing her deep, stiff nipples. She used her pointer and thumb fingers to pinch her nipple as she pulled them, rotating them.

Aiyden was enjoying the show. That was apparent by the slow nod along with the seductive way he licked his lips. Tyree watched in amazement as Aiyden grew stiff and ready for her. He was a grower and a shower, proud and unimpeded, as if he were on display at show and tell. Tyree heard him suck in a quick breath at the sight; her center pulsed.

This little joke just may backfire, Tyree thought. Her arousal heightened as Aiyden began to put on a show of his own. He continued licking his lips while he took his soapy washcloth and began to focus on his penis. The water ran down his chiseled body. He stroked slowly, using the towel as a buffer between his hand and his stiffness. His shaft good in his grip, he stroked, twisting his hand to cover all nine inches as he worked from the tip to the base. Now, it was Tyree who licked her lips.

"So, you wanna play dirty, huh?" Tyree had something for that. Thinking quickly, she thought of the perfect get back. It was time she threw her trump card.

Tyree walked to her vanity and pulled a hair tie from the drawer. Using both hands, she pulled her hair into a messy top bun. Her eyes met Aiyden's in the mirror and just like she figured, she held his full attention. As she took a deep breath, her back arched and she bent over slowly, teasing Aiyden as the top half of her body inched closer to the floor. Once she was bent all the way over, her man got a perfect unobstructed view into her smooth southern lips.

That was the game point; Tyree: 7 Aiyden: 6.

Woosh.

She felt a warm breeze rush her body seconds before strong slippery arms wrapped around her waist.

"Aiyden!" she squealed as he lifted her up and carried her into the shower.

"That's it. We are not doing shit today!"

After two rounds in the shower, Tyree and Aiyden used it for what it was intended for and washed each other. Being spent from the passion they released on each other, they decided to order delivery from a hibachi restaurant up the street. They laughed at reruns of *Martin* until their sexual hunger resurfaced. The two took the party to Aiyden's room, where they fed off each other into the early morning.

forty-three

One Saturday in early December, Toni and Tyree rode down Moncrief Avenue. They crept through bumper-to-bumper traffic as they headed toward Raines High School. As usual, the ladies were running behind and they couldn't get there before the parade began, causing them to ride the last three miles at a snail's pace. After sitting in traffic for over an hour, they finally reached their destination. Aiyden stayed behind to broker a few loads to his drivers, and he was going to link up with them around halftime.

The entire city and surrounding areas came to support the Northwest Classic, an annual matchup between two of the biggest high school rivals in Jacksonville: the Vikings, and the Trojans. It was the last hoorah before students began their Christmas break, and it was a good time for all ages. Older generations came each year to represent their alumni. Students came to cheer their teams on to victory. Even those who hadn't gone to either school came to chop it up and have a good-ass time. The stars of the main event, the football teams, worked hard each year to get here and earn a year's worth of bragging rights.

"This is our lot right here," Toni announced as she parked at an older brick house on the corner. Residents in the neighboring areas would rent their yards and driveways out for attendees to park and tailgate. The arrangement was considered a luxury as it saved you from walking blocks down the road in the heat, and the residents kept an eye on your car.

After parking, Toni and Tyree did a last once-over in the mirror and got out of the car. The game wouldn't start for hours, but the real fun was the tailgating that started well before kickoff.

"I love these shirts your family made." Tyree complimented the custom tees that were ordered for today. They were a heather grey with "Straight Out of Ribault" printed on the shield belonging to the school's mascot, The Mighty Trojan Soldier. It paired perfectly with her ash-denim jeans and black and blue Roger Viver Viv pull-on sneakers. The weather peaked in the mid-seventies, true Florida style for a few weeks before Christmas, so jackets weren't needed.

The ladies crossed the street and walked through the car show section of the classic. Chevy Donks, candy paint, and old schools covered every inch of the three-block radius the display area spanned. This was where the guys showcased their big speakers and even bigger rims, as everyone competed to be the biggest and the loudest on the block. Everyone who participated in the show had their aftermarket radios turned up to the max. The tweeters were crisp, and the music was clear, but when the bass dropped, it shook the car from the hood to the trunk. The intensity of the bam even made license plates rattle, which also added a razzle-dazzle. It was a goal to have the hood hear you before they saw you, and just about everyone who participated could cross that feat off their list.

The ladies roamed through the street until they reached the end of a long line. Tyree had expected a wait because they had shown up late, but this line seemed endless.

"If this is the ticket line, we can bypass this because we have our wristbands already." Toni shielded her eyes with her hands and peered toward the entrance gate to see if there were any quicker options to get inside.

"This isn't the entry line; this for the food truck," the woman who stood in front of them turned around to advise them.

"*This* line is for food?" Toni asked incredulously.

The woman nodded with a simple shrug of her shoulders. "It's good chicken, the best in Florida."

"Obviously," Tyree added as she pulled her rope twists up into a bun. "Damn, now I want to stay and get some and see what this is all about." Tyree may not have had the truck before, but a line of people this long waiting when there was tons of food waiting inside told her she wanted to be a part of that number. She told Toni she planned on checking it out when the crowd died down.

Check in and the security point went by in a breeze, and they proceeded to Toni's family's tent.

"Hey, isn't that Jordyn who you used to work with? I haven't heard about her in a while." Toni nudged Tyree and pointed in the direction ahead of them.

"Yeah, that is her. We keep in touch. She has a book club and blog channel I follow. You should join; I think you'll like it," Tyree confirmed. "Jordyn!" she turned and yelled through cupped hands.

The woman who was driving a golf cart turned around and waved at Tyree before pulling up to them.

"Hey, Tyree!" Jordyn parked the cart and stepped off to embrace her. "How are you?"

"Hey, hot girl! I can't complain." Tyree turned to Toni. "You remember my friend, Toni?"

"Yes, I remember. How have you been? That cut looks great on you." Jordyn commended Toni's hair that she'd recently cut a few inches shorter. Her silky curls were now cropped closer to her scalp, which gave her a chic look.

"I've been good, girl, and you are rocking those braids. I may have to grow these edges out a little more to get like you!" The interaction between queens was always a pleasure to watch. The goal was always to uplift the other as much as one could. "You think we could bum a ride with you to our spot?"

Jordyn nodded. "Sure, hop on."

Tyree sat in the passenger side next to Jordyn, and Toni stretched her legs out across the backseat bench.

Tyree took in the scenes as they passed them by. People were everywhere. Smiles were on everyone's faces. Kids huddled around each other as they played and danced. She laughed at an older man who overzealously slammed a domino on the table and announced that he'd won again. The man beamed as his opponents groaned while begrudgingly pulling their losses out of their pockets. It felt like a family reunion, familiar and contented.

"So, Jordyn," Toni began. "What's the move for tonight?"

"We're going to hit a hookah lounge then head to the Foxx. We have a section at both."

Tyree laughed. "Damn, a lounge and the strip club tonight?"

"Yeah, girl, our ghetto can only be on a low level here. It ramps up to medium ghetto at the after party. Then, when we get to the strip . . . all bets are off!" The ladies laughed.

"Sounds like my cup of tea," Toni said with a chuckle. "This is us right here."

Jordyn pulled off to the side next to Toni's family. Tyree and

Toni thanked her for the ride and said their goodbyes, promising to call her later. The white canopy tent stood over the food area. The tables were lined with aluminum pans that were filled with barbeque, fried chicken, and an array of side dishes. The family sat at tables below the blue tent neighboring their food area.

Toni announced their arrival to the group and went around to greet everyone individually with Tyree following suit. With TNT being so close, she had met everyone before and even spent time at a few of her cousins' houses. Tyree caught up with Toni's cousin, Elise, who Tyree assumed she would be staying with when Toni offered her "cousin's" place.

"Hey, T-baby, you looking good!"

Tyree's pulse quickened as recognition hit her. She hadn't expected the woman here, not that there was a reason she wouldn't be, but she just hadn't thought about it. Why would Aiyden nor Toni mention it to her to give her time to prepare? Reena Hughes had been a gem when Tyree was younger. She understood Tyree's loss and supported her even before she and Aiyden became involved. Reena had been someone who Tyree found it easy to talk to, and she missed that interaction after her breakup with Aiyden. While Toni's mom, Norah, always looked out for her and treated Tyree like she was her own, it was her sister Reena who Tyree was most comfortable with. She was the cool elder who listened more than she judged. She was her Aunt Viv, the dark-skinned one.

Toni walked to Reena, who stood stirring a long-netted scoop in a large pot full of blue crabs, potatoes, corn, shrimp, and crawfish. Not wanting to seem disinterested or awkward, Tyree followed, bracing herself for an icy welcome. She stood to the side while Toni hugged and caught up with Aiyden's mom. When the two separated, Reena's eyes found her. She didn't seem surprised.

"Well, hello there. It's been a while, hasn't it?" Reena asked with a raised brow.

Tyree pursed her lips and swallowed. "Yes, ma'am, it has."

Tyree fought to not falter under the woman's intense glare. She hoped her panic didn't seep out. She didn't know that to do. She avoided a lot of gatherings at Toni's parents' for this reason. The relationship she had with Aiyden's mom ended the moment she and him broke up. Just as she did with him, she excommunicated anyone tied to Aiyden except for Toni. Everyone else received the deuces from her.

Tyree blinked, and Reena's stoic expression softened into a smile.

"Don't be shy. Come give me a hug, girl."

Tyree released the breath she'd been holding and walked into the woman's open arms. She hugged her briefly and went to pull back, only for Reena to squeeze her, keeping her there. Tyree didn't fight it and relaxed. Reena had that effect. It was as if she'd sensed Tyree's resistance and reason for her absence. Unable to explain it, she felt Reena telling her she understood and that there were no hard feelings. The power of a mammy bosom hug was astounding.

"You reneged, renigga! Give me books! Uno, dos, tres. I need that!"

"Excuse me, baby. Let me see what these folks got going on over here. You get you plenty of food. Toni, keep an eye on those crabs for a second." Reena walked around Tyree to the card table to join in the banter.

"Those are the only books you have? Don't let 'em run a Boston on you, Earnest!"

They all talked and laughed over food. Tyree sat back and took in the happenings around her. After being welcomed by Aiyden's mom, she wished she hadn't stayed away. Toni and her family were precious. It saddened her because she knew she had missed out.

"One time for the birthday bitch!"

Everyone turned as Toni's coworkers, Nique and Danielle, walked up. Nique held a portable Bose speaker in her hand, blasting the Jacksonville natives' hit song. It replaced the traditional birthday song. It was a part of Duval culture. Thou shalt fuck it up for your birthday.

Black people and music, that was the cue. The younger generation harmoniously began the ritual chanting of "Ayeee" while Danielle put a hump in her back and gave a slight pop—not too much since elders were present.

Tyree and Toni walked over to the duo, and they, along with Nique, surrounded Danielle as they motivated her with their chorus.

"Lemme stop!" Danielle giggled. She thanked her audience, who took turns hugging her and giving birthday wishes. When she turned to Tyree, she paused as if contemplating if she would accost her or not.

"Happy birthday, Danielle," Tyree bit the bullet and began. "I want to say sorry for how childish I was at Ray's."

Danielle shook her head while waving off Tyree's words. "It's OK, girl. I won't lie, I wanted to fire off on you for making my fall more embarrassing, but Toni told me about the cookie. I get it. One day, I'll tell you my brownie story. I cringe every time I think about it." Memories from Danielle's experiment with edibles had her shaking in mirth. "Hey, at least you had a good time. I saw you tearing that stage up!" They both laughed. Tyree's cheeks turned a deeper brown; she was still getting over the humiliation from that night but was glad they could laugh about it now.

"Speak of the devil."

Toni's friend Jon-Jon walked up. He held up his hands in surrender.

"The devil? Not me? I'm just out here doing the Lord's work."

Danielle's neck snapped backward. "By selling edibles? I think not."

"I think so. It is *He* who blessed us with the tree. I'm just spreading His gifts," Jon-Jon jokingly argued. "If y'all need anything, just come holla at me at the trunk. Don't sleep on me. I will sell out before the battle of the bands."

"You selling out here? Security gon' get you. They said they are not playing with that this year."

"Shit, security can get right too!" He pulled his phone out of his pocket. "Welp, money is calling. I'll get at ya later."

"Let me get one of those cookies before you go," Toni asked quietly. Jon-Jon pulled a sealed package from his MCM belted bag that he wore across his chest. He pulled a second package out and told her to have a good time with her girl. Toni walked up to Tyree offering up the treat.

"Naw, you enjoy it. I've had enough of that."

Toni shrugged. "Suit yourself. Let's get to the field so we can get a good spot for the battle."

They made it to the football field in enough time to get a good spot right in front of where the bands were setting up. Tyree jumped when she felt a pair of arms snake her waist from behind. The soft scent of the Prada cologne she recently grew an obsession with calmed her, and she settled back against Aiyden's strong chest.

"Hey, baby." Aiyden bent down and nuzzled her neck.

Tyree turned in his embrace and jabbed her finger in his strong chest.

"Don't 'Hey, baby' me," she feigned aggravation. "Why didn't you tell me your mom was coming?"

Aiyden chuckled. "'Cause I didn't want your scary ass to run." He pecked her lips.

She scoffed after returning his kiss. "I am not scary!"

He squinted, clearly not believing her. "Would you have come had I told you?" Tyree nodded her answer, which Aiyden answered with a sucking of his teeth.

"K."

Tyree opened her mouth for another rebuttal when a speaker announced the host of the halftime festivities.

"Duuuvalll!" Sherwood T, the personality from Jacksonville's hip-hop and R&B radio station, called out. As expected, the crowd repeated the sentiment. "That's what's up! It's the weekeeeeend, baby! Let me hear you if you're ready to see these bands battle!" Cheers and claps were sent up. The anticipation was readable; everyone was ready for a showdown.

"Before we begin, we have some great news. The Jacksonville Jaguars have been so generous to send two students from each band on a full-ride scholarship to Edward Waters College, where they will join the Triple Threat Marching Band!" Sherwood waited a moment to allow the ovation to sober. "Here to announce the winners is Mr. Duval himself, Kamaal 'Mack Truck' Duval!"

To say that the crowd went wild would be an understatement. The surprise visit from the golden boy had been well received. Those who had been sitting stood.

"Mack Truck! Mack Truck! Mack Truck!" the crowd roared as passionately and clamorous as the crowds she heard many times at the stadium.

Tyree went still. First, Aiyden's mom and now Kamaal. She'd

had enough surprise appearances from the past for one day. Sensing her discomfort, Aiyden leaned down and spoke in her ear.

"You good?"

Tyree gave a slow nod. "That's nothing."

Aiyden regarded her for a few moments, and she was sure he was looking for clues to determine the validity of her response. Tyree offered what she hoped was a convincing smile.

Kamaal took the microphone from the DJ and smiled at the crowd full of his admirers.

"Thank you, thank you. As Miss T indicated, two members from each band will be receiving a scholarship today, courtesy of your Jags."

Kamaal's words were lost on Tyree as she watched him. His attire was understated compared to his normal drip. He sported a franchise team polo shirt that seemed to be tailored for his muscular torso. The ridges and bulges of his body were so pronounced. His khaki chino pants were snug on his powerful thighs that she had ridden many times. What she hadn't remembered was this beard. It was longer than he ever wore it when they were together. The hairs of it extended until it met his chest. Why did he have to look so good?

The spectators ushered into another round of applause, snapping Tyree out of her trance. She hadn't realized that he had finished his spiel. The four band members, one young lady and young man from both schools, accepted the certificate from Kamaal. Tyree joined in on the clapping as she, along with everyone else, watched them take their pictures.

Kamaal gave one last thanks before introducing the bands. The majorette squad led each band out to the track. As the groups assumed their positions, he walked off to the side. Tyree's eyes followed him the entire time. As if he could feel her, Kamaal turned her way and immediately found her gaze. His amber gaze widened in surprise at seeing her before traveling upward to take notice of Aiyden. He shifted his attention downward and noticed Aiyden's arms that circled her waist. The squint that appeared told of his disapproval. Tyree felt the grip around her tighten. She looked up and saw that Aiyden's attention was just where hers had been. Kamaal watched them watching him for what seemed like forever. His stare didn't avert until a man tapped him, garnering his attention. Tyree's breathing returned normal when he was no longer in eyesight. Not wanting to mention the awkward encounter, she focused on the happenings on the track.

The drumlines faced each other where they met on the track that surrounded the football field. Everyone watched the beasty battle between the Vikings and the Trojans. They weren't competing in front; it was like medieval times. The crowd that circled the competition were like the spectators who cheered and booed just as onlookers historically egged on gladiators who fought to the finish.

The squads took turns showcasing their talents. The crowd went wild as they recognized Raines playing a classic for the 904: "I'm A Freak" by Young Cash featuring T-Pain. The horns were blown with perfection, the notes matching the octave of the song. The crowd joined in, adding the lyrics. Once the last count ended, each drum major held their right drumstick high in the air before dropping it on their instrument, the thumping sound as the stick met the batter head created the final beat of the song. This was their mic drop.

Ribault stepped forward to perform their finale. Not to be outdone, they too had chosen a song made by a Jacksonville native. The stadium encouraged the ensemble with their applause as the instrumental to YK Osiris's "Worth It" began.

"You just got to be worth ittt!" everybody sang while waving their hands in the air. Some even turned on their cell phone flashlights and hung them in the air as if they were lighters. Some even raised lighters toward the sky. The song trailed off to a natural end. There wasn't any flamboyant ending. The confidence in their performance itself had been enough.

"All right, everybody! Let's give it up one more time for both teams and the amazing job they did today!" Sherwood T instructed over the speakers. "We have one more surprise for you. Instead of a normal sendoff, we have two of our very own. Welcome, Trap Beckham and Tokyo Jetz!"

"Hit It" began booming out of the speakers as the crowd got hype once again. Toni looked over at Tyree.

"If we want to beat traffic, we should head out. You ready?"

Tyree looked up at Aiyden who gave a nod.

"Yes, let's go. I've had enough excitement for today." She looked forward to getting cleaned up and winding down with her man. She needed a quiet evening to balance out the commotion of the day.

forty-four

"Isn't that Ms. Homewrecker right there?"

"Yeah, that's Ms. *Hoe*wrecker all right."

Tyree and Toni both turned to see the urban Doublemint twins. Just like most in attendance, they wore matching shirts. Not as if they needed anything else to resemble, they both even wore the same grimace.

"Hello, Cherise, Channing," Tyree greeted.

"Hello, Tyree. I see you're still slumming with side bitches. Maybe I should have invited Simone out," Mrs. Watkins spewed as she sent deadly daggers to Toni.

Tyree gave a questioning look to her best friend who refused to look at her. Toni was uncharacteristically reserved compared to her "beat a bitch without a moment's notice" attitude Tyree was used to seeing from her in hostile situations. She could go as far as to say she looked bothered, even frightened. How had Cherise found out about their affair, and why was she in the dark about it? Understanding that now was not the time and she would, without a doubt, be getting her answers later, Tyree tried to diffuse the situation before it detonated.

"Who are you here with today, Cherise?"

Cherise's chin and nose inched up as she tilted her head back. "I'm with my man. Who else would I be with?"

Tyree lifted her palms as she shrugged. "Exactly. That's my point."

Channing scoffed. "What is that supposed to mean?" she asked for her sister.

Tyree rolled her eyes before settling them on Cherise. "She knows what it means. C'mon, T, let's go."

"That may be best," Channing chimed in just as Tyree, Aiyden, and Toni moved to walk by them.

Having enough of her slick mouth, Tyree stopped. Aiyden must have sensed trouble because he tightened his hold on her hand, and Tyree could feel that he was trying to calm her. She shifted and looked up at him.

"It's OK, babe. We're just talking.

"You both are dear friends of mine who I love and respect. But this right here is my sister." Tyree alternated her eyes between the splitting images before her. "Please don't make me put these twists in a rubber band." Her expression was calm and pointed, not to be misunderstood for an empty threat. "I hope that one day, you and I can sit down and have a talk. You're owed that."

"All right, I see you, Ty." Cherise nodded knowingly as if she read Tyree loud and clear.

The three amigos proceeded to the park's exit. Aiyden grabbed Tyree's hand and patted it, his way of assuring her that everything would be fine. She looked up into his tawny face and smiled softly. She appreciated his reminder; she needed it.

"Hey, Aiyden, your phone been broken?"

Tyree, Aiyden, and Toni turned to find Brandy standing there, hands on her hips and a chip the size of a bowling ball on her shoulder. Tyree took a deep breath and looked toward the sky. This is why she preferred staying at home.

What the fuck was this? she thought. *A ratchet reunion? Ay yi yi.*

"Brandy? What are doing here?" Aiyden's hand tightened on Tyree's, a move that Brandy hadn't missed.

"I've been calling you. I had a layover and thought we could hang out. But I see you've been preoccupied. I just find it funny that all this time, you've been telling me you weren't looking for anything serious, ya know? No titles because you were working through your things.

"Me and you were just having fun," she used air quotes to emphasize his words. "But you're walking around with the bitch that's bumming around on your arm like a proud suitor."

Toni stepped up before Tyree could react. "OK, Brandy, that's enough. Just walk away, love, you're sounding really bitter."

Aiyden's ex-lover scoffed. "If I sound bitter, I could only imagine what your wife sounds like."

There goes that record scratching again. Tyree snatched her hand from Aiyden's grip and turned to stand before him with her back to Brandy.

"Wife? What is she talking about?"

Brandy's sour face lit in amusement. "I'm sorry, did she not know you're married, Aiyden?"

Tyree saw red. *Wife?* She shook her head and tried to make sense of the word. She knew what it meant, but hearing Brandy mention it sounded like a foreign language.

"That's enough, Brandy," Aiyden stepped. "You should just go.

I'm sorry you aren't able to accept that our run is over, but this won't change that."

Tyree felt like a fool watching Aiyden fight with his fuck-friend about his wife. She wanted to believe that Brandy was just grasping at straws to save face, but Aiyden hadn't done anything to help her determine the validity. He hadn't gone right into denying the woman's claim and that was telling.

She looked around for cameras and set crew because Tyler Perry had to have been in the midst. She didn't want to be a part of this, and she damn sure didn't want either of them to witness her tears that were at bay.

"Ty!"

Tyree heard Toni call from behind her and continued her stride. They could talk once they got inside Toni's car. "I know you're mad, but just let him explain. It's not what you think it is."

Tyree stopped in her tracks and pivoted to face her best friend. "You knew, didn't you?" Toni remained quiet, but her hesitation was loud and clear. She felt like Julius Caesar, stumbling with blades in her back. Et tu, Brute?

"Really, Toni? I'm over here defending your slimy ass to my friends just for you to do the same shit to me. 'Fuck Tyree' must run in your blood." She shook her head in disgust. She needed to get away from Aiyden and Toni, the conniving cousins.

"Everything all right over here?" The deep timbre paused Tyree. For the first time in months, she was glad to hear it. She spun and found Kamaal there next to his teammate Jeremiah.

"Yes!"

"No!"

Aiyden, who had caught up to them, and Tyree answered at the same time. Kamaal's brow raised at the discord. She knew he was inwardly questioning what caused such a contrast to the loving embrace he witnessed earlier.

"Ty?" Kamaal asked.

"Could you give me a ride home?"

"I think the fuck not," Aiyden snarled, garnering Kamaal's attention.

Kamaal stepped toward Aiyden. His arms that were across his chest were now at his sides. His teammate must have read the move because he stepped ahead of Kamaal.

"Let's go, Ty," he ordered from behind Jeremiah.

He wasn't her first or second choice, but Kamaal was her only option in the moment. She needed to get away from this place before she lost her shit. Without looking at Aiyden or Toni, she fell in step beside Kamaal and left the field.

Tyree fumed as she sat in the passenger seat of Kamaal's truck. She didn't get it. All she'd asked for was a nigga who would hold her down and not embarrass her. Why was that shit so hard to come by? Were millennials programmed to say one thing and do the other? *Shit!* She'd just gotten over Kamaal's deceit just to tumble back into a love triangle.

"You're going to be just fine," Robert Morris tried to console his daughter.

"I know I will, Dad." Tyree tried to keep a brave face for her father. She knew he worried a lot about her. Losing his wife led to an extreme paranoia that lasted a while. Robert would only let Tyree out of his sight when it was necessary. She always had to check in with him whenever she wasn't home, and her phone always had to stay on; one missed call could send him into a panic attack.

"OK, Miss Morris, your X-rays are normal. Your appendix and kidneys are fine." Her primary care doctor reentered her exam room.

Both Tyree and her father breathed a sigh of relief. The pain she felt in her side and back reminded her of what her friend complained about years ago, which turned out to be appendicitis.

"That's great, doctor. Were you able to find out what's causing this pain?"

The doctor stood between Tyree, who was on the exam table, and her father, who sat in the visitor's chair in the corner of the room.

"Yes, your urine sample confirms you are pregnant, Tyree."

"Pregnant!" Both Tyree and Robert shrieked at the news.

"Yes, the levels detected in your sample do indicate this. Now, I need to do an ultrasound to check on the fetus. Please disrobe and lay down here at the table. I will be back in a few minutes." Her doctor turned to Robert. "A word outside, please?"

The next moments flew by in a blur for Tyree. In a daze, she took off her clothes and waited for her doctor to come back. How was she pregnant? How could she not know? She wasn't one to track her cycles, but had it been that long since she'd had one? What other symptoms had she missed?

Two soft raps at the door alerted Tyree, who straightened the drape at her waist.

"I need to do a transvaginal ultrasound, and your father thought it best to wait outside," she said, explaining Robert's absence with an apologetic smile.

Tyree nodded. She understood him wanting to give her privacy, but she preferred he be in there with her.

"Could you scoot all the way down for me. Yes, just like that,"

Doctor Johnson coached. *"OK, I'm going to apply a serum for lubrication, and you may feel a little pressure."*

Tyree flinched at the squeeze as the probe was inserted.

"Here goes your baby," the doctor pointed at the ultrasound monitor. Tyree was frozen as she saw the little lumpy shape. She couldn't make out any noticeable limbs or other body parts. The doctor clicked on the screen and measured. "By the size of the fetus, you're between six and eight weeks. We can do further tests to narrow down your exact gestation."

Tyree remained silent and nodded. She didn't need further tests. She knew she was with Aiyden four-and-a-half weeks ago when he visited for a day. He drove to town for his uncle's retirement party, and they had spent the night together.

"I'm going to turn on the microphone and check the baby's heartbeat."

Another nod.

After a few seconds, she could hear the mic. There wasn't any sound she could make out as a heartbeat. The doctor adjusted the probe to catch the rhythm, to no avail. The physician switched to an abdominal ultrasound.

"Let's see here." The instrument resembling the microphone on an infant's karaoke machine was pressed down on her stomach. Five minutes later, the doctor had to announce there was no heartbeat.

Tyree gained and lost a baby at the same time.

"That's why you refused to get pregnant before we were married." Kamaal listened to Tyree as she spilled her heart to him. As soon as she was inside of his car, all it took was him asking if she was OK for her to break. She bent over in Kamaal's passenger seat as she cried from her gut. She wrapped her arms around her middle to soothe the pain there. Thinking about Aiyden betraying her again and reliving her miscarriage caused her physical pain. She could actually feel it. It was reminiscent of the cramping she'd endured when she learned about and lost her baby.

"Yes, I felt that the assurance of a marriage would mean that I wouldn't go through anything like that again, all for history to repeat itself."

Kamaal waited a few moments before he asked, "Are you pregnant now, Tyree?"

Tyree shook her head. "No, I'm not pregnant. Just left in the dark by the one I love."

forty-five

Three hours later, Kamaal pulled into Aiyden's driveway. Tyree hadn't been ready to face Aiyden and asked that he ride around before bringing her there. They rode around for about an hour before he pulled up to St. Augustine beach. There, they just sat on the sand and listened to the waves crash onto the shore.

Tyree sighed when she saw Aiyden's white Camaro parked in its usual spot. It was his home, but she hoped he wouldn't be there.

"Are you staying here tonight?"

Tyree turned and met Kamaal's amber eyes. "I can't." She shook her head.

He nodded, satisfied with her answer. "You can always come back home, Chelle."

She flinched at her nickname. It felt good being able to vent to him. She needed someone familiar to get out what she'd held on to for so long, and he fit the bill in the moment. But just like the Titanic on April 10, 1912, that ship had sailed.

The front door to the house flung open, and Aiyden rushed

out, concern etched in his features, until he noticed the driver. Having Kamaal bring her here was a penalty.

"I'm fine. I'm just getting some things, and I'm going to a hotel. Thank you for the ride, Kamaal."

Kamaal frowned at Aiyden through his windshield. "I'll just wait out here until you get your things."

Tyree nodded before getting out of the truck. She didn't have any fight left in her, and she would be on her own soon enough. She walked up to the front door, ignoring Aiyden's inquiring eyes. She could see the many queries swimming about his orbs, and she intended to ignore each one.

"Take your time, Ty. I will be right here waiting for you. Always." The words were spoken to her, but his eyes had been fixed on Aiyden. His not-so-subtle warning that he would remain lying in wait, lingering so he would be available when Aiyden fucked things up, appeared to not sit well with her old so-called friend.

"What up, Quavo?"

Tyree paused.

"You probably want to put a leash on John Coffey over there. I know he's a jock, but he can't be that dumb." Aiyden's boorish request was spoken over her head. His dark eyes gawked into Kamaal's emerald ones. "But then again, maybe he is. I've been watching the news. It's not smart to walk around without your helmet, young man."

Kamaal leaned his head to the side. Tyree was sure he'd caught the verbal gauntlet Aiyden tossed his way as if it were a screen pass. His nose twitched, a sign that the beast inside the giant was emerging. She watched his body prepare for a battle just as it did each Sunday. With determination, Kamaal urged forward as he closed in on the battlefield.

Aiyden didn't seem scared and appeared to perk up at the

challenge. There was no hesitancy as he advanced toward the titan. Kamaal's physique was more robust, but Aiyden damn near met his height.

"No! Please don't do this!" Tyree pleaded at the top of her lungs. She intercepted Aiyden and walked sideways, holding both her arms in either direction, hoping that would keep the men apart.

"Get a collar and a muzzle for that mutt, Tyree."

Her eyes bulged. She was surprised by this side of Aiyden. She'd never met the cantankerous version of him. It was different than his usual cool poise.

"I'll agree, I made some stupid decisions that I'm paying for dearly." Kamaal's amber gaze found Tyree's eyes for a moment. She sucked a quick breath at him owning up to mistakes. "But you aren't a hard act to follow . . ."

Tyree's mouth dried. She knew this man. The evil smirk on his mouth mirrored the malevolence in his gaze. Mack Truck was a by-any-means-necessary kind of guy. That's how he was bred to be both on and off the field. Just as football teams studied game tapes of their opponents to find a weakness, Kamaal had his intel and was ready to spew it, even if that meant she was taken down as collateral. She knew what he was going to say next. His eyes were a fierce hunter green, darkened by the fury behind them.

"No, Kamaal," she urged quietly. Her eyes pled with his. He wouldn't do this to her; he couldn't. Kamaal was a lot of things, but capable of using her loss as ammunition was a low for him. But...

"It was pretty dumb of you to play off on your girlfriend the day she lost your baby."

Tyree wanted to shrink when Aiyden's dark eyes shot to her for her to deny what he'd announced. The grimace he wore softened as, without words, he silently begged her to relieve him and tell him it wasn't true. That, she couldn't do. No longer interested in brawling with Kamaal, Aiyden resigned and retreated into his house.

Tyree called after him as she followed, ignoring Kamaal who called out after her. Aiyden's stride hadn't broken; he walked as if he couldn't hear her. She placed an arm on his shoulder, and he jerked away from her with a force that made her stumble. She caught herself and straightened. His rejection hurt. She hated him for deceiving her again, but she didn't want him to find out this way. That wasn't why she told Kamaal. She knew she didn't use her best judgement telling Kamaal about her history with Aiyden. She was so pissed at finding out he was married, and she needed to vent.

Seconds ticked into minutes, which turned into an hour. Time and their diaphragms had been the only things moving since the lake of fire and brimstone had broken loose with Kamaal's word vomit. The ill-mannered decision to weaponize her miscarriage was the lowest one Tyree had witnessed from her *almost* fiancé.

The fucking nerve!

Aiyden sat on the edge of the sofa, his head bowed and his eyes trained on his tented fingers held right above his lap. She sat in the recliner on the other side of the living room. She wanted to retreat, to look away, but she had to face him. Their cards were face up on the table, and it was time for them both to face their hidden truths.

"Why didn't you tell me?" His voice sounded foreign to her. The tremor in his tone touched her behind the wall she erected.

Tyree's phone began to ring, and she ignored it. There were more pressing matters at hand, and the caller would have to wait.

She pulled in a deep breath and let it out slowly, counting to five as she did.

"I tried to tell you that day. I called you over and over and got no answer . . . until *she* picked up."

Her phone rang again, and Aiyden turned to look at her. *Finally, he sees me.* His eyes were rimmed in red. His face scrunched in angst.

"You better not answer that motherfucking phone," he growled. A cool chill snaked up her spine. She'd never heard him speak so harshly. His cords were heavy with anger, a stark contrast from the adoration he normally spoke with. "Who picked up?"

Tyree rolled her eyes and settled on him. This was what he wanted, and she would give it to him. "The girl you cheated on me with."

Aiyden's shoulders slumped. His gaze averted to the space beside her as if the news was too much for him to face head on. The conversation he wanted to have and she declined because she knew it would get them here, apart when they were just so close. They couldn't have a future if they didn't settle the past. So many pieces were missing from the puzzle, and Tyree needed to see the picture in its entirety.

"What happened to her?"

She was fearful of what caused his sunken demeanor. She'd been hit by the blow of learning he had a wife. She knew another one was coming to complete the combo. His words were low, defeated. Tyree had to strain to hear the three words he spoke next.

"I married her."

Her chest heaved as the walls spun and caved in on her. When she learned of Aiyden having a wife, she envisioned some nameless, faceless woman she didn't know, a person who hadn't come about until years after she and him had ended. She needed to take a seat; her legs felt wobbly. The lip lover.

He. Married. Her.

While she was home healing from a broken heart and the loss of their child, he was whisking the next bitch—the one he told her she didn't have to worry about, that it was her who had his heart—away in the sunset. Just as Kamaal did, Aiyden gave away what belonged to her to the next willing body. She didn't know which would have been worse.

What prayer had she gotten wrong? She jumped at the sound of her phone ringing again.

"Tyree," Aiyden urged as she grabbed her phone. She needed something else to put her mind on, something to steady the spinning. She boxed Aiyden out as she tried to pass her security system. Her trembling hand made it hard to capture her full thumbprint for access.

"We are not done talking," Aiyden barked. He marched over to her and tried to grab the phone from her hand.

"Just give me a second!" She snatched from him. The only contact between them was the spit that sprayed from her mouth. He took a cautious step backward. Happy that he retreated, she opened her messages and screamed.

"What is it?" he asked in a low voice.

If Tyree heard him, nothing about her countenance showed that. Her vision was tunneled on the phone in her hand as she clicked and swiped ferociously. Her face was contorted into an anguished scowl. "No, no, no. Please, no," she pled in a low mumble. Her fingers typed in a frenzy as she searched for answers.

"Is everything OK?" His voice was absent from the bass it possessed a moment ago.

Everything went silent. It felt like her throat was closing.

Perspiration coated her forehead. She was so lost in her phone that she hadn't noticed he closed the gap until she felt his large hand on her arm.

"I need to call Toni."

Tyree swallowed. She read the words again while trying to fix her mouth to speak them.

"It's Karl. He was hit by a car and is in critical condition."

She choked back a sob; she couldn't open those gates as the dam would surely break then she wouldn't be good to drive.

"I need to go."

Not waiting for a response, she picked up her purse from the table and headed to the door.

"Ree!"

Her fingers that gripped the handle went still. She didn't need Aiyden telling her she shouldn't go or, even worse, that they needed to talk. Not right now. It was best that they didn't speak right now. She turned her head to the right, only giving him her profile until she heard his words.

"Please, be careful."

Three moments passed, and she proceeded out of the door. She hit the highway and put her truck in sport mode; her speed neared 100 miles per hour the entire way. She was relieved he'd been taken to a nearby hospital.

Here she was racing down the highway to be there for the family she fought hard to keep her distance from. She'd made so many strides over the past months just to be right back here, running back to save the day. She shook her head at the realization. The soul ties hadn't loosened like she believed.

Tyree parked in the garage and grabbed her phone just as it rang. Thinking it was an update on Karl, she quickly unlocked it and saw the notification from the Bible app.

**Philippians 4:6-7. Be anxious for nothing, but
in everything by prayer and supplication, with
thanksgiving, let your requests be made known
to God**

A calm that came over her couldn't be explained. Knowing
what needed to be done, Tyree sat her items down and bowed her
head.

"God, I'm begging you to come through for my guy." Her lips
trembled. Her grip on the steering wheel squeezed tighter, causing
her knuckles to crack. "He means so much to us, and we wouldn't
make it with—"

She snapped her lips shut. The emotion building was too great;
she couldn't say those words. Thankful that God could hear her
thoughts, she silently continued. She called on the Lord and all His
angels to be in the midst and see her baby boy through. Wanting
to seal her deal with God, she continued with the prayer she'd
prayed at a young age.

"Our Father in Heaven, hallowed be your name. Your king-
dom come, your will be done, on earth as it is in heaven. Give us
this day our daily bread, and forgive us our debts, as we also have
forgiven our debtors. And lead us not into temptation but deliver
us from evil."

When Tyree made the decision to move on from Kamaal, she
knew she needed to sever all the ties. There was no way she would
lead a prosperous romantic life while the umbilical cord was still
attached. She needed to be delivered from the man and the place
that wore the same name. She needed to amend her request to
Heaven.

"With all the glory and the power, in Jesus's name. Amen."

Tyree exited her car and headed inside the hospital to meet

Kamaal. Once again, her past had transformed into her present, and she just knew it was going to be a part of her foreseeable future.

Thank you for reading *Deliver Me from Duval*
If you enjoyed this book, please help spread
the word by leaving an online review.

deliver me from duval playlist

1. "So Anxious" - Ginuwine
2. "Get Up On It" - Keith Sweat ft. Kut Klose
3. "Smile (Living My Best Life)" - Lil Duval ft Snoop Dogg and Ball Greezy
4. "It Kills Me" - Melanie Fiona
5. "Stranger in My House" - Tamia
6. "F**k Boy" - Trina
7. "I Remember" - Keyshia Cole
8. "Ice Melts" - Drake ft. Young Thug
9. "Unbreak My Heart" - Toni Braxton
10. "Stay" - Rihanna ft. Mikky Ekko
11. "Brokenhearted" - Brandy
12. "Hit Em Up Style (Oops!)" - Blu Cantrell
13. "Tootsee Roll" - 69 Boyz
14. "Can't F**k with Me" - Trick Daddy
15. "F**k the Other Side" - DJ Khaled
16. "Knuck if You Buck" - Crime Mob
17. "Pray You Catch Me" - Beyoncé
18. "Safe with Me" - Sam Smith
19. "Twerk 4 Me" - Kamillion

20. "John Redcorn" - SiR
21. "Permission" - Ro James
22. "No Problem Remix" - Tokyo Jetz ft. Trina
23. "Summer Rain" - Carl Thomas
24. "Walked Outta Heaven" - Jagged Edge
25. "Start Over" - Beyoncé
26. "Birthday B*tch" - Trap Beckam
27. "Worth It" - YK Osiris
28. "Freak" - Young Cash & T. Pain
29. "Me, Myself and I" - Beyoncé
30. "I Need You Now" - Smokie Norful

ME FROM
DUVAL

Eyes Wide Open

A Sneak Peek

Tyree Morris rode down I-295 with the windows down as she headed to visit Karl at the hospital. It had been a week since he was involved in a hit and run, and he was still unconscious. Her chest ached for the little man who had stolen her heart and continued to own its pieces, even after his father had shattered it.

The wind whipped through her car and curls as the Jhene and H.E.R.'s acoustic tune oozed out of the speakers. Her head bobbed to the beat as she felt the words of the song. This was her anthem. She was back on her bullshit.

Always get caught up in love, but I'm done with that.

She'd tried love, then tried it again, and *another* time after that. Each time ended the same—her being made a fool of and heartbroken.

"Boy, I tell ya." She shook her head as she recalled all the details of the melodrama that was her life. *It's cool,* Tyree thought. *I got me. From now on, nothing else matters.* She continued with her F-boy playlist until she reached her destination.

After parking, Tyree proceeded to the elevator and headed inside.

"Good afternoon, Miss Morris," the attendant at the check-in desk greeted.

"Hi, Megan. Doing alright today?" Tyree asked as she signed the check-in list. They were on a first-name basis since she was the one usually on duty whenever Tyree came to visit.

"Better than I should be," Megan answered while handing her a visitor's sticker.

"I hear that. Thanks." Tyree placed the sticker on her shirt and walked to the double doors. Once the buzz sounded, she pushed the door and walked to the end of the hall. She took a deep breath as she reached room 516 and pushed it open.

A figure sitting beside the bed made her stumble. Had she known he would be there she would've come another time. "I thought you were going to be at practice today," Tyree observed, trying to hide the disdain and surprise in her voice.

Kamaal looked up from the book he was reading. A brightness flashed across his sad expression at the sight of her that caused her to believe he didn't know she would be there. "I was, but I couldn't focus, so Coach let me leave early."

She nodded. "I understand. I can come back another time." She pivoted and began to walk toward the door.

"No," Kamaal said quickly as he stood. "You stay; I'll go."

Tyree stopped and turned to him, shaking her head. "I couldn't ask you to do that, Kamaal. Karl is your son. I'll go." She placed her hand on the door handle.

"Tyree."

The commanding bass in Kamaal's voice paused her. Slowly, she turned around and looked at him, and this time, she really saw him. His emerald eyes were dim and sunken into dark bags. He looked like he hadn't slept since she'd seen him. She had been dealing with the blow-up Kamaal caused when he used her loss as ammunition against Aiyden on the day she learned Karl was hit by a car. When she rushed to the hospital, Tyree waited outside the room, refusing to be in there with Kamaal. Her hatred toward him kept her on the other side of the door, but the love she had for his son wouldn't let her go too far away.

To keep things mess free, with the help of Kamaal's aunt Brenda, they coordinated her visits. Usually, Tyree would show up to spend time with Karl while Kamaal went to freshen up at home or attempt to handle some business.

"I need to make a run, and then Aunt Brenda will be back

up here for tonight's shift. Please stay. I know he wants to hear from you."

Tyree gnawed on her bottom lip before nodding slowly. "Okay, but only if you're sure it's not a problem."

Kamaal held out his hand toward the seat by Karl's bed. "It's nice and warm for you," he said, attempting to lighten the mood.

Tyree offered a tight-lipped grin before taking cautious steps toward the bed. She twisted her shoulders as she passed Kamaal, careful not to touch him. Once settled into the chair, she pulled out a children's book she'd brought to read to him. "Thank you," she called out to Kamaal, who was about to open the door.

Kamaal nodded his response and slipped out of the room.

"Hey, my guy," she crooned. "I picked up the newest Dog Man series. I know you'll like these." Tyree opened the first book of the series and began reading. She took ahold of Karl's hand and tenderly rubbed as she read the pages, unaware of the spectator in the hallway.

Kamaal felt a pit in his stomach as he watched Tyree read to Karl through the rectangular window. He didn't know what he did to deserve such a compassionate person in his son's life, but he was thankful.

He knew Tyree hated him, and it moved him even more that she put her feelings to the side to be there for Karl. Just as she had the night they met over two years ago when she found his son, who had gotten separated from him at the Jacksonville Fair. She'd put his child's needs before her own. She, once again, proved to be a better mother than the woman who'd birthed him. He felt like he'd blown a three-score lead at the Super Bowl. With the biggest victory clenched in his grip, he'd lost it all because he'd gotten too comfortable and lost sight of his prize. He'd gotten cocky and behaved as if a win was guaranteed, as if his status, the trips, and the gifts were head starts, sure to keep him ahead of the competition. All of that just to fumble and have another man scoop the ball and sprint in the other direction. He'd been trying to catch up ever since.

The buzzing in his pants pocket tore his attention away from Tyree and Karl. Kamaal pulled his phone out of his pocket and checked the caller ID. As if she could read his thoughts regarding her, Marie was calling—something she'd been doing a lot these days.

Kamaal walked down the hall and answered. "Shouldn't you be calling my attorney?" he barked into the phone, forgoing any pleasantries for the woman who was trying to take his son from him now that she'd decided her twelfth attempt at rehab was going to be the one that broke through.

"Dammit, Kamaal! I deserve to be there. He's my son too!"

Kamaal pushed the exit button and walked through the double doors to the guest check-in area. "No, he's your inconvenience, remember?" He spat her words back at her, the words she'd said when she was mad because he and their son blew her high one day. He was sure she didn't even remember saying that, but they were words he could never forget. After ignoring the obvious signs and sweeping her neglectful ways under the rug with foolish hope, Kamaal had to accept it for what it was. He'd lost her. Their son was a motherless child.

"Maal, I'm not like that anymore," she resigned. The bite of her words had dissipated. "I've changed, and I want to be a part of his life. I just want to be there and see that he's okay."

Kamaal rolled his eyes at the tremble he heard in her voice. Her apparent pain had no effect on him; he'd heard it all before—too many times. "Just like he's been while you were too busy popping pills and smoking your life away, he's okay. If you have anything else to say to me, say it to my lawyer." Kamaal hung up and proceeded to add this number to his block list. Marie had somehow gotten ahold of his number when news of Karl's accident hit the airwaves. Karl being in a coma was sending him into a black hole that he tried to fight his way out of daily. Marie and her bullshit didn't make the cut for matters that he needed to be concerned with. He had enough on his plate. Nursing his son back to health and winning his woman back left no room for anything else.

KEEP IN TOUCH WITH CHASSILYN HAMILTON

Website: www.chassilynhamilton.com
Instagram: @authorchassilynhamilton
Twitter: @authorchassilyn
Facebook: facebook.com/authorchassilynhamilton

Made in the USA
Columbia, SC
28 May 2021